Tell-TAIL Sign

A forbidden Love Romance by

TIFFANY ANDREA

Paperback ISBN: 978-1-990724-33-6
eBook ISBN: 978-1-990724-31-2

Cover Design by: Burden of Proofreading Publishing featuring Graphics by Msanca, Levente, and A7880S via DepositPhotos

Interior Graphics by Design & Beyond via Canva

www.boppublishing.com

To my first friends in life, my cousins

*As we've grown older, distance and responsibilities have
led us down different paths, but that has never meant
a lack of love or support when it matters.
Thank you all for being a part of my life, and allowing
me to be a part of yours.*

TABLE OF CONTENTS

PREFACE

I know what you're thinking. Tiffany, this is a rom-com. It's supposed to be light-hearted and fun. An escape from the world. Well, I hear you; I really do. We need escapism right now, and I hope you find it in Sophie and Boyd's story.

However, I don't like to do things the same way as everyone else. As much as I love fluffy rom-coms with unrealistic plot lines, perhaps my imagination isn't that great. This one borders contemporary romance/rom-com. Point of all this, is that Sophie and Boyd's story is fun. It's quirky and laugh-out-loud funny (I hope). But there is also an underlying theme that could be triggering for some people. If you have any potential triggers that could be harmful for you, please read ahead. If not, skip on to the emotional roller coaster Sophie and Boyd ride.

Also, remember this is a fictional story with some realistic elements, so take a second now to suspend reality.

This book addresses issues regarding having a narcissistic parent. That includes emotional manipulation, blackmail, and narcissistic abuse.

coffee's for Closers

"Andy, where's my one o'clock?" I ask my assistant through the intercom.

"Sorry, Miss McNamara. He just called to cancel."

How considerate. Five minutes after our meeting was set to commence, he has the decency to let me know he isn't coming. Not that I expect anything less from a VIP member to my father's *Good Old Boys'* club. A group of men in Henry McNamara's world who all subscribe to the mentality that women are inferior. As if this same group's entire business model isn't built on making deals over whisky and crude jokes.

Little do they know, I can play with the old guys when I have to, but none of them take too kindly to being slaughtered on the golf course by a shapely brunette. That's one of the many points of contention between my father and me. He thinks I should inflate a man's ego by letting him win. I'm of the mentality that it's not my fault their short game isn't up to snuff.

"Andy, can you come in here, please?"

Seven seconds later, Andy swings open my office door. As far as assistants go, I hit the jackpot with him. He has also become a good friend.

"Yes?"

"Did Mr. Newton explain why he cancelled, rather than rescheduled?"

Andy looks at the floor, not walking any farther into my office. "He wants to meet with Mr. McNamara instead."

Knew it. I'd call him back to prove a point if I wasn't well aware it would be an exercise in futility.

"Thanks." I huff an aggressive sigh, resisting the urge to roll my eyes. This is a frequent occurrence and is becoming more common the longer I'm in this role as senior import and logistics executive.

Andy spins to leave, but turns back to add, "If it's any consolation, I told him he was making a mistake."

I nod a terse smile, not wanting to let on that it bothers me. I knew from childhood that my role in this company would be secondary to my father or brother. Thankfully, my twin brother, Caleb, doesn't have the same archaic way of thinking as our father does, but that's not the only thing that sets him apart from Henry. Caleb has no interest in this job or company. He's settled into his career as a chef, with no intentions of being a part of *McNamara Enterprises*, so that leaves me, the female half of the McNamara twins. The *lesser* half, if you ask Henry or any of his associates. He's going to have to accept that he can leave the company in my capable hands when the time comes, or he'll have to hire someone else who hasn't worked toward this career since childhood. It's the second option that scares me.

A problem for another day.

I respond to some lingering emails from our tenth-floor shipping division, requesting changes and making suggestions for improvements. At least most of the employees in that department are reasonable professionals who respect my position and expertise, which helps to lessen the sting of Mr. Newton's snub.

Upon completion of my last message, I reach for my mug, anticipating the last sips of my room temperature coffee. I'm disappointed to discover I already finished it. There's nothing worse than going to savour the last bit of caffeinated delight, only to realize it's gone. I didn't get closure, and I'm not ready to conclude that chapter on my day quite yet.

Instead of having another disgusting breakroom coffee, I opt to get out of the office and go for a drive. Not that I can get far in under an hour with Toronto traffic, but I need a change of scenery and my schedule is suddenly wide open.

A café catches my eye on the south side of Queen Street West. *Just Add Coffee.* Cute.

I park my SUV along the curb several yards from the sidewalk seating area, adorned with pastel umbrellas over wrought-iron bistro tables. The front door is rustic, and the outside has a shabby chic aesthetic, which normally I find contrived and played out, but for today, I'll appreciate it for the creative vibe it presents.

Inside, there are ten patrons seated on wood-topped metal stools surrounding wooden tables affixed to the wall around the perimeter. A long L-shaped butcher block counter stretches along the left side of the room, with multiple coffee machines in behind. It's simple, cozy, and chic. A perfect combination. The air conditioning is on, so it's far more comfortable than the scorching late summer temperatures outside. I wait in line behind a tall woman with orange skin—after what I'm assuming was a self-tanning session gone wrong, or she's been surviving on a diet of carrot juice for years—and scan the chalkboard menu for inspiration. Who am I kidding? I'm going to get the same thing I order everywhere.

My turn comes, and I ask for a flat white. The added espresso shot is a necessity to survive the remainder of my day. The petite blonde behind the counter, whose name tag reads Tessa, can't be more than eighteen. I tell her my name for my order, drop a five-dollar bill in the tip jar, and give her a reassuring smile.

I stand at the drink receiving area behind the orange woman and when the other employee turns to pass the lady her drink, I lock on to the most captivating hazel eyes I've ever seen. They are set in a serious face surrounded by a perfectly groomed short beard, and caramel-coloured hair that's as animated as his movements.

His expression doesn't change when he spots me, but he doesn't look away as he sets the drink down for the other woman. She grabs her beverage and retreats out the door.

Before I can come up with something clever to say, he spins to fulfil my order. I shamelessly check him out as he fills the takeout cup with a double shot of espresso and steaming hot milk. In addition to his coffee-making skills, I like what I see. Maybe I've been spending too much time with the old perverts, but I can't stop myself from drinking him in.

"Sophie?" His deep timbre doesn't match his appearance. He looks like a hipster and sounds like a lumberjack. Who knew that was a combination hotter than the drink he's handing me.

"Thanks." I grab the cup with one hand and tuck a stray strand of hair behind my ear with the other. I'm blushing like a love-struck teenager. I can only hope my makeup is doing its job.

"It's hot."

"Yeah, you are." My eyes widen, and I nearly drop my drink, clutching my fingers around it just in time. Can I melt into a puddle now, please? "I mean, yeah, I know." Okay, time to high-tail it out of here. This has surpassed mortifying. Before

I run off, I lift my coffee cup up in a thank you gesture at the man and read his nametag: Boyd. He doesn't look like a Boyd. Maybe Beau or Hayes or Dax. Something punchy and hot. Not *Boyd*.

I exit through the door as fast as my three-inch heels can carry me, straight to my car. Once I secure my drink in my cup holder, I ease into slow-moving traffic, back toward *McNamara Enterprises*, determined to never return to that café again.

My level of mortification is almost as high as the time I walked onto the subway and my jersey skirt had stretched out enough that it just fell off. It was so hot out, I was trying to minimize the clothes I had on and... well... I put every dime I had saved into a car down payment the next day and haven't returned to the subway since. And that's a system with tens of thousands of daily riders and hundreds of miles of track. It's far less likely I'll run into anyone who remembers seeing my pasty cheeks than Boyd in that coffee shop.

Plus, I've learned my lesson from pursuing men who work in minimum wage jobs, because they're never interested in *me*. They're more curious about my potential inheritance or think because my name is on the side of a multi-million dollar company that they can get a job with no qualifications. Job by association.

It probably makes me a sucker for punishment, but despite my track record, I enjoy the dating process. Not online dating. Meeting people in real life and seeing if there's an organic connection. That's the fun part. The anticipation. Not knowing if sparks will fly or it will feel like being doused in ice water. More often than not, it's the latter.

Still, I've met some colourful people who have given me plenty of stories to tell my best friend, Ashlyn, over drinks. I'm done with trying to create more material for my eccentric friend to laugh over, though. If—and that's a big if—I decide to settle down, it needs to be with someone who is hardworking and understands what it's like to be married to their job. One where they constantly have to prove themselves to feel even remotely appreciated. Maybe they don't need to understand that part. For now, it will just be me and my labradoodle, Wilson. And my seventy-one-year-old widowed neighbour, Celeste, who dog-sits while I'm slaving away to be under-appreciated.

I arrive back at work with the same desire I have each time my SUV lands between my designated parking spot lines: go in, kick butt, and prove that I've earned my place here.

2

BOYD

Eternal Summer

People come in here, day in, day out. Most don't give me a second glance, short of a few middle-aged women who give me a wink instead of a tip. Winks don't pay the bills. But when the shapely brunette stood on the other side of the counter, waiting for her order, I almost forgot how to make one of the most common drinks on our menu.

Good thing I'm not interested in pursuing anyone. She doesn't look like the type to give a barista the time of day, anyway. This job allows for a lot of people reading, and I've gotten pretty good at it. A woman like her is committed to her job. Interested in brand name clothes and expensive restaurants. She's gorgeous, but not my type. Not anymore.

Chances are I'll never see her again, and that suits me fine.

The rest of my shift is marked by more customers coming and going. Some are friendly, while others are too absorbed in their devices to look up. None stick in my mind like Sophie. I'll blame that on her Freudian slip, which I am counting as a confession.

My days are jam-packed and long, so after a full shift at the café, when I pour myself in the front door of my house at

10pm, I'm exhausted. Even as a morning person, several years of early days, long hours, and no time off are taking their toll.

"Hey," my brother, Holden, calls from his perch on the sofa, his nose stuck in a copy of Tolstoy's *War and Peace*.

"Hey. Have you been here all day?"

"No. I went out for a bit. Stopped over to see Grace and Phoebe. Picked up groceries for Mum. Went to the library." Holden's mouth quirks into a slight smile at the mention of the library.

I stifle a groan. How anyone can be *that* much of a library nerd is beyond me. "Right. I'm beat, so I'll see you tomorrow."

He doesn't even look up as I leave the room, too consumed by his Russian literature.

My bedroom is on the second floor, at the back of the house my brother and I share. I don't spend much time in it—or in our house in general—because I'm always on the go. When I am home, I'm sleeping more often than not. My life is a constant grind, working on multiple things at once, trying to strike a balance. So far, the only things I have on the other side of my work scale are a standing family dinner arrangement every Sunday and my best friend, Monica, who happens to work at the café. Though, instead of providing any balance, the three-hour window I spend with my parents and siblings usually weighs me down.

That leaves me counting down the days of the week until I have to suffer through it again.

We're down to two.

I strip off my work clothes, despite the protest from my muscles, climb into bed in my boxers, and can't count to ten after my head hits the pillow.

Each shift I've worked for the past three days, I've gone through the motions, fulfilling orders and catering to customers. But with each chime of the door, I find myself glancing up, looking for a gorgeous brunette. It's ridiculous. I know nothing beyond her first name and her onetime coffee order. She looks like the kind of woman who gets the same thing every day, but I can't know for sure. Not when she hasn't returned—at least not while I've been here. Then again, she probably works nearby and has weekends off like a normal person.

When she walks in again on Monday afternoon, I have to stop myself from gawking like an idiot. She's wearing a form-fitting dress with a high neckline and a hem that reaches to just above her knees. It's a blush colour, which would almost match her skin tone, but she's got a tan, accented by the light pink. Her fresh-brewed coffee coloured hair is down and straight, reaching midway down her back.

It takes seconds for her eyes to lock on mine. When she smiles, I nearly pour scalding hot coffee over the back of my hand, instead of in the intended paper cup. Workmen's Compensation Benefits probably don't pay out very well for failed flirting accidents.

As expected, her name pops up on the order screen a minute later, next to *10oz flat white - Sophie*. No fuss, no muss. I work at completing her drink because I pride myself on being efficient in everything I do. No one is going to come in here and get between me and my work. It doesn't matter how jaw-dropping her figure is in that dress.

Once bitten, twice shy.

She's standing in the pickup area when I spin around to place her drink on the counter.

"Sophie?" I ask, like I don't know with absolute certainty.

"That's me." She holds up her hand at chest level with one finger raised.

I pass her the cup with the paper sleeve around it. "It's hot." My smirk is unmistakable as I say those simple words I repeat hundreds of times each day—but they don't have the same double meaning with anyone else.

Her face flushes so bright, I wonder why anyone would call the light pink of her dress "blush". A thrill of satisfaction rushes through me, knowing she remembers.

"Yeah, thanks." Without any more slips of her tongue, she grabs her drink and walks out the door, stopping on the patio to sit at one of the bistro sets.

I serve one more customer before I gesture to Monica that I'm going to make the rounds to clean off vacated tables. Including the ones outside. She raises an eyebrow at me that suggests it's not usually my job, but I brush off her suspicious stare.

The humid air hits me as I step outside. It's late summer, but we've been suffering through another heatwave. Why anyone would choose to sit out here is beyond me, but I've always been partial to climate control.

I start at the table behind Sophie, wiping down the surface, lifting the seat cushion to clean underneath, and checking if the umbrella is secure. Then I move on to the table diagonal to where she's seated, giving me an opportunity to eye her as she sips her drink and scrolls through her phone.

When I move to the table beside her, the last of the empty ones, she looks up from her cup and smiles.

"Aren't you hot?" That's the best icebreaker I could think of. Not a smile, like a normal person. I already used up my one smirk for the month.

She chuckles, setting her cup down on the plexiglass tabletop. "You tell me."

Her playful response catches me by surprise, almost making me laugh. My body probably forgets how to make that sound.

Instead, I offer a practical response. "It's about a hundred degrees out. I think everyone is hot."

"Hm."

The vague, one syllable reply doesn't offer much clarification. If anything, it makes me think she doesn't want to pursue this conversation any further.

"I just needed to get out of the office for a bit. Clear my head. This beats sitting in my car." She takes another sip of her drink, drumming the table with her left hand.

Apparently, I was wrong. "Not if your car has AC."

She chuckles again. "Yeah, I guess." She clutches her drink and stands, but because the chairs are so heavy—an intentional choice to deter thefts—she has to shimmy out from the table. "Thanks for the drink, Boyd."

"Any time, Sophie." I'm so used to being dismissive around people, the weird desire to converse with her has thrown me for a loop. The more frustrating thing is that I don't *want to* want to talk to her. It's pointless. I don't waste my time on things that don't serve a purpose.

"This is the best coffee I've ever had, by the way. And I've tried a lot."

That's a huge point of pride for me. In my humble opinion, we do have the best in the clty. Probably the country, but I haven't tried them all to say for sure.

"We're the only place in Toronto that gets our coffee from a privately owned farm in Indonesia. They age their coffee for a few years after harvesting, which is what gives it the rich flavour and makes it less acidic."

She didn't ask for any of that, yet here I am nerding out over coffee production.

"Interesting."

With most people, I'd assume they were patronizing me or just being polite, but she looks genuinely interested in the topic.

"You'll be seeing me around, then. Now I'm hooked." She's still standing five feet away, not making any effort to move. Until she does. "Bye, Boyd."

I'm disappointed she's leaving already, which surprises me more than my incessant need to glance at the door every time someone has walked in over the past three days. She's not my type. Why do I care? All that has resulted from this conversation is frustration.

The woman standing in front of me is the epitome of why I've put off dating for years. The *princess* who skirts by on her flashy smile and sunny disposition. A woman who covers herself in designer clothes and expensive perfume that smells like citrus and flowers I can't name. A bombshell who ropes people in with her charms, only to let the trap snare them when it suits her best.

My disappointment washes away as she exits the patio and disappears down the street amongst the foot traffic.

Back to work. Always back to work.

3

SOPHIE

I'm Not Afraid

I promised myself I wouldn't return to *Just Add Coffee*. When I got in my car earlier and started driving back there, it was because I had just finished a frustrating meeting where I was cut off, spoken over, and dismissed a record number of times. Neither of the men in the room cared to hear a word I had to say. That didn't stop their lewd comments or lascivious looks, though. Safe to say, I was ticked. I wanted one of those amazing flat whites to take my mind off of the percentage of my clients who treat me as less than human.

Of course, Boyd had to bring up my little slip when he handed me my drink. He looked amused. I was mortified, but not enough to stop me from going back like I had initially thought. Yes, the coffee is *that* good. In my capacity organizing shipments from overseas for large companies, I've arranged plenty of coffee orders—never from a privately owned Indonesian farm. Hearing him talk about their niche market was really interesting.

My head is a jumbled mess when I return to work, running through potential contacts and options to look into more specialized farms to offer unique products to clients. Unique often means more expensive, but *Just Add Coffee* is evidence that also means superior.

"Sophie, your fath… uh, Mr. McNamara requested to see you immediately. I wasn't sure where you were, so I bought you a little time," Andy rambles as I walk past his desk toward my office.

Just what I needed. "Thanks, Andy." I don't ask what he said to placate my father, but it doesn't matter. He will find something to be disappointed in me about, regardless. I could be in a hospital bed after having an emergency heart transplant and he'd be bothered by my lack of work ethic.

I walk down the corridor toward Henry McNamara's office, stopping to ask his assistant, Joel, for permission to enter. He gives me the go-ahead, so I swing open the wide oak door.

"There you are. I've been waiting fifteen minutes. I trust you sorted out your lady troubles?" My father points a vague finger toward my abdomen.

Not cool, Andy. Not. Cool.

"I'm fine. What do you need me for?"

"Clarence and John stopped in to see me after your meeting with them. They weren't very pleased, Sophie. They requested another sit down with me."

Of course they did. Now, I could fly off the handle in a fit of rage and blame it on PMS or uncontrollable lady hormones, but that only perpetuates the stereotype my father has created of women in business. That we're delicate, unhinged, sensitive, emotional, and essentially useless. Instead, I say nothing. Defending myself to Henry is a lost cause, which I discovered before I even got my first period. I've had practice with this. You never anger the beast.

"You have nothing to say for yourself?"

Would it matter if I did? "There's nothing to say. They weren't happy, and you're going to 'handle it', right?" I use air quotes because that's what he says every single time.

"I'm never going to be able to leave this company to you if *you* don't start handling it, Sophie."

My jaw clenches as I dig my nails into my palms. The harder I work, the more I get the impression he's not planning to leave me in charge, anyway. He's just looking for excuses to make it sound more reasonable to freeze me out. Anyone who feels that their father's love is unconditional is lucky. I'm pretty sure my father's love is non-existent for anything other than his business.

"I went into that meeting prepared, and my presentation was on point. No matter how prepared I am, I can't make people listen to me." Should have stayed quiet. I regret my defensive words as soon as my brain processes them.

My father fiddles with a pen, tapping it against his opposite hand. "That's your problem, Sophie. You don't *make* people listen to you. If you're going to succeed in this business, people need to trust what you're saying and hang on to your every word. If they have questions, answer them without hesitating. Know the industry inside and out, and if there's something you don't know, pretend you do."

Trust me, dear father, I *know* this business inside and out. I've made it my life. Given it my all. And for what? So my father can keep telling me I can never know enough because of my second X chromosome? If he wants me to prove I'm fierce enough to command attention, so be it.

"Yes, sir."

I stomp back to my office, not bothering to check in with Andy upon my return. We'll discuss my menstrual cycle as a defence at another date. For now, I have work to do.

It's after seven before I leave the office. I was lucky to find a townhouse condo only three kilometres from the location my father moved *McNamara Enterprises* to, so the commute is minimal. I could walk, but the extra hour a day that adds isn't something I can budget in. Plus, I need to walk Wilson when I get home.

Before I get to my door, I pass by Celeste's and knock. I hear faint barking from the other side and smile. My little guard dog.

Celeste's muffled, "Who do you think it is, huh?" makes me chuckle. She loves the little fur ball and talks to him like he's going to reply. She swings the door open, greeting me with a smile. Her white hair is stylish in its pixie cut, and she's dressed in a leopard-print blouse and burgundy capris pants. There's never a day she doesn't wear makeup and put herself together. In her words, 'you never know who you'll run in to.'

"Sophie, dear. Come in. I've made you dinner."

I bend down to pet Wilson as I shuffle inside her home. "You didn't have to do that. I could have whipped something up."

"Nonsense. Not after working a full day. Let me make sure you're fed properly. You're far too skinny. Men like a woman with some meat on her bones." The septuagenarian ambles toward her kitchen, waving off my comments.

I stop myself from pointing out that my goal in life is not to please a man with my figure, but I let it slide. She's from a different era and most of the time, I love that about her. She reminds me of my grandmother, who thinks happiness lives and dies with a relationship. Though, clearly her eldest daughter didn't inherit that way of thinking, because she's stuck with my father for thirty years.

"Did you two have a good day?" I ask, slipping out of my shoes and walking into the small, open-concept space.

"Same as usual. We had a great round of *Jeopardy!* today. There was a category on crochet stitches and another on Elvis songs. Would you believe it?"

"Wow. Right up your alley." I giggle to myself as I drop on her floral sofa. I know better than to ask if she needs help in the kitchen; she slapped my knuckles with a wooden spoon a few months ago when I tried to lend a hand.

Wilson climbs on my lap as soon as I'm seated, waiting for me to give him some attention. Not going to lie, it feels good that he still knows I'm his person. Celeste only has one estranged stepson and a granddaughter a few years younger than me, but they haven't seen each other for more than a decade. Wilson has become her surrogate grandchild. She spoils him like any good grandparent would.

"Dinner won't be but a minute. Tell me about your day. Anything interesting happen?" she asks in a sing-song voice.

My throat goes dry, causing me to cough as I'm scratching under Wilson's chin. Interesting isn't the word I'd use. Weird, sure. Being dismissed because I'm not a middle-aged man, so I can't possibly be good at my job. Returning to my new favourite coffee shop for more reasons than the delicious drinks. Or having my tardiness excused because of fake period issues. I could tell Celeste about any of them, but because I don't want to address the drama of my day, I oversimplify things. "No, nothing. Same old phone calls, emails, spreadsheets, and male chauvinists."

"Oh, dear. I do wish you'd think about working somewhere else. You're young and a real whipper-snapper. You don't need that toxic place."

She's right. It is toxic, but it's also my birthright. My obligation. I've invested too much into this job to go elsewhere. It would be like taking out a mortgage on a house, paying it for twenty years, then up and leaving it behind to take on a new mortgage somewhere else.

Anyone who has a hint of jealousy over children born to parents with a successful business, I wish they understood the flip side. The grass isn't always greener. It's not always guaranteed opportunities and trust funds. The only money I have comes from my paycheques. I'm not banking on an inheritance or having my income supplemented by "daddy dearest." Mostly, the familial business connection has limited my potential, not enhanced it.

"Pay no mind to that now. It's time to eat." Celeste exits the kitchen with two steaming pasta bowls.

We sit at the small kitchen table with ivory upholstered chairs, eating mushroom stroganoff, drinking the remaining white wine Celeste didn't use in the recipe. It may sound crazy, but aside from Ashlyn, my elderly neighbour is my best friend. I'm happy to say I'm hers, too.

By nine o'clock, I need to get home and prepare myself for tomorrow, so I say good night to Celeste, then Wilson and I walk fifteen feet to my front door. We only stop inside long enough for me to change into yoga pants, a T-shirt, and sneakers, then I take him for his nightly walk.

The entire three kilometre trek, Fall Out Boy pounds through my headphones, and all I can think about is my coffee break tomorrow. But it's not just because of the coffee.

Tuesday afternoon, when I finally make it in for my shift just before 4pm, Monica isn't wearing her usual *you're late* face. She's got a suspicious grin that tells me I'm in for an earful. We've been friends for seven years, since she started working here the same week I did. Because of my busy schedule, it's nice having a built-in friend in a co-worker. The convenience aspect is secondary to the fact that she's a good person and we've always gotten along well. She puts up with my grumpiness, and I tolerate her perpetual optimism. I guess that's one area I have some balance.

It doesn't take long after the last customer in line makes their way to a table before Monica spills. "She came back. The brunette with the—" She makes an hourglass shape with both hands.

I don't allow my face to betray the little swirl in my stomach. "So?"

"That woman came in here, wearing a dress that... whoo. And heels that could be the star in any fantasy."

Part of me wants to hear more about this dress. The rational part, however, has no interest. "Is there a point to this?" I ask, tying my apron around my back.

"She looked disappointed. Like she wanted a coffee, but wasn't *really* here for the coffee. You know?"

"No, I don't. It doesn't matter, anyway. She's too much like *her*, and you know my policy."

One factor that bonded me and Monica has been our strict no-dating rule. We've both been burned in the past and refuse to put ourselves in that position again. For her, being a single mom to a thirteen-year-old son has been a constant reminder of what trusting the wrong person can do. Granted, she loves her son—as do I—but raising him on her own hasn't been easy. For me, my life is too busy to make room for anyone else. Sunday dinners are enough of an inconvenience.

"I do. But I also think it's time you stop letting *her* rule your life."

"She's not." My already foul mood sinks to new levels and *her* name hasn't even been mentioned. Just reminding me of how stupid I was, being blinded by a nice smile and charming personality, is enough to turn me more sour.

"You can tell yourself that all you want, but she is, because you're not living your life for you. Your resentment is making choices before your heart is."

I scoff. "You're one to talk."

How mature. Next I'll stick my tongue out and say 'I know you are, but what am I?'

Mercifully, we're interrupted by a pair of girls in their early twenties walking in and placing elaborate orders. I get to work making a trenta green tea frappuccino with a banana smoothie base, two pumps of hazelnut syrup, two espresso shots, topped with light whip and caramel drizzle. No one can convince me this is a better tasting option than plain coffee. The second order is equally ludicrous. I hand off the drinks to the giggling duo, happy to rid that ridiculous list of instructions from my screen.

Before I can get into any sort of work groove, Monica picks up our earlier conversation. "I also have a kid to consider. My bad relationship didn't just impact me, and I couldn't sit around feeling sorry for myself until I got over it. I had to be strong and put my kid first. So no, I don't want to risk bringing anyone else into the dynamic I've worked hard to protect." She levels me with a glare that only mothers are capable of.

Like my mother, Monica also has the ability to make me feel like an idiot for holding onto a grudge for as long as I have—even though neither of them will forgive *her* either.

"Besides, she may dress nice, but I get the impression Sophie has worked for it. If she was a snooty, stuck-up type like *her*, she'd come in here and order some obnoxious concoction like those two just did. She might surprise you."

The problem is, I want her to be different, but I have a hard time trusting my instincts outside of my job. My professional instincts are finely tuned. Personal instincts are deranged. Monica's instincts are more trustworthy.

"I'll think about it."

That satisfies my best friend. She ends the conversation with a smile and a victorious nod as she unties her apron to wrap up her shift for the day. Lately, our shifts have only had a slight overlap, so we haven't seen each other much. The least I can do in exchange is consider what she's saying. She hasn't steered me wrong yet.

Wednesday, I walk into the café just after lunch. It's chaotic and loud, with every table full. Monica, Shawny, and Tessa are behind the counter, fluttering around in a choreographed routine to fulfil orders.

"Oh good. You're here," Monica says, her shoulders slumping as she exhales. "We got slammed. Did you know there was some big conference happening at the hotel, and apparently they don't have coffee to offer?"

"Shoot. Sorry, Mon. I didn't know. Everything okay?"

"It is now. We ran out of a few things and it was a nightmare to grab stuff from the back while we were so busy, but we managed. Tip jar makes up for it." She winks and turns back to make another customer's drink.

I jump on the line to pick up the slack until there's a lull. Several items are nearing empty by the time the bulk of the crowd clears out. I go to the stockroom to grab a few new syrups, and when I return to the counter, I find Sophie standing opposite the cash register, placing her order with Tessa. She's wearing a powder blue pencil skirt and a floral blouse, which makes her look like an actual angel. She doesn't appear pretentious or extravagant. Just poised. Polished. Fierce.

Maybe Monica is right.

Her name and order appear on the screen again—same as always. I pop the syrups in place and remove the empty containers, then get to work on a flat white. The espresso machine hisses as it expels the last of the two espresso shots, and the milk has reached the appropriate temperature, so I add the ingredients to the takeout cup and snap on a lid.

"Sophie?"

"Thanks." She steps forward. "Looks like it was busy in here today."

I follow her eyes, turning to look over my shoulder. My co-workers all look beat. Frazzled hair, defeated body language, and filthy aprons. "Yeah, I guess so. I just got here thirty minutes ago."

"Oh." She moves to take a sip of her drink, stopping herself before her lips hit the lid. "Right, it's hot." Her cheeks flush, which almost makes me smile.

"Sure is."

She clears her throat and lowers the cup with both hands to her waist. "I came in yes—" She's interrupted by the door chime, and several people dressed in tailored suits file inside. "I'll let you get to work."

Work is always my focus. There's never a day I come in here and don't give it my all. I should be happy to get back to doing what I'm good at. But once again, I'm struck by conflicting feelings as she walks away. Like she did on Monday, she exits the café and finds a seat on the patio.

Ten minutes later, we've successfully navigated another influx of caffeine addicts—thankfully, most of them just wanted plain coffee—and Sophie is still sitting outside.

"Go 'clean the tables,' would ya?" Monica jokes, using air quotes to call me out on my excuse from two days earlier. She sends me off with a rag, a bottle of cleaner, and a trademark wink.

I walk onto the patio and pick up some trash previous customers left lying about, then clean off the tabletop opposite Sophie.

"Is Boyd a family name?" Sophie asks from behind me as I wipe down a chair.

"Uh… no. My parents just thought it suited me." Though, how anyone looks at a baby and thinks 'yep, he looks like a Boyd,' is beyond me. "Apparently it means blond. My parents are from the UK… it's a Scottish name." That was far more information than she asked for—again. Why does she have that effect on me?

"Hm." She tilts her coffee, draining the contents, and wrestles with the chair to stand.

A lot of this encounter is feeling like a routine... and I don't hate it.

"I have no idea what my name means. Or why my parents chose it." She tosses her cup in the garbage can, then walks toward me.

There are a lot of things I'd like to say right now. Like how I associate her name with complete mental paralysis. How she's synonymous with *flat white*. But I surprise myself by saying the words Monica encouraged me to. "Hey, Sophie? Would... I'm sorry if I'm off base here, but do you want to go out sometime? A drink or dinner?"

She glances at the table to my left with an unreadable expression. My stomach sinks because if she was interested, her face wouldn't look like that. Serves me right for stepping out of my comfort zone.

"I... I'm seeing someone, actually. It's serious."

Now there's a shortage of oxygen. I'm not sure if the choking feeling I have is from being suffocated by humidity, or if embarrassment feels that much like having a bag pulled over your head. If it were possible for me to leave with my ego intact, I would bow out, but it's already obliterated. Apparently, I should have trusted my head. Monica's radar is off.

"Well, he's a lucky guy."

"Thank you." She offers me a kind—pitying—smile. "And thanks again for the coffee." Then she walks away. She hops into a white Cadillac SUV parked along the curb, and I return to cleaning tables as she drives away.

There's a reason why work is my comfort zone. It never leaves me with annihilated dignity. I'm never left berating myself for being presumptuous. So I'll stick with what I know best. Work hard and stay single.

SOPHIE

The Break's Over

Why did I say that? Why did I lie?

I got in my head. Too concerned about what people would think—what my father would think—if I went on a date with another guy with a dead-end job. In any career, there are ceilings to what you can achieve. A barista's ceiling isn't very high. Not compared to my capacity at a multi-million dollar company. Instead of following the same route I've been going down for the last decade, I let my fear and past experience dictate my answer.

What's even more frustrating is that I wanted to say yes. He's a bit of a mystery and the broody, serious personality thing is like a code to crack. I'm curious if he's like that everywhere or just at work. Maybe he's only cranky because customers are frustrating. I know that feeling. Dealing with infuriating clients is part of the reason I ended up back there on Monday. And Tuesday.

Driving away from the café, I feel even more angry with myself than I was at the sexist jerks I had to deal with. Now I'm afraid I really have screwed myself over. Either I can never return, or I have to go and cultivate the lie, or tell the truth. None of those options seem very appealing.

I march out of the elevator and walk past Andy with a percussive tempo to my steps that amplifies my *don't-mess-with-me* mood, but he stops me anyway. All so he can tell me a client I'm supposed to meet with tomorrow morning insisted my father join us. Andy is trying to make arrangements with Joel, but it irks me that I'll once again have to play second fiddle when I've done all the legwork. Not that I expect anyone to sing my praises for doing my job, but some basic respect would be nice. An acknowledgement that I'm capable, even though my testosterone levels are significantly lower. Hard to imagine for these men my father attracts, unfortunately. They must have some secret club I don't know about—since I am a lowly woman—because I know for a fact that most men don't share their views.

Why can't I just stand up and be honest? Fight for what I deserve?

Oh, right. Because Henry doesn't like to be questioned or second-guessed. He certainly doesn't like to be challenged, so it's easier to just stay quiet.

So I do what I always do. Buckle down and do the hard part so my father can swoop in to take credit. Another opportunity to pad Henry's ego and inflate his already bloated self-esteem. Yay.

I settle into my office and review my presentation for a meeting I have at 3pm, resolved to prove myself while I have a chance.

Saturdays are usually my favourite day of the week. A full day off work, and I don't have to think about the week ahead. Yet, after three days without a proper flat white, the only thing I *can* think about is visiting *Just Add Coffee*. The single serve coffee maker at work and the instant coffee I have here are abominations by comparison.

Just as I build up the determination to drive to the café, my phone rings, stopping me in my tracks. Wilson lifts his head from his spot on the couch, tilting it like he's asking if I'm going to answer.

"Hi, Mom."

"Hello, my darling. I haven't heard from you for a while."

Immediately with the guilt trip. Go figure. It's not like phones work both ways or anything.

"I've been busy with work. Late nights. Then I get home and have to take care of Wilson." I feel guilty using my dog as an excuse; especially because I talk to Ashlyn on the phone all the time when I take him for walks. It never crosses my mind to call my mother.

"Right. Your father said he had to sit in on a meeting with you this week."

I clench my jaw, recalling the disastrous meeting Henry joined me for. One where, once again, I was interrupted, dismissed, subtly insulted, and hit on in a matter of minutes. "The client requested him."

"He's never going to be able to retire at this rate." She sighs, piling on the guilt.

But I don't feel guilty. I'm angry. "Is that what he tells you? That he's going to retire?" I know for a fact that my father has no interest in being a retiree. Zero desire to give up the clout that comes along with his CEO position. Certainly not so he can tour the continent's golf courses and *winter* in Florida with other retired rich people. He doesn't want to be seen as an equal. In his mind, he's an alpha, and belongs at the top of the food chain. He'll stay there as long as he can.

"He promised once you were ready, he'd retire and we could travel more. I miss those days."

Ah, yes. The days when our parents jetted off to random countries across the globe on business trips and left me and Caleb at our grandparents' for weeks on end.

I want to ask her why she's stayed with him all this time. It can't be the money, because that only serves as a Band-Aid for so long. Their mansion in Forest Hill is nice, but not enough to sacrifice the prime of her life. In her mind, though, she'd rather be an eighty-five-year-old widow than a fifty-four-year-old divorcee.

The sad thing is, I get it. Every thought I've had about my mother and her perceived weakness for staying with Henry, I could say about myself. No doubt she stuck it out because she thought it was the easier choice, even when it was hard.

So, after far too many seconds, I ask, "Do you really want him home every single day?"

Silence. I wonder if the call disconnected because Mom replicates my long pause with one of her own.

"Have you spoken to Chelsea or Hollis recently?" That's a sharp turn in the conversation. Clearly she's sidestepping my question. Whether it's because she doesn't want to answer me or she doesn't want to admit the truth to herself, I don't know.

"I spoke to Chelsea a few weeks back, and Hollis and I went for dinner two weeks ago. Why?"

"Just curious. Zara calls to check in like I'm *her* little sister, but I don't often talk to Lexi. Her and Lorenzo are probably having issues."

My mother's speculations about her sister's marriage do not appeal to me—like she has any right commenting on someone else's relationship.

I really just want a coffee. "Sorry, Mom. I have to go. I've got plans with Ash this afternoon." No point in signing off with pleasantries I don't mean. I've already lied once... something that seems to be a new habit.

"Way to make your mother feel important. It's not like I carried you for nine months and birthed you or anything."

Not to split hairs, but she carried us for seven-and-a-half months and had a c-section. Not saying that wasn't a painful sacrifice on her part, but... details. It's yet another way for her to make me feel guilty.

"Have a good day, Mom." I hang up the phone before she tries to smother me with more shame and culpability for things I never asked for.

Instead of walking out the door and going where I had planned, I drop onto my couch and slouch against the back. As always, Wilson takes the opportunity to show me how capable he is as a lapdog and settles atop my thighs. I rake my hands through the curly hair at the side of his ear and make a mental note to book a groomer's appointment for him. For now, I soak in the love of my shaggy dog and try to decompress from the phone call with my mom.

Somehow, my thoughts drift to Boyd and his offer to grab dinner or a drink. It loops in my head several times, making me question my response. That is something I feel guilty about. For lying to him. But I've learned the hard way, and I refuse to wind up with another guy who treats me as a stepping stone instead of a person.

5

BOYD

Alone Together

To say my mood has been foul the past few days would be putting it mildly. I don't have a legitimate reason why, but my usual crankiness has reached new lows. Now I'm being forced to gather with my siblings and parents, and put on a happy face over dinner.

"Let's go. I don't want to show up late," I snap at Holden as I walk to the door. He doesn't deserve to be on the receiving end of my bad mood, but unfortunately for him, it's a position he's become accustomed to.

"You could have gone without me. I'm sure I can find my own way."

I roll my eyes at him—an admittedly juvenile response—and sigh. One of the two actions prompt him to head for the door. He walks out first, so I follow and lock the door behind me. Within the ten seconds it takes me to do so, Holden has already made it halfway to our parents' place, two houses over.

Every Sunday since we each moved out, this has been our standing arrangement. And no one dares defy our mother. She's a tough old bird who could stir a pot of boiling pasta with her bare hand and not flinch. She's never been particularly warm or affectionate, but she has always been a dedicated mum. Sometimes too dedicated. Aside from her interest in her kids and the Princess of Wales, little else captures her attention. I thought she'd relax once she became a grandmother last month, but nothing has changed.

The newest addition to our family, Grace, is a tiny little thing whose personality is already starting to show. She's a girl who knows what she wants and won't take no for an answer—much like her mother and grandmother.

Phoebe is walking up the front stoop to Mum and Dad's place as we approach. Her husband, Aaron, is cradling their infant, standing behind her.

Holden stutter steps before climbing the step, and I almost crash into his back. I realize he's checking his phone, so I chastise him for texting and driving, trying to make a joke. He doesn't see it as one; or at least, he doesn't acknowledge it, too consumed with whatever he's reading. I bypass him and walk into the foyer behind Phoebe. Dad has already claimed Grace, and he's cooing over how beautiful she is. I kiss my sister and the baby on their foreheads before shaking hands with Aaron and greeting my father. He doesn't seem enthused to see me. Apparently, once you stop pooping your pants, people don't gush over you anymore. I don't have any memories of my father ever being as excited to see me as he is with Grace. I'm not about to start soiling my pants to see if that's the trick, though.

Holden walks in behind me and, as soon as my dad starts chewing him out for his poor manners, I exit into the ornate living room. Phoebe and Aaron join me, followed by Dad and Grace. Holden detours into the kitchen in search of our mother.

We spend the next hour catching up on anything pertinent to share since this time last week, which is virtually the same as everything we discussed last Sunday. Aaron, as a Toronto police officer, always has the best stories to share. This week he had to arrest a naked man in Nathan Phillips Square, who was performing "the helicopter", asking random women if they were ready for takeoff. Dad sheds a tear or two over Aaron's animated re-enactment—fully clothed, thankfully. His description of the takedown is comedy gold, but still does nothing to boost my mood.

My mother's unamused voice cuts through the laughter to call us into the dining room. She's never ventured out of her comfort zone when it comes to Sunday dinner preparations. I'd like to say that means she's perfected the Sunday roast, but we're not so lucky. Forty percent of the time, it's fine. Another forty percent, it's not great, but you can choke it down with enough gravy. Twenty percent of the time, it's dreadful. Like eating the sole of a sneaker. One that's made the rounds through an entire NBA team during playoffs.

My father, being the loyal, supportive man he is, compliments our mother for everything. But on those twenty percent days, even he stays quiet. Aaron, on the other hand, takes every opportunity to suck up to his mother-in-law, even though we all know he's lying through his teeth.

Tonight's meal, mercifully, is in the top forty percent category, so we're all able to maintain conversation throughout dinner. We hear all about what kind of achievements Grace should be reaching next, and listening to my sister talk about her daughter almost makes me crack a smile.

Both of my siblings knew what they wanted from a young age. Holden read a biography by a renowned history professor when he was a teenager and decided from that moment he wanted to pursue an advanced degree in history. He's working toward his PhD with the goal of becoming a professor someday. Phoebe knew from an even younger age that she wanted to be a mother. Other girls had lofty dreams of being

CEOs or actresses, but to Phoebe, nothing was loftier than having a family. Our mother always worked, and worked hard, so it wasn't that she ingrained the mentality that a woman's place is in the home into us. That was just Phoebe's dream and, from what I can tell, she's never been happier.

It's been a source of pride to see them both achieve their dreams. Even though I don't tell them that.

As for me? I don't know what I want exactly, but I'm willing to work hard to figure it out.

I don't consider myself a proud man, but after six days, Sophie hasn't returned. My coffee-making skills are top-notch after doing this job for eleven years, so I know that's not the reason she's opted to get her caffeine fix elsewhere. Plus, she admitted it was the best coffee she's ever had. She's avoiding me.

Nearing the end of our morning rush, I'm just about to take my break when I see her walk in with a bearded brunette. Their arms are linked together as they smile ear to ear. She's wearing a black floral sheath dress and strappy heels. The smart thing to do would be to save myself from witnessing young love and slink into the back room.

But I don't.

Instead, I continue making the drinks on order and glance up at Sophie's other half while he studies the menu. She says something to him, dragging him to the cashier. He replies with his head tilted toward her and one eyebrow raised, but I can't make out his words.

Then, before I can force myself back to my current task, Sophie's eyes lock on mine. Not just hers, but the angry eyes belonging to the man on her arm. He stares at me a few seconds longer than what's comfortable, so I raise one hand

and shoot him a friendly wave. One that I hope reassures him I'm not after his girl. She made sure of that.

The two of them exchange words again, leaving Sophie with slumped shoulders, but after a few more verbal exchanges, she's laughing. The entire interaction is so confusing, there's no deciphering it from where I'm standing. Not that I should even be trying. She's a customer, and I don't get invested in customer's conversations. Ever.

They step up to the counter, just as the man says, "I love you too," and kisses the top of her head. I've never considered myself the jealous type, but... no. I'm not jealous now, either.

Sophie and her boyfriend each order a flat white, which restores a little of my pride. At least that's one thing I can always do right. The entire time I'm crafting the perfect caffeinated beverages, I feel eyes on me. I carry on, doing my job, eventually turning around to pop on two plastic lids and hand them to the waiting customers.

That's all she is. A customer. A sentiment I will keep repeating to myself until my head gets the message.

The man thanks me as he grabs both cups and turns, giving me a bit of a side eye. Not an angry look; he seems more curious.

To ease my suffering, I decide to take my break now. I inform Monica, who gives me another suspicious glare before she nods. When I told her about Sophie's response last week, I could tell she felt a little bad for pushing me. Even though it stung, I needed a little shove to move out of the slump I'd been stuck in. Though, I'm firmly back there now and will remain in that slump for the foreseeable future.

I waste my break time sorting through order forms that don't need to be sorted, trying my best to find a distraction. The ten minutes aren't long enough and don't help me avoid the scene I was trying to. I return to the dining area and something possesses me to approach Sophie's table. It's one of those moments where your brain is screaming at you to stop because you know it's wrong and bordering on skeezy, but your feet take you there anyway.

I watch as she places her hand on top of his, not paying any attention to my arrival. Until she does. The guy spots me first, which draws her attention. Both of them staring leaves me struggling to explain why I'm standing here. This is not a full service café.

Finally, I choke out, "Sorry to interrupt. Can I get you anything else?"

The guy looks from me to Sophie, then scans the room. His furrowed brows greet me as he replies, "Thanks, man, but I'm good. Soph? You see anything *you* want? Anything at all?"

Sophie jolts in her seat, which makes her boyfriend laugh.

"No, I'm good, thanks, *Caleb*." She narrows her eyes at her tablemate.

I'm totally lost in this conversation. "Right." I look at Sophie for any kind of clarification, but get none. "Well, let me know if you change your mind."

My feet cooperate this time to retreat to safety. There's a small line forming at the counter, so I breathe a sigh of relief I can immerse myself in work and suppress my curiosity over this girl who I have no right to be curious about.

She's *just* a customer.

I look up after the crowd disappears and find an empty table where the happy couple was moments earlier. They left at some point while I was busy doing my job, which is exactly what I should be doing.

Staying in my comfort zone.

Ashlyn and I haven't seen each other for more than three weeks. She's a busy medical and health services manager who dedicates her time off to CrossFit and her fiancé, Jim. Seriously, her two hobbies are gym and Jim. Sometimes I question which she loves more. Between our jobs and her training, our free time to catch up is in short supply. So today, we're setting a few hours aside to have a girls' day. Except Wilson is joining us. That point was non-negotiable for me since he's been with Celeste every day this week. Ashlyn isn't an animal lover, though. Not unless they're seasoned and in a low-carb burrito.

We meet at the entrance of *Froning's Farmers' Market*, where she greets me with a radiant smile. She's wearing casual leggings and a cropped sweater. She looks like an Icelandic goddess, with her long ice blonde hair tied in a ponytail, bright blue eyes, and muscles that are the envy of many—myself included. Her six-pack abs are a sight to behold. This girl is never asking a man to open a jar.

"Giiiiirl, I've missed you so much." Ashlyn pulls me in for a hug, nearly choking me with her python-like arms.

When she releases me, I have to shake out my shoulders. "You've got to stamp a warning on those guns of yours. Squeezing people like they're sandbags. Sheesh."

She chuckles, grabbing my hand to pull me into the market. "Sorry, I'm three weeks out from my first competition in Montreal."

"That's exciting. Do you feel ready? You *look* ready."

We stop at a booth that features fresh flowers and produce, and Ashlyn replies, "Yes and no. I'm as ready as I can be, but I don't think I stand a chance. It will just be a fun experience to say I did."

"I think it's amazing. You've put in a lot of work."

She picks up a bundle of spinach, inspecting the leaves. "Thanks. So what's new with you? That hot brother of yours ready to take me on a date yet?"

"Those are two entirely different questions, and I'm not sure Jim would appreciate the latter." I laugh at her longtime crush on my brother, whom she's met once in person because of his extended time in Europe, but asks about every time I see her. "You'd be hard pressed to find Caleb outside of work for long enough to date."

"What is it with you McNamara people and your work hours? Do none of you know there's more to life? You all make me feel like a slacker because I *only* work forty hours."

I shrug because that's just how we are. Long hours, working toward goals, smashing the competition. We may not stand on the podium for the CrossFit Games, but we're competitive in our own ways.

We each purchase some items from various booths through the market as we maintain easy conversation. I hear about the last few dates Jim has taken her on—mostly fitness themed—and their plans for a destination wedding in Jamaica next year. She asks about my dating life and insists I'd love *Embers*, the dating app of the future. I maintain my strict anti-online-dating position. I also wrestle with the idea of telling her about Boyd, but that would also require me confessing to my little—okay, big—lie.

Wilson is capturing the attention of so many people as we stroll, we're stopping every twenty feet for him to greet someone and get some stranger loving. Before I know it, we've walked through the entire market, and we're headed south toward Queen Street.

After checking her phone, Ashlyn asks, "Do you want to grab a coffee or something?"

"Sure. If we can find somewhere with a patio still open. I can't take Wilson in." There's really no question if somewhere nearby has an open patio. I know there is. I know this because I've been there multiple times.

Just Add Coffee comes into view, as do their patio tables.

"Oh, look. That one's cute." Ashlyn claps like she's created the café out of thin air and she's celebrating her accomplishment.

Again, she grabs onto my hand, even though I'm juggling fresh flowers for Celeste and Wilson's leash with one arm and a bag full of market fares in the other. Her conditioned grip strength allows her to hold all of her purchases in one hand and squeeze mine with the other. I'd say she's ready for her competition. Especially if friend-dragging is an event.

Once we cross the street, we stand side by side, looking into the café windows.

"Do you want to go in and look at the menu, or should I just get you a flat white?" Ashlyn asks, holding her hands over her eyes to block the sun's glare on the windows.

If I'm being honest with myself, it's not the menu I want to check out. But I hold back from being truthful with my best friend. "I'll go in to look. I'm not sure what I want. You go first, though. I'll save us a table and tie up Wilson."

"Ugh, I guess I'll have to watch your beast. You owe me." She flicks her long ponytail over her shoulder and walks inside while I chuckle at her back.

As I wait, I set down my market purchases and tie my curly labradoodle to the base of one of the heavy tables. He plops down at my feet, panting like this is the best day of his life. I love that about him; every day is a new day, and each one has the potential to be amazing. I wish I could absorb some of his optimistic nature. For now, I'll just scratch his ears and enjoy his for a moment.

"There is a tall, broody, tan, drool-worthy drink of water in there that could have me leaving Jim at the altar." Ashlyn drops into the chair across from me and fans herself with a stack of napkins.

My stomach clenches when I take in what she's saying. I mean, that pretty much sums up my impression of Boyd from the few times I've been here. There's also no lineup inside, so if I go in, I'll have to interact with him. Last time I was here with Caleb, things were awkward. I was so worried Caleb would blow my lie wide open, because he kept teasing me. Brothers.

Just go in, order a drink, and get out.

I stand and brush off my skinny jeans—more to dry my palms than fix my pants. "Okay, I'll be back in a second."

"Girl, get his number. If not for you, for me."

"Poor Jim." I laugh as I walk inside and see the back of a familiar head. I make it all the way to the counter before he turns around.

"Hey." His voice is an octave above normal. He clears his throat and tries again. "Hey."

"Hi." I pause for a few seconds, staring at him. "It's quiet in here today."

"Usually Is on Saturday afternoons." His face shifts from cordial, at best, to indifferent. "What can I get you?"

The change in his demeanour is weird, but when I think back to previous encounters, considering I shot him down when he asked me out, I can't expect him to give me a welcome hug. We've exchanged little more than pleasantries otherwise.

"What do you suggest? I always get the same thing, but I could use a little variety." I attempt to appeal to his love of all things coffee, hoping that will improve our interaction.

"Cold or hot?"

"Hot." It's October. Only a lunatic would sit outside and drink iced coffee.

"How do you feel about pumpkin spice?"

"I'd rather you gag me with a toilet plunger," I deadpan. That came out before I put any thought into it, and now I'm ready to flee. Again.

Boyd's boisterous laughter stalls me in place. He continues for far too long. "I'm sorry. That's a new one. Pumpkin spice is a polarizing option, but…" He trails off as he starts laughing again. Like he's bottled it up for the last decade, and it's finally bursting out.

We're interrupted by a loud, "Oy, girl! What's taking you so long? Your *dog* keeps trying to make me pet him, and I. Don't. Want. To."

I glance back at Ashlyn, who is half in, half out of the door. She is incapable of expressing indifference, so her annoyance is clear.

"I'm coming. Just discussing my options." I direct a pointed look at her, hoping she'll slink back outside.

"Yeah, you are." She releases the door, but before it closes, she shouts, "Get it, girl!"

I turn back and grimace at Boyd, hopeful he didn't hear that. "Don't mind her. She's high on endorphins."

Boyd's residual laughter is fading, but a small smile remains. "This is the most entertainment I've had all day. All month." He spins around, toward the coffee paraphernalia, and continues, "How about salted caramel? Vanilla? Hazelnut?"

"Any of the above."

He hums a response, then starts fiddling with the equipment, pouring, shaking, and sprinkling. "You have a dog?"

"Yeah. My baby, Wilson. He's a labradoodle."

"A what?"

"Labradoodle? A cross between a labrador and a poodle."

He hands me a takeout cup he just filled with a mysterious concoction and replies, "Water?"

I feel my eyebrows collapse together as I swing my shoulder bag around so I can grab my wallet. "Water?"

He didn't just do all that work to hand me water.

"For Wilson. Does he need water?"

That offer is really touching. "Yeah, that would be great. Thanks."

He brushes off my attempt to hand him cash. "My treat. You don't even know if you like it. I'll bring water out in a second."

Instead of arguing, I tuck the cash in the tip jar, smile, nod, and walk outside before Ashlyn gifts Wilson to the next pedestrian to pass by. He's the only guy I'm seeing, and it *is* serious. I better not lose out on him, too.

8

BOYD

What's This?

Today has been the most boring day at this job since I started. The tips are usually garbage on Saturdays unless there's some kind of street festival or parade happening, but the worst part is the amount of time alone to think about everything else I could be accomplishing.

When the door opens and a muscular blonde woman walks in, I'm both relieved and annoyed that she is interrupting my inventory reporting. I make her a black coffee, then attempt to refocus on my paperwork. When the door chimes again a minute later, I never would have guessed it would be casual Sophie with a timid look on her face. Dressed in dark jeans and an oatmeal-coloured cashmere sweater, she is almost hard to recognize—or she would be if I hadn't committed the curves of her cheekbones and arch of her almond eyes to memory. A departure from the business-savvy woman I've seen every time before. Still as captivating. Still unavailable.

It doesn't take me long to remember that she was here not too long ago, holding hands with and sharing intimate conversations with the man she says she's serious about. Our confusing dynamic *isn't* confusing as long as I remember that truth. But then she makes me laugh, flipping my determination on its head.

Now I'm filling a mixing bowl from our back kitchen with water for Wilson. I haven't been around many dogs in my life, but I know they need water. I'm not sure if they can eat donuts, but I've heard of pup cups enough times to make him one.

I step outside and glance down the road in both directions to see if any customers look like they're planning to stop in, but it's clear. Sophie and her friend are having a hushed conversation as I approach. Before I can greet them, Wilson greets me.

He's not what I expected. He's pretty small, with copper coloured curly hair that looks like it's been cut recently.

"Hey there. I brought you something." I hold up the make-shift dog treat and ask Sophie if it's okay to give it to him.

She grins and nods.

Wilson is thrilled with his coconut whipped cream, slurping up the entire thing, minus what he splatters on my arm. I pat his head, so he moves closer to my legs, but instead of standing still, he spins in a circle, stopping with his butt against my knee.

"Are you a butt man, Boyd? Because it looks like your furry friend there wants you to scratch his. If you're offering..." The blonde shrugs one shoulder and looks over at Sophie, who is blushing again.

It's not often I'm left speechless. I am now. Not because I *can't* think of something to say, but because I know I shouldn't say it.

Before I can come up with a work-appropriate reply, Sophie chimes in, "Excuse her. She's just been released into society. She's on a learning curve." Then she boops her friend's nose, like she's chastising a dog. "Don't ask people about their butt preferences, mm-kay?"

Casual Sophie is funny. She's silly and relaxed. More than just her clothes have changed from the other occasions she's been here. She's got a gleam in her eye that she's never had on any of her previous drop ins.

Before I'm busted for studying her, I turn my focus back to Wilson, giving him the butt scratches he's asking for. I'm afraid to look at the expression on the blonde's face, so I train my eyes on Wilson's black leather designer collar, trailing my eyes up the matching leash. My knowledge of high fashion is limited, but I can guess what that cost. Certainly more than I make on a Saturday shift at the café.

Like a jolt of lightning, that reminds me of my position here. I'm the guy who serves coffee. I'm not supposed to be fraternizing with customers. Especially not taken customers I asked on a date and got shut down faster than a malfunctioning coffee maker. And I already learned my lesson with women like her. Ones who pay people to make their coffee instead of making it themselves. Ones who drive fancy cars. Ones who have designer dogs and buy them designer collars.

I straighten myself without looking at either woman. "Let me know if you need anything else. I'll grab the water dish after you leave." I give the dog one last pat on the head and return to my task.

Inside is quiet and isolated. It feels like there's a bustling metropolis on the other side of the glass, but I'm trapped in here with the permanent aroma of fresh-ground coffee beans and cinnamon buns.

Could be worse.

Fifteen minutes later, Sophie, Wilson, and the blonde vacate the patio. Of course they leave their cups on the table, so I have to clean them up. When I pick up one cup, which I'm sure was the blonde's, there's a note on it.

Call me! 416-555-7674.

I stare at the cup for a few seconds, contemplating whether I should put the number in my phone just in case. In case of what? I'm not sure. Maybe a cataclysmic event and all human race is destroyed except me and this blonde. I'll never know if I don't have her number to check.

What is wrong with me? I'm a rational guy. A logical one. I don't deal in a world of hypotheticals and what ifs. That's not my arena. The reality is, I'm not interested in the blonde, and it would be shady of me to take her number, knowing the woman I asked out is her friend.

Still, I find myself snapping a picture of the cup before I toss it in the trash. I pick up the bowl I used for Wilson and return inside.

The rest of my shift passes with a few more customers. None with dogs, which I find disappointing, even though I only have one dog on my mind. Wilson seems sweet, but deep down, I know my disappointment isn't related to him.

Something I need to rectify, because even if she wasn't in a committed relationship, I'm not going down that road again.

Mondays are always insanely busy for me. They result in the creation and consumption of a lot of caffeinated beverages. I'm exhausted by the time I walk in my front door at the end of the day. Holden is staring at his phone again, moping on the couch.

"What's wrong with your face?"

He gives me a side-eye glare when he looks up from his device. "Genetics. You're one to talk."

I stop behind the sofa, untying my apron. "No. Why do you look like you just sat on a toilet seat that someone else warmed up?" My attempt to add some levity to the conversation fails.

"That's... oddly specific," Holden deadpans. He missed the note of humour.

"You know what I mean. You look like you're trying to decide between two uncomfortable situations."

He doesn't reply as I take off my dirty apron and work shirt and drop onto the couch beside him.

"I know things have been a little weird between us, but I'm still your brother. I still care."

Again, he remains silent for several seconds, as if he wants to talk about whatever is bothering him, but doesn't want to confide in me. An error of my own doing because I haven't given him the impression he *could* talk to me for a long time. Holden and Phoebe are a lot closer with each other than they are with me, and that's my fault.

Finally, he replies, "It's nothing. I'm just brain fried from studying and stressed about these exams. So I guess you're right. I have to choose between studying more, or staying here for this conversation." The animosity in his response makes his words sting, but I can't be angry at him. He stands and walks up the stairs, leaving me to slump back with my face in my hands.

Another relationship I've failed at. That's something I should dedicate some work ethic to.

My office phone buzzes from the intercom, and Andy's hesitant voice broadcasts from the speaker. "He wants to see you."

He doesn't need to clarify. I know who he's talking about.

"Thanks, Andy. I'll go in a sec."

I wrap up an email to one French man who is happy to deal directly with me, which I can largely attribute to my time in France. We connected over French cuisine, and that opened the door for me to impress him with my business expertise. I do have a lot of contacts who respect me, and I'm grateful for them. I just wish I could say the same about all of them. Or at least more than forty percent. That mentality starts with my father, though.

The man I now have to face.

I walk past Andy's desk area and remind him to hold my calls until I return. An unnecessary reminder, but it gives me a pathetic ego boost to say it as I walk down the corridor.

"Can I go in, Joel?" I ask, giving him a smile.

"Yes, ma'am. He's waiting for you."

I take a deep breath and push the door open, finding Henry McNamara sitting at his desk underneath the six-foot wide *McNamara Enterprises* logo affixed to the wall. Just in case anyone was confused where they were by the time they made it all the way to the CEO's office.

"You wanted to see me?"

He doesn't look up, but gestures for me to come closer. Not to sit down, which means this will be a quick chat.

After he finishes whatever he's writing with a flourish, he addresses me. "The annual dinner for our Alma Mater is next Wednesday. Your mother and I will be attending, and I expect you to come too. I already bought a table."

I stifle a groan; the thought of spending the evening outside of work hours with my father and *his* associates isn't pleasant. Whether they'll ever consider me as an equal remains to be seen. At this point, I'd be surprised if they saw me as anything more than an object. Doesn't matter if I graduated from the same program as them or that I've been *McNamara Enterprises'* senior import and logistics executive for three years. It's not nearly as impressive as being a middle-aged man with narrow world views in an international industry.

"Is that all? I'm assuming Joel can send Andy the details?"

"Who?"

"Joel. Your assistant?"

"Sure. Or you could call your mother."

My resolve is faltering because I can't stop an audible sigh from escaping. I nod, then spin on my heel to leave.

"Sophie?"

I wonder if other grown women have the same visceral reaction to their father saying their name in that authoritative tone. It's like a hand around my throat. "Yes," I ask as I turn back to face him.

"I expect you to bring a suitable date." Then my father—no, my boss—waves his hand to shoo me out of his office.

Apparently, it's evidence of a fatal business flaw if a female shows up to an event without a date. Not just any date; a "suitable" date. Meaning someone who has a pedigree or a bank account to impress complete strangers. Someone who can have the personality of drywall dust, as long as their career sounds impressive.

When I return to my office, I park myself behind my desk so I can sort through my options for a date. The list is not long. Non-existent, really.

How pathetic is it that after fifteen minutes, my options boil down to my assistant—who has no interest in going on a date with a woman—or my twin brother?

"Andy? Can you come in here, please?" I call through the intercom.

My finger is barely off the button before he walks through the door. "Yes?"

This is humiliating. "Did Joel send you details for an event next week?"

"He did. About sixty seconds ago. Do you need a dress?"

"Well, I need a dress, but I need something else, too."

Andy appears apprehensive. He looks a lot less enthused than he did at the prospect of dress shopping. "Okay?"

"I need a date, Andy. Not a boyfriend. Not a carriage ride through the park. No hand holding. Just someone to sit in the seat beside me and schmooze with people we'll likely never see again."

"Okay…"

He's really going to make me spell this out for him, isn't he?

"Don't feel obligated to say yes. Saying no will not impact your job or my opinion of you. But…" I blow out a breath. "Will you be my date?"

My assistant, all five-foot-ten of handsome Baltic man, appears lost for words.

"You can help me choose a dress." I flash him a smile, despite feeling at my peak for pathetic.

"I have a standing Wednesday evening volunteer thing, but I can—"

"No." I put my hand up to stop that sentiment before he can even consider it. "You are not rearranging your schedule or anyone else's. Not to worry. I'll figure it out." My smile fades at the realization I have to ask my workaholic brother. It's hard enough to find a dress in seven days. Let alone a real date.

Even if Caleb wasn't working 100 hours a week, the chances of him showing up at an event, knowing our parents are going to be there, are slim.

Worst-case scenario, I show up alone, disappoint my father, and lose any ground I've made up in my job because I'm single. No big deal.

I arrive at Caleb's restaurant, hunting down another employee who looks like they'll be able to take me to him. Sure, I could have called, but a question like this requires finesse. Not to mention begging and puppy-dog eyes.

A woman walks past in a uniform, so I wave and call out to her, asking if I can see Caleb. Maria, according to her nametag, turns up her nose at me and tells me I can't. I assure her he'll want to see me, and after a bit of back and forth, she agrees to go ask him.

Three minutes later, she stomps back to where I'm waiting and instructs me to follow her.

My brother is hard at work when I walk in. "Hey. Give me a couple minutes. You can wait in my office if you want." Like our father, he doesn't look up from his task when he speaks to me. But I'd never tell Caleb I noticed that similarity.

"No, it's fine. I'll stay out of the way over here." I lean against a stainless steel table, taking in the flurry of activity in the humid kitchen. Not wanting to stay in here longer than necessary, I blurt, "I have a favour to ask."

He's silent for a second and I'm not sure if he's worried about whatever he's cooking or he's considering what I said. I don't like asking favours of anyone, and I know this one is a particularly tall order. If I told him I needed a kidney, he'd probably grab a filet knife and hand one of his to me on the spot. Asking him to spend an evening with our parents is less likely to be an automatic answer.

"Okay. What is it?" He slides out some scallops onto a pair of plates, then flicks a towel over his shoulder.

"I need you to come to a gala with me next week."

He gestures for me to walk toward his office. "My staff are not on their games today, so I only have a minute." He opens his office door, but I stall in the doorway when I look inside.

"Caleb? What the hell is this? You call this an office? This doesn't even qualify as a... dumpster."

"I know, but I haven't had time to sort through everything. I've got my necessary contacts, contracts, and purchase orders, so beyond that, I don't care right now." He squeezes past me to walk inside, then sits on the edge of his cluttered desk.

"This is not okay. You need someone with good business sense to get this organized for you." Time to implement the puppy-dog eyes.

"In exchange for?"

"Baby brother"—I scoff—"I am offended you think I would only offer help, expecting something in return." I walk in to inspect the damage. Maybe I can hire someone to clean this up and we can call it even for being my plus one.

"Soph, I can't take an evening off right now. We're booked every night, and none of the staff here are ready to handle it."

That statement deflates me, so I sink into the extra chair in front of his desk. "I was afraid you'd say that. I don't have anyone else to ask, as pathetic as that is, and Dad made it clear I need to bring someone. The male-dominated world of international business is already bad enough. Showing up as the poor single girl is even worse."

Caleb doesn't answer. He leans against the desk, arms crossed, his face going from one emotion to the next so fast, I can't get a read on them.

"What is happening to you? You just stared off into space and made the full range of emojis," I ask, studying his face for answers.

He finally directs his attention back to me, a smirk turning up the corner of his mouth. "Why don't you ask the barista? You obviously have a thing for him. Just give it a go."

"I can't ask him!" Even if I hadn't lied to him and told him I was in a relationship. "Could you imagine Dad's reaction?" The thought of facing my father's wrath for bringing a barista to an important event makes me nauseous. I scrunch up my nose, battling with the upset stomach. "It would be worse than if I brought you!"

The look on Caleb's face makes me laugh. It shouldn't but it does.

"Gee, thanks."

This is obviously not accomplishing anything. I stand from the tacky vinyl chair, using my purse as a shield for my churning stomach. "We both know it's true. I'll let you get back to work, though. Someday, I hope you'll make me something spectacular to eat."

My big little brother pulls me in for a hug, resting his chin on my head. "Once my staff is settled in, I'll make you something amazing. I promise. Love you, Soph."

"Love you too, little brother."

I exit the office before him and end up running into an old acquaintance, so I take a few minutes to catch up with her.

When I leave, I'm no closer to finding a 'suitable' date. No closer to pleasing my father, and I'm not sure I ever will be.

10

BOYD

My List of Things To Do

Once upon a time, I had lofty dreams and goals. My parents have afforded my siblings and me with more opportunities than we could ask for, even though they came here as immigrants with high school educations. They were determined and worked hard to achieve what they have. So I may complain about my mother's overbearing nature, my father's willingness to turn a blind eye to said overbearing nature, or their insistence on maintaining a strict family dinner schedule, but I am grateful to them both.

On the flip side, that comes with a lot of pressure. The unrelenting need to make their hard work pay off. The never-ending feeling that you have to be an even greater success because that's what they sacrificed for. For us. For me. It all has to be for something.

It took me a lot of years and a major detour to figure out what that something would be for me. Holden and Phoebe both decided on their "something" and never wavered. They both committed to their chosen purpose and haven't changed course. I envy that about them, but at the same time, my detour has led me here, and I'm proud of what I've accomplished.

"Boyd?" My sister draws my attention, breaking the same train of thought I have every time I enter my parents' house. "Do you want to hold her?" She gestures to Grace.

"Uh, sure." No, I don't really want to because she looks fragile and temperamental, but my sister can be terrifying, so I'm not about to turn her down.

She passes me Grace, instructing me to make sure I hold her head. I look into her piercing blue eyes that have already guaranteed she gets whatever she wants from my father and her father. The tiny thing has Phoebe's fierceness already. It doesn't take long before she begins fussing, but everyone else has left the room when I break the trance Grace had me caught in.

"Guys? Hello?"

No answer. Grace is getting louder and more determined. Whatever is upsetting her is out of my area of expertise. Which, when it comes to babies, I *have* no expertise.

"Phoebe? Aaron? Holden? Anyone?"

Grace is morphing from a beautiful little angel into a fire-breathing dragon in a hurry, and I'm too afraid that if I stand up, I'll drop her.

I try rocking and softly bouncing her, but it's not helping. Suddenly, I feel a vibration on my forearm, and she goes silent. I stare at her for a second, wondering if what I think just happened actually happened.

"You good?" Holden peeks his head around the corner. I know he's put a lot more effort into bonding with Grace than I have, so he's comfortable with her.

"She just farted on me. Is that normal?"

Before Holden can answer, she lets another blaster go, and I'm not convinced it was just a fart. My jaw drops, but I keep Grace held close to my chest. Even once I'm *certain* it wasn't just a fart.

Holden chuckles—because farts are a cheap comedic ploy no matter how old you get—and confidently lifts Grace from my arms, placing her head on his shoulder. "Phoebe can deal with this one. Apparently, the full-on butt explosions are normal. It was news to me too." He leaves the room with Grace and heads toward the back of the house.

Here I was thinking I got a defective niece because little girls are portrayed as sugar and spice and all things nice. There's no way pigtails and bows are going to mask that kind of firepower.

I suffer through dinner, once again listening to my mother discuss Grace's liquid bowel movements while she pours gravy on her food. If I don't choke this down, Mum will be on my hide asking what's wrong, oblivious to the real cause of my appetite loss. How does no one else see the connection?

Stop thinking about it. Focus on something pleasant. Coffee. Boston Legal. Free shipping. Sophie.

I drop my fork, surprised Sophie came to mind. Everyone except Holden looks at me, questioning me with their eyes. They'll have to try a lot harder than that to get the truth out of me.

"Sorry. Dropped my fork." I pick it back up to wave at them, as if they need clarification what a fork is.

Slowly, each family member returns to their disgusting conversation, while I return to my thoughts. Unfortunately, the comedic dynamic between James Spader and William Shatner doesn't consume my focus. Nor does the benefit of Amazon Prime. No, I focus on the brunette I shouldn't be thinking about.

Mercifully, my dad is distracted by Grace, and Mum is distracted by Holden. That means I escape my parents' house an hour later without being grilled about my day-dreaming and lack of conversation.

It turns out, returning to my empty house doesn't alleviate my torturous thoughts, and my head is too much of a whirlwind to sleep. What kind of masochistic moron continues thinking about a woman who is in a committed relationship? I'm not a home-wrecker. Right and wrong matter to me. Self-respect and integrity matter.

I head upstairs to my office and sort through some mail. I've been staring at this event information for two weeks, debating if I want anything to do with it. For my career's sake, I should go. But I need backup. I pick up the phone and dial my best friend's number.

"This better not be work related," she answers.

"Would you hang up if it was?"

She huffs. "Shut up. Aren't you supposed to be at your parents'?"

"I was. I got home a little while ago. What are you up to?"

"*Trying* to tell my son that we can't afford season tickets to Toronto SC next year." She groans, which is met with a grumble from Phoenix in the background. "He seems to think going to a few soccer matches is worth the trade-off for our apartment."

I collapse against the back of my office chair. "How much are tickets?"

"Nope. Don't even think about it. He needs to learn to accept no as an answer sometimes. You've done enough."

I've always had a soft spot for Phoenix. He was in first grade when Monica and I started working together, and I think part of me still sees him that way. The shy little kid who was trying to make sense of the world after his dad left. Monica's family disowned her when she got pregnant because that didn't fit into their plans for her, so she's been on her own since she was seventeen. And she's never once complained about it. She's always worked hard and been an amazing mother.

So as much as I'd like to swoop in and cater to Phoenix's wants sometimes, I've always tried to respect her word as final.

"Fine. But maybe we can catch a match sometime."

"That would require time off." She calls out something to Phoenix, but must have her hand over the phone because it's muffled. Then she returns to our conversation by asking, "Did you call for something?"

"Not really. Just to say hi, I guess."

"That bad, huh?"

I freeze. "What do you mean?"

"Boyd, you know I love you like my best friend and family rolled into one. But you never call just to say hi. You call for work schedule updates, to make plans for something, to check on us… never just for a chat. So, are you going to tell me?"

A huge part of me wants to confide in her that Sophie is stuck on my mind and she shouldn't be there. Confess that I keep thinking about someone who is in a committed relationship. But Monica would hate me for it. Phoenix's father cheated on her for years before she found out and they ended things. Even though I'd never step in between a happy couple, just knowing I've thought about the 'what ifs' would make Monica see me differently. So I keep it to myself until I can push thoughts of Sophie from consciousness. Permanently.

"Will you come to this stupid gala with me?" I blurt.

Over the years, we've catered several events together and Monica always makes them tolerable. She has a way of patronizing people with compliments they're too self-absorbed to see the irony in.

Silence.

"Mon?"

"Just trying to wrap my head around the word 'gala'. Gag. Sounds miserable."

That's almost the exact reaction I had when I found out about it. If it wasn't an important career move, I'd have shoved the paperwork through the shredder and slept soundly. "Please?"

"You know you're the only person I'd consider this for?"

"And I adore you for it."

She groans. "Fine. You owe me. Send me the details and I'll figure something out for Phoenix."

He shouts in the background, "I'm thirteen! I don't need a babysitter!"

"This child. I hope he realizes I'm saving up embarrassing stories about him from his potty training years."

"Like when you were teaching him to pee standing up," I prompt.

Monica starts howling. "But he didn't understand and his little poop dropped on the floor."

More evidence that bathroom humour never loses its lustre. Even I almost crack up. Phoenix shouts something in the background, but I don't understand over Monica's cackling.

Once she's breathing at a normal rate, I revert her attention back to the made-up reason for my call. "I'll text you the details. I'm sure Phoebe can hang out with Phoenix for a few hours. As long as he doesn't give Grace any potty training tips." Really, after the blaster on my arm earlier, I'd hate to think how that scenario would play out with her.

Monica starts babbling, attempting to form words through her laughter. Finally, with no sign of it letting up, I bid her good night and end the call when she huffs an acknowledgement. I hear Holden stomp in a moment later, so I tiptoe into my room and close the door in case he needs to use the office.

And instead of going to bed and falling asleep from sheer exhaustion like I normally do, I think about her.

11

SOPHIE

Of All the Gin Joints

I challenge every man who has ever complained about the discomfort of their "penguin suit" to spend several hours wearing an adhesive bra, pantyhose, and an elaborate gown. Not a single one of them would have anything bad to say about their bowtie and pants after suffering through an evening with silicone stuck to their under-boob. All in an effort to make themselves more appealing for someone else. Who ever decided a track suit gala was a bad thing?

On one hand, I enjoy getting glammed up—having my hair and makeup done, wearing a fancy gown and sky-high heels. It always makes me feel beautiful. On the other hand, I have a mild adhesive allergy, so this particular outfit could be catastrophic for my boobs.

After a quick glimpse in the mirror, I check my phone to confirm my car is here, then make my way out. Wilson is spending the evening with Celeste, but I'll pick him up the second I can escape this wretched event. He's slowly becoming more her dog than mine, but it's nice knowing they have each other. Especially with my long work hours.

The black Town Car is at the end of the walkway, the driver already waiting with the door open.

"Good evening, Miss. I'm Elton. Pleasure to be at your service."

"Elton, please, call me Sophie."

He smiles and nods, gesturing for me to get in the car.

Before I slip inside, I stop at the door. "This other stop we're making is to pick up a blind date I got sucked into bringing to this thing. I'll pay you an extra hundred dollars to bring him home when I say the word."

Elton chuckles, but clears his throat to recompose himself. "At your service, Miss… Sophie." He hands me a card with his cell number and instructs me to text or call if I'm ready to ditch my date. Worth every penny. It always pays to have a backup plan.

Twenty-two minutes later, Elton pulls up to an apartment building in Oakridge. We chatted like acquaintances the entire way. I appreciate his willingness to distract me. He's a new grandfather to a toddler his son and daughter-in-law adopted from Haiti. It's clear he's a proud Papa. Unlike my father, who is the reason I'm here to pick up a complete stranger Ashlyn set me up with. She met him at her gym, and insists he's "perfectly normal."

As my date strolls down the path in front of the dilapidated apartment complex, flicking a burning cigarette onto the path, I have half a mind to tell Elton to make a break for it.

"Don't go far tonight, Elton. I have a feeling I'll be needing you sooner than later."

"Now, Miss Sophie. Don't judge a book by its cover."

Sound advice in most instances, but I can't rationalize why someone would commit to an intense exercise regimen just to zap their lung capacity with cigarettes. Not only that, but he seems to think "black tie" meant he had to wear a black tie. That would be fine if his suit fit properly. It looks like he bought it his senior year of high school before he started working out.

Elton steps out of the car to open the opposite door for my date. As soon as the blond slides into the backseat, the cigarette smell wafts off of him.

I'm going to strangle Ashlyn.

"Wow. I figured you'd be hot if you're friends with Ash, but damn. The picture she showed me didn't look like this." He whistles long and low. "I'm Chad."

He must think he's irresistible, because he leans toward me and tries to plant his lips on mine. I refrain from choking him out with his black tie as I push him away.

"No, thank you. No. There's no kissing. This isn't a date, Chad, and even if it were, it wouldn't start with a make-out session." I hold my hand to his firm chest until I'm sure he'll keep his distance. "Tonight, I just need you to stay by my side. Don't speak. Just... look pretty, okay?"

He smirks, creating creases around his left eye. "Being pretty is my specialty."

Elton directs us southbound on Warden Avenue, toward the country club that's hosting the event tonight. He's making eye contact with me in the rear-view mirror every few seconds, and I feel like he's an adorable protective grandpa. He wouldn't be able to do much against this mass of muscle beside me, but aside from his forwardness, he seems harmless.

"Tell me something about yourself, Chad. What do you do for work?"

He squints his eyes, as if he's recalling something from deep within his memory vault, or he's debating if he wants to tell me the truth. "Right now, I'm doing security."

You have got to be kidding me. Ashlyn may have been my friend since our freshman year of university, but things are looking bleak for her right now. She knows how critical my parents are and my checkered dating history.

I mutter some words I wish I could say to my so-called best friend, then turn to Chad. "This night is a big deal. So when I say just look pretty, I mean it."

"Ashlyn didn't tell me you were such a crank." He rolls his eyes and turns to look out the rear passenger window.

All is well. It's too late for a crash course to get to know each other, and I have a feeling anything he told me would waste space in my brain, anyway. I'll just hope his skin-tight suit deters anyone from talking to him. Including my father. Even if I'll hear all about it from my mother in a lengthy phone call tomorrow or from my father in the office. Probably both.

But when I work sixty hours a week, spend my time off with my dog and elderly neighbour, and evidently have friends who attract guys like Chad, when do they expect me to find someone? Part of me wants to stay single just to spite them.

We pull up to the country club, so Elton opens my door and waits for Chad to slide out behind me. I brush my dress flat, trying to smooth out the wrinkles from sitting the last thirty-five minutes, then glance over my shoulder to make sure my reluctant date is following.

I walk a few strides before I feel an arm slip around mine.

"Part of looking pretty." Chad winks, and the playfulness on his face makes me relax with him a little.

"Thank you."

That earns me a smile, which displays his yellowing teeth, covered in nicotine stains. And just like that, the moment is gone. I face forward and continue to my destination, trying not to curse my brother for being too busy with work to accompany me tonight. One of these days, I'm going to show up at an event with someone who can hold a conversation and look the part. Chad here is oh-for-two.

As soon as we enter, I spot my mom. She's wearing her trademark red dress with crimson lipstick. She has one particular shade she's worn to every event since I was a kid. I lock eyes with her and a smile makes it halfway across her face before she spots my date and her shoulders slump. Perfect.

But next event, the option for me to come alone won't be presented. I'm still only half a person without a date. Not worthy of any accolades until there's potential for me to take on someone else's last name. I have a lot of sympathy for women who lived in the Middle Ages. My father still does.

Chad and I walk toward my parents, and I find myself clutching his arm until I see a familiar face. With a wide smile, I'm welcomed into an affectionate embrace.

"How are you? You look gorgeous." My Aunt Zara holds me at arms' length to look at my face. "No, you look ready to take on the world."

"I didn't know you were coming. You've just made my night. Are you sitting at our table?"

She nods her head. "Zach and I were last-minute seat fillers, so we're across the table from you. If anyone"—she leans in to whisper—"and I mean *anyone* gives you a hard time tonight, you know where to find me."

When I was young, Aunt Zara and my mom weren't very close, but I spent so much time at my grandparents', she was a staple of my childhood. Since then, she's been an endless source of support. Having her here tonight makes it more tolerable.

I pull her in for another hug as Zach walks up behind her, so I greet him and introduce my silent date.

"Nice to meet you, Chad." Zach holds out a hand.

Instead of shaking it, Chad stares at me as if he's awaiting permission. For half a minute, I was hopeful this wouldn't be so bad. But this buffoon has to make it seem like I dragged him here under threat of death. I give him an adamant, eyeball-bulging look that approves his silent request.

With that out of the way, I continue making the rounds, greeting important contacts and avoiding my father's displeased stare.

But as I make my way toward the tables near the stage, I'm met by another stare, which doesn't look displeased at all.

12

BOYD

It's a Small World

Just like in the coffee shop, I spot her as soon as she walks in. The difference, the distance between the counter and the door at the café is about twenty feet. Here, she's standing at least eighty feet from my spot by the stage, but I know it's her. She's next to some muscled jock with a neck bigger around than his head. It's not the same guy I saw her with at *Just Add Coffee*.

She is stunning. Like a mermaid in her human form. She's wearing a black sequin gown with the thinnest straps I've ever seen and a plunging back. It shimmers on her beige skin as she passes through the room. Her silky hair is cascading over her shoulders in loose curls, with some pinned into a fancy twist. Whoever the blond beefcake is, he's lucky. Not just because she's the most gorgeous woman in the room, but because when she walks in, she commands attention. And that has nothing to do with her looks. It's her confidence and air of authority she possesses.

I attempt to walk toward her, but I'm stopped by a few schmoozing couples who need me for one thing or another. My words are directed back at the people speaking to me, but my eyes are on her. I know it's wrong. She's taken. She turned me down when I asked her out. I shouldn't be focusing on her laugh as she speaks to a middle-aged couple, nor on the sway of her hips as she makes her way around the room.

"Boyd, are you listening?"

I rattle my head to free the distraction, so I can reply to Mr. Nicholls. "Sorry, Sir. What was that?"

Instead of repeating himself, he turns to see what my eyes were focused on. Once he makes the connection, he lets out a quiet whistle. "Miss McNamara. I can't fault your taste, but her old man is a tough nut to crack."

McNamara. As in *McNamara Enterprises*? As in the multi-million dollar import-export company that expanded into Toronto after starting with humble roots in a small town no one outside of it had ever heard of? *That* McNamara?

No wonder he whistled.

Not that I needed any more incentive to stop gawking at her, but that little tidbit of information makes the decision for me. "Sorry, Sir. You were saying?"

Mr. Nicholls drones on as Monica returns to my side. She gives me a questioning look, but doesn't interrupt the steady stream of memorized quarterly progress reports Mr. Nicholls is sharing. Like I care.

I see another couple waving me over, so I interrupt Mr. Nicholls and turn to walk toward the elderly pair. But before I cross the twenty feet to get to them, I lock eyes with a stunning brunette and forget how feet work. We gawk at each other for a few seconds as she steps closer. Monica tugs at my arm, which is all it takes for me to compose myself.

"Sophie." I nod and hope I can play this off as a casual encounter. I'm not sure what is more intimidating. Her family business or her.

"Boyd." She glances down at herself, smoothing her form-fitting dress.

The brief flicker of her running her hands down her body is an image that will live rent free in my mind until I die. The pink dress she wore to the café showed her soft curves, but this gown is a creation straight from Heaven.

"This… um… this is Chad. Chad, Boyd." She grabs the arm of the muscular guy tucked behind her, pulling him forward until he's a step in front of her. There's not an ounce of affection in the gesture. It's almost as if she's using him as a shield.

Still, my parents raised a gentleman. "Chad, pleasure." I acknowledge him, but don't offer to shake his hand. Instead, I turn my focus back to Sophie. "Is this a *new* boyfriend?" My tone is more accusatory than I intended. I meant to sound curious, not like a judgemental jerk.

"Aren't you going to introduce me to your…?" Sophie nods to Monica with a slight tilt of her head. "I recognize you from the coffee shop. Nice to officially meet you. Sophie." She one-ups my response to Chad with an enthusiastic handshake.

"Yeah." Monica draws out the syllable, dropping her hand back to her side. "I recognize you. Monica." She turns her head to me, intimidating me with one raised eyebrow.

Chad disregards the awkward introductions, turning to face Sophie. "Do you want a drink, Babe? I've got to go launch a butt shuttle, but I'll grab you something on the way back."

The three of us stare at Chad. I don't know about the women, but I'm trying to figure out if the term "butt shuttle" just left his mouth at a black-tie event. Judging by Sophie's scrunched up nose, she's asking herself the same thing.

"No… thanks. I'm good." Sophie redirects her focus to me and Monica as Chad walks away. "Sorry. This isn't really his scene."

Go figure. Never would have guessed that based on our brief encounter. Or his outfit.

"He seems… nice." An involuntary grumble escapes me when Monica elbows me in the ribs.

Sophie pulls her shoulders back, straightening her posture. I have no right to look at a woman—especially not a taken woman—like I do, but I can't stop myself from consuming every bit of her on display like a sculpture of my most specific dreams. Again.

"He is. Yeah, he *is* nice. And… pretty."

I mumble a combination of "good grief" and "kill me now," earning me a scowl from Sophie and another elbow from Monica. This evening is getting more insufferable by the second, and the thought of seeing Sophie on the arm of this moron for the entire evening is driving my mood south—which was already in Antarctica.

Without relaxing her eyes, which are framed with a deep, smoky eye shadow, Sophie starts, "What are you do—"

"Edwards, we need you over here," Mr. Benton interrupts. He steps beside me, and recognition lights his aging face. "Miss McNamara. Lovely to see you, as always."

"Good to see you, Professor Benton," she replies, her face morphing from irritated to receptive in an instant. Every hint of her scowl disappears as she addresses the portly professor.

"How have you been? Still kicking butt and taking names?"

Sophie looks down at the swirl-patterned carpet. "Something like that. You taught me well."

"You are too kind. I'm sorry to interrupt, but if you'll excuse us, I need Mr. Edwards for a few moments."

"Of course. Nice seeing you." The woman who flashed through half the emotions on the spectrum in a matter of minutes is the picture of poise as she spins to walk away. She only makes it a few steps before another middle-aged woman in a red dress with bright red lipstick clutches her arm and pulls her aside. A woman who looks like an older version of Sophie, I assume is her mother.

Monica makes her way toward the bar as Mr. Benton directs me into the corridor adjacent to the convention room, instructing me about what's coming for the evening. I nod and agree, but find myself wondering what happened to the guy Sophie brought to the café two weeks ago. Did they break up and she moved on to the blond? She said they were serious.

But whatever her relationship status is, it's not my business. I need to refocus on what is.

Forty minutes later, we've listened to countless speeches. Everyone else is seated at elaborate tables, enjoying a five-star meal, while I wait in the shadows. Monica flags me over to where she is enjoying her meal, but I don't have an appetite. I can see Sophie and her parents from my position, but I don't linger on her. She's seated between Chad and her father. I do look at Henry McNamara as he speaks and can feel the authority radiating off of him from here.

Another round of applause booms and fades as one speaker finishes, and Mr. Benton takes his place at the podium. He's a charismatic speaker with plenty of experience captivating a crowd. That much is obvious by the attention of everyone in the room.

He gives a brief introduction of who he is and why he's here, touching on his experience as a professor and board member at the *Montgomery Centre for Business and Law*. His reach in the business community is wide and esteemed. People hang on to his every word, coming to him for advice, prospects, or a pat on the back. Where Henry McNamara thrives on intimidation and brute force, Edwin Benton operates in a world of consideration and support. That's why he moved into a teaching capacity, because he admits he lacks the "bulldog" mentality needed to run a successful enterprise.

What he lacks in cut-throat business instincts, he makes up for with his analytical approach and a wealth of legal knowledge. I have deep respect for the man, and if the look on his face is any indication as he calls me out on stage, I'm one of the many recipients of his mutual respect.

It's not the look in his eyes I'm focused on, though.

13

SOPHIE

Hot To the Touch

My boobs are so itchy, I think I might die. The fabric in my dress doesn't have enough give for me to sneak a graze along the edge of the table or scratch with my clutch. I'm just stuck here, listening to endless speeches, picturing the raging allergic reaction my skin is having to this stupid "bra". Again, no man would ever complain about a suit if they had to deal with this malfunction for the ages.

Chad is finishing my meal—because I'm not a fan of rare prime rib—and informing me about the benefits of calorie tracking. He's convincing enough, I consider downloading an app so I can track my coffee and pastry consumption, but I'm distracted by a familiar name mentioned through the speakers.

"Boyd Edwards." Mr. Benton is clapping and smiling as Boyd makes his way out onto the stage. "This young man was my pleasure to instruct over the past few years. Now, it is my honour to present him with the Medal for Academic Excellence in our Masters of Business Administration/Juris Doctor double major program."

Everyone claps, some standing to show their support. I remain in my seat, frozen, trying to close my mouth. He's... a barista.

Except he's not. He is, but evidently that's not all of what makes up Boyd Edwards. *Boyd Edwards, MBA/JD*, to be more specific.

Boyd doesn't speak. He just stands beside Mr. Benton, who rambles on about how Boyd is "one to watch" and sells him as the greatest legal-minded business student he's seen in the last twenty years. Apparently Boyd will be ripe for the picking after his call to the bar.

I look at my father, who is practically drooling over the prospect.

Once Mr. Benton completes his speech, everyone applauds as they exit the stage. Seconds later, the servers bring out dessert. Here I thought Boyd was here to bring main courses and appetizers to the mass of people filling the tables, but joke's on me. He's here to be the star of the show. With a beautiful woman on his arm.

Around a bite of crème brûlée, my father points out, "You were speaking to him earlier."

Of course he was watching my every move.

"For about twelve seconds. I don't know him."

"I suggest you *get* to know him. We need someone like him. Make it happen."

My jaw tenses with a spoon in my mouth, sending a shooting pain through my teeth. My position at *McNamara Enterprises* already feels fragile. I'm doing the work, and doing it well, but people on the outside looking in assume I have the job because of my last name. No way am I going to let some random guy show up and risk my future just because he's part of the boys' club.

"Sophie, this is non-negotiable. I expect him to be in my office by the end of the week. After tonight, everyone will be gunning for him."

I want to scream at my father, 'So let him go work somewhere else. You already have someone to ensure the success of your company.' But I'm too afraid of burning a dilapidated bridge. One that splinters a bit more each day. "Fine."

"And get rid of your date. He's an embarrassment."

I'm not Chad's biggest fan, but he doesn't deserve that. He's still a person, and he came here as a favour. I apologize to him quietly, but he shrugs it off—my father's crass comment falling right off Chad's broad shoulders. He didn't touch his dessert on account of his strict competition diet, which apparently only leaves room for near-raw red meat, so he slides his chair out without a word to either of my parents. Not that my mom was any more receptive toward him than my father was. He waves at Zach and Zara across the table, tosses his napkin on his plate, and turns to leave.

"Let me walk you out, at least." I stand to follow Chad outside, texting Elton as I walk. We step outside and I apologize again for my father.

"Don't sweat it. I'm used to people like him. Guys with money who think the rest of the world is beneath them. I'm sure once I become a cop, he'll beg to use his money to get out of a speeding ticket."

"A cop?"

He raises his light blond eyebrows in an expression that says 'duh' without a sound. "That's why I'm working security. And why I work out so much. I've got a physical to pass."

I'm so stupid. Elton was right. It was wrong of me to judge Chad based on his appearance. After seeing Boyd on stage and hearing the accolades he's accumulated, it seems this is a bad habit of mine.

Speaking of Elton, he pulls up the Town Car in front of Chad and me, getting out to open the back door.

"I really am sorry, Chad. Thank you for showing up for me tonight."

He nods and disappears into the back of the car. Elton assures me he'll return once he drops Chad back at home and will wait for me as long as I need. Hopefully, it won't be too late. I miss my dog.

Instead of rushing back inside, I take a moment to chastise myself for being no better than my father. His judgemental superiority complex has always infuriated me, and Chad just made it clear that I've been guilty of the same thing. I breathe in the air blowing off of the lake and allow the breeze to whisper over my clammy skin. Now I just need some relief from my bra situation. I scan my surroundings and deem it safe to shift the fabric of my dress and reach my hand inside to scratch some intimate places.

"Did your boyfriend leave?"

I freeze, much like I did when Boyd was introduced on stage. This time, he's standing behind me and I have my hand inside my tight gown, cupping my boob. Awkward.

I consider my options, and they're no more appealing than they were when I blurted a lie because I made an assumption about his job. I slip my hand out and turn to face him, hopeful he couldn't see what I was doing. "Yeah, he had to work. He's… a cop." What am I doing to myself? Digging a bigger hole, evidently. "Where's your date?"

"Oh, a pretty cop. That's cool." He doesn't acknowledge my question about the woman he's here with.

I'm starting to discover that Boyd has a very dry, sarcastic sense of humour. I'd find it endearing if I wasn't so annoyed about my father's demands. "Congratulations… on the medal. That's a big deal."

He shrugs off my compliment. "Thank you. Everyone else thinks it's a bigger deal than it is."

I want to hate him for being so blasé about an achievement I narrowly missed out on with a *single* major. But I can't.

I'm too impressed. "No, it is. Being top of your class in a double major is a huge accomplishment."

He brushes off my praise again. "How long ago did you graduate?"

I don't want to talk about myself. Nor my academic pursuits. If I'm going to appease my father, I need to make this about Boyd. "I didn't know you were a student."

"You never asked. Technically, I'm not anymore. I'm doing my LPP… Law Practice Program. Four months training; four months placement." He scrubs his hand over his trimmed chin stubble. "Working at the café gives my brain a forced break. Making coffee and talking to customers kept me sane through school."

Having been a student who ate, slept, and breathed the information being thrown at me, I can respect needing that break. "And now?"

"Now what? Staying sane?"

A smile threatens to appear, but I need to stay in business-Sophie mode. "No, what are your plans for work now? Surely you don't want to work as a barista forever."

His eyes narrow, and he takes a half step back. "I like my job."

I close my eyes and exhale, resenting how much I'm sounding like my father. "Sure, but I doubt you worked toward your JD so you could serve coffee."

His facial expression doesn't relax at all.

As much as I don't want Boyd coming into my family business, leapfrogging me in a position I've worked hard for, my father won't take no for an answer. I've got to sell this and hope Boyd aspires to a different career path. "Point is, your skill set would be beneficial to *McNamara Enterprises*. If you're interested, we'd love to have you come in this week and talk about career opportunities."

He pauses for a beat before he replies, "It's Wednesday."

I stare at him, trying to figure out how that's relevant. "And?"

"I'm working the next two days. Long days. Training and the coffee shop."

At least he's a loyal employee, committed to his job.

"Okay. Why don't I come into the café? We can figure out a time that works."

He steps toward me, narrowing the gap he created a moment ago. "You can tell me the truth, you know."

"Wha—" I swallow hard and straighten my posture, just as my mother taught me. Shoulders back, chin out, stand tall. "I don't know what you mean."

With no readable expression on his face, he states, "You just want to have another one of my world-class flat whites."

The flood of relief I feel is startling, prompting me to "Ha!" an obnoxious laugh. "I'll hand it to you, there. Your coffee is fantastic. That's why I keep coming back." That's another lie. Coffee was fantastic, but it had very little to do with my repeat business.

For the first time all evening, I look at Boyd—really look at him. His tux fits him perfectly, with the black sateen lapels flat against his chest and not a wrinkle to be seen. His white shirt is crisp, with a neatly executed bow tie. He could be on the cover of Forbes and not look out of place. There's no sign of a hipster barista here tonight.

He interrupts my gawking by asking, "Who was the other guy at the café?"

My face twists of its own accord when I realize what he's asking, combined with his inquiry earlier about my 'new boyfriend'. Eww. "That was Caleb. My brother. Twin brother, actually." It never occurred to me that any on-lookers would think Caleb was my—gag—boyfriend. Did Boyd seriously think I'm that self-absorbed, I'd date someone who looks just like me? I just wanted Caleb to taste the coffee.

Whatever Boyd thinks about that revelation, he doesn't express it with facial cues or body language. He's going to make an excellent lawyer.

"Everything okay out here?" Aunt Zara steps around a teardrop-shaped boxwood bush that adorns the country club entrance.

Just the excuse I need. "Good, yep." I walk toward my aunt, looping my arm through hers. "I'll see you tomorrow around 5:15," I call over my shoulder, looking at the man who I'll do anything to stop from taking the job I've earned. And deserve.

14

BOYD

Cold on the Inside

Sophie disappeared last night and left me in her wake, contemplating her offer. I've never considered working at *McNamara Enterprises*, but I'd be foolish to pass up getting my foot in the door. My LPP will take until April to complete, then I have to wait for the call to the bar. If they're willing to hold a position for me until then, it could be a good option.

The entire morning, I've been sidetracked, weighing the pros and cons. The greatest pro? Seeing Sophie every day. The greatest con? Seeing Sophie every day.

Monica has asked no less than eighty questions about Sophie—most of which I don't have answers to. I told Monica that Sophie rejected me when I asked her out, but never explained more than that. At the time, she told me she was glad I put myself out there, but I disagree. I would have preferred to stay in my comfort zone. It's *comfortable* there.

Sophie walks into the café at 5:20, looking unsure, but as soon as I meet her gaze, she straightens and pulls her shoulders back—a habit I've noticed. She does it often, as if she's putting on a persona.

I nod her over to bypass the line. "Already have your drink. I'll be out in a second. Do you want anything to eat?"

She stretches herself to look at the pastry displays around the corner. "Oh, no thanks. Too much crème brûlée last night."

"Kay. Give me thirty seconds."

I turn to remove my apron and grab our drinks I made moments ago, then inform Monica I'm taking a break. She smirks as her eyes dance between me and Sophie. My expression back to her makes it clear this is not what she thinks it is. That ship has sailed. Never mind. It sank in the harbour... still tied to the dock.

Outside is the perfect temperature to enjoy a coffee. Sophie is at the same table she was seated at when I made my failed attempt at asking her out. I'm assuming she doesn't see or hear me coming, because she's furiously scratching her chest as I approach, much like last night. I set our drinks down and sit opposite her, watching as her face turns pink.

"Um, hi. Sorry... I—"

"Don't let me interrupt... again." I hold my hands up in surrender, hoping to lessen the unexplainable tension between us.

"That's embarrassing." She slides her coffee in front of her, gripping it with both hands. "Okay, moving on. Henry was really impressed by everything Professor Benton had to say about your potential and academic prowess." She says the last bit through gritted teeth. "He'd like to meet you to discuss job opportunities."

"Your father?"

She narrows her eyes and presses her lips together, but her face relaxes as fast as it tensed. "My boss, ye—"

"Why didn't he speak to me himself? It seems a bit weird he's sent you to fetch me."

"The big boss never gets his own coffee. He has lackeys to do that."

"You're a lackey? I thought you were a senior executive."

She scoffs. "We're not here to talk about my job title. I can see you're committed to your work, which is a necessity in our company. You have to be married to the job. If you have a problem with that, don't waste time pursuing this further."

"What about you? Are you married to the job?"

She sets her coffee down hard enough, some splashes out the opening. "I have to be. It's my legacy. I'm fully committed to my work and this business. So much so, I barely have time for a social life. " Her eyes shoot wide open, and she stammers, "I mean, every time Brad takes me out, it's to work events for one of us."

Who is Brad now?

"You mean Chad? Your boyfriend?"

Her face looks more surprised than it did when I caught her scratching herself. "That's what I said. Chad."

"Chad, Brad. Same difference."

We stare at each other for a moment. She's avoiding eye contact and I'm struggling to read her. Each time her eyes dart up toward the small canopy over the door, I get a stronger impression she's lying. Her story has so many holes in it, if it were an alibi, it wouldn't hold up in court. Failing to make eye contact is a telltale sign someone is being dishonest.

That's why I press her, like I would with anyone in a mock trial. "So, the guy you came here with is your brother? Chad Brad, the nice, pretty cop, is your boyfriend? And your blonde friend—"

"Ashlyn." She finally looks at me.

"Ashlyn," I repeat. "She's... intense." That's the most polite word I can think of.

"Too many endorphins." She waves with her hand as if she's wafting away that topic of conversation. "Anyway, what do you say about getting an appointment on the books to meet with Henry? Tomorrow?"

I'm not ready to give up my line of questioning yet. Time for a redirect. "Tell me about Chad. How did you two meet?" I do my best to feign interest in her love life.

She seems even less interested than I am, but she looks at me with confidence in her eyes. "Through Ashlyn. They workout at the same gym. CrossFit."

That explains why Ashlyn looks like she could bench press me and the iron chair I'm seated in. Chad's physique was also obvious under his ill-fitting suit, but his personality gives me the impression I'd stand a better chance against him in an arm-wrestle than I would against Ashlyn. She appeared both strong and intelligent. In my experience with lawyers, strategy and intelligence win out over brute force every time.

"What about you? You asked me out, but you and Monica were pretty cozy."

I lean forward and say softly, "Were you watching me, Sophie?"

"No! I just… noticed."

"Monica is a good friend. Has been for years. I asked her to tag along to make it less miserable. Like Brad Chad, those things are not my scene."

"Oh." She looks like she's warring with herself over pressing the subject further.

"So, tell me more about your friend Ashlyn. She left me her number, and I think I might give her a call." I won't, but I want to circle back around to her connection to Chad and get to the bottom of this.

Sophie's eyebrows pull together. "She's engaged. Like final stages of wedding planning, engaged."

That doesn't make any sense. Why would she leave me her number, then? I doubt the butt scratches I gave Wilson were enticing enough to call off an engagement. I pull out my phone and open the photo I took of the takeout cup. "See? She left a note for me to call her."

Sophie looks at my phone, then at me as if she's studying both. "That's a baby."

I spin the phone back to look at the image. Sure enough, a recent photo of Grace covers the screen. "Sorry. Must have swiped by accident."

"She's cute. She yours?"

I shake my head, then make a second attempt to show Sophie the message Ashlyn left. "See?"

Sophie examines the number for a split second, and her narrowed eyes return. She mutters, "You can delete it. Trust me. That number won't do you any good. Jim is her soulmate."

Something about her reaction tells me I should hang on to it.

"Anyway, you're not inspiring a lot of hope with your legal genius, Boyd. You can't stick to the topic at hand."

"On the contrary. My legal genius has helped me redirect the conversation back to what I want to talk about."

"If you're not interested in the job, I'm wasting my time here. You could have just said that from the get go." She attempts to stand, but the heavy chair trips her up, so she drops back into the seat. Before she can shimmy out, I place a hand on her forearm.

Our eyes zero in on the contact, then I refocus on her face. She draws her gaze up from my hand and gives me a questioning glance.

"Sorry. It's not that I'm not interested, but I've heard murmurings about your father, and I'm not sure it will be the right fit for me."

"Murmurings?"

"You can't be blind to his reputation. He's cut-throat and not well liked. That's not the kind of company culture I want to get sucked into." I hope she doesn't take offence to my very watered down description of her father's reputation.

She blows out a breath, then tips her cup to drain the contents—though I'm certain it was already empty. "I know what people say. My only concern right now is what you're going to say to my request."

Props to her for staying on point. I commend her determination. But if she wants something from me, I want something from her first. I don't know why I care, but I ask anyway, "What's the deal with you and Brad Chad? Honestly."

This was a mistake. Coming here was a mistake. Talking to him again was a mistake. Lying in the first place was a mistake. I'm on a roll. So I can keep rolling, or I can put an end to the charade.

I prop my elbows on the table and rest my face in my hands. That lasts for two seconds before I paint my confidence back on. "Fine. He's not my boyfriend."

Boyd's expression is a mixture of victorious and hurt. "So, this serious boyfriend you have?"

This is not going to bode well for getting him into Henry's office.

"I lied."

Boyd leans back in his chair, all traces of victory having disappeared. "Why? I mean, if you didn't want to go out with me, you could have said no."

"It's complicated. Not to be cliche, but it's not you. I have…" No, I'm not going to dive into my dating history or my perpetual need to maintain my father's approval. "My reasons."

"Reasons. Ones that justify lying instead of being a decent adult?"

His characterization of my response makes me clench my teeth. With them still gritted, I reply, "In all fairness, I don't know you from Adam. So as far as I know, women are within their rights to refuse a date, however they see fit."

"That's my point. You could have said no for any reason. Why did you lie?"

He won't understand. Unless someone has direct experience with someone like my father and all of his cronies, they don't get to judge me for my decisions. I can't exactly say 'because you're a barista,' because that lacks a lot of context. Saying that makes me sound like a pretentious princess who won't date outside of her tax bracket. That's not the reason. Well, it is, but it isn't. And yes, I could have just said no. I wish I did. But at the moment, I was more concerned about sparing his feelings and thought that was the safest bet. Apparently not.

"It's complicated."

He leans forward, resting his elbows on the table, mirroring my gesture from moments ago. "So uncomplicate it. You want me to meet your father? I want the truth. Or is that something your family is incapable of?" Boyd cringes at his words and starts to sputter a lame apology, but I cut him off.

"You've obviously made up your mind, and I'm just wasting my time here." I fish out a five-dollar bill from my purse and drop it on the table because there's no way I'm allowing him to pay for my drink. I will not owe him for anything. "I'm sure you have more important things to be doing than wasting your time with a liar."

"Soph—"

"No, you've formed an opinion. About me, the job, and my father. But he's the one thing you're *not* wrong about." I stand with enough determination this stupid thousand-pound chair can't stop me. The iron scrapes across the brick patio, punctuating my movement with a wretched metal grinding sound.

Boyd doesn't move or say another word. My inner monologue is screaming to rip into him about why I lied. Why I turned him down, even though I wanted to say yes. There's no way I can formulate the words to make them sound better. It's not a situation that can be explained in a few words, because my family dynamic requires a college-length essay to summarize the complexity of it. My dating experience is its own psychological journal, awaiting analysis.

But my traitorous mouth can't rein it in. "I've been in a lot of one-sided relationships. Ones where guys in dead-end jobs see me as a meal ticket or an easy route to a better job they don't have to work for. I promised myself *and* my brother that I wouldn't get sucked into another situation like that."

I watch as Boyd flashes through a few unreadable expressions before he stands and levels me with a glare, his jaw protruding forward slightly, which makes his feelings *very* readable. "You said no because you thought I was a deadbeat who would use you for a job?"

"Not exactly, no. I said no because I learned the hard way that most guys aren't interested in me. They're drawn—"

"Guys in *dead-end jobs*?" His words drip with so much anger, I'm worried we're attracting a crowd, but only a few passersby turn their head our way and continue walking.

I knew if I tried to explain, it would come out wrong. "That's not the whole—"

"Wow. I can't believe I asked you out in the first place. Thanks for helping me dodge *that* bullet. Since I'm a lowly barista." He scoffs and steps back, turning to face the sidewalk.

Surprisingly, tears burn my eyes, but they're nothing to do with Boyd. They're because I fear failing my father, and I've royally screwed up. Just like he probably anticipated I would.

"That's not fair." My voice is weak, trying to defend myself. "What do you want from me? You're mad I lied; okay, I get that. But you're mad I told the truth, too?"

He takes another step away, then spins back to face me. "I'm not mad at you for either. I'm mad at myself for thinking you were different."

There's a note of anguish in his voice that spurs my outrage over the situation. He's talking as if our brief conversations warrant me being labelled as a villain. "It must be nice to live in a black and white world, Boyd. Not all of us have that luxury. You have *no* idea what it's like for me. Why I reacted the—"

"You turned me down because you assumed I didn't have a six-figure job. Got it."

We stare at each other for a moment, but a couple exits the coffee shop to find a seat on the patio.

Despite the hurt and anger I'm feeling, I won't leave without saying one last thing. I step forward so I can keep my voice low. "You have no idea what my life is like or what I've had to overcome. What I *still* face every single day. You might see one thing, but I promise, it's not the entire picture. So yeah, I'm sorry I lied, but it was never because I'm a wretched gold digger who can't see beyond someone's job."

He scrubs his hands over his face before tucking them both into the pockets of his pants. "I never said you were."

"You implied it," I snap.

Whatever my feelings are about this interaction, I do respect that this is his job and I won't put that in jeopardy.

"Thanks for the coffee." I brush past him towards the opening in the ornate iron railing separating the patio from the sidewalk, and march down the street to my SUV.

I'm upset about the interaction, but another thought dominates my consciousness. Henry McNamara is not going to be happy.

I don't know how to face my father. Rather, my boss. If he was just my father, I wouldn't fear him as much, but it's a different story when he holds my future over my head. Like I'm strapped into a guillotine and I don't know when it will drop.

Andy pokes his head back in my office after leaving moments ago to complete the task I asked him about. "He's expecting you in five minutes."

"Thanks, Andy."

To give myself extra time to gather my thoughts, I stroll down the hallway earlier than necessary. The hours between my disaster meeting with Boyd yesterday and arriving at work this morning have only amplified my anxiety. I brace myself for the uncomfortable conversation that needs to happen, but I'm not prepared for. It will just get harder the longer I put it off, though, so I better break the news.

"Hi, Joel. Can I go in?"

"Yes, ma'am. He's expecting you." He leans over and whispers, "He's in a good mood today. Try not to spoil it."

I swallow hard. Joel is a nice guy. I don't have the heart to tell him I'm about to make his day a whole lot worse, so I give him a weak smile and scurry past. I take a deep breath as I open the door, and find Henry McNamara smiling as he hangs up his phone.

It's unnerving.

"Sophie, come in." Not only is he smiling. He's welcoming me.

My good sense says I should take off at a run in the opposite direction, pack my bags, and move to Nunavut. I'm sure their remote areas could benefit from my expertise, and I've always loved polar bears.

My pride won't allow that. "I went to speak with Mr. Edwa—"

"I know. He told me you were persuasive. He's coming in to meet with me at four."

16

BOYD

We Are Enemies

I rearranged my schedule so I could meet with Henry McNamara today. If I'm being honest, I don't want to work for him based on his reputation, but the pragmatic part of me decided I should see what he has to say. Still, even if he offers me a six-figure starting salary, I'm not going to make things easy for him. Maybe it's cocky, but I know there are plenty of companies gunning for me. I don't have to take a job I don't want. And I don't *want* this job.

But I felt bad for how Sophie and I left things, and I know, from the ever-churning rumour mill, Henry McNamara doesn't handle not getting his way very well.

"He'll see you now." A friendly man with black hair and thick-framed glasses nods to his left toward the oak door.

"Thank you." I push up from the leather club chair in the waiting area and enter the large office.

Henry looks just as serious as he did two nights ago at the gala. He's not the kind of guy you get a warm fuzzy feeling from. I'd imagine if he ever hugged anyone, it would feel like being surrounded by a cactus. Or like an iron maiden from medieval times. Kind of like my mother.

"Take a seat. Can I get you a coffee or anything to drink?" Henry stands from his chair and gestures to one on the opposite side of his desk.

I cringe at the thought of drinking office coffee. "No, thank you."

"Very well." He unbuttons his suit jacket and sits back down.

For the next twenty minutes, Henry briefs me on *McNamara Enterprises'* mission statement, goals for the future, and employment benefits. What I hear is a business entirely driven by profits, and they use those profits to bribe their employees to put up with the poor company culture. I immediately recognize areas I'd make changes, but even if I were to accept a position, I'd be on the bottom of the totem pole. My opinion wouldn't matter for years.

Henry tells me about the "ideal" job, and the benefits for me and the company if I were to accept it. He's willing to offer me part-time hours until I complete the requirements to fulfil my JD, then I can start immediately into a full-time position. He lays it all out, making it seem like an opportunity that's too good to pass up.

He's an effective salesman. Until he says, "I'm not leaving this company in the hands of my daughter. I know you've spoken with her, so you probably understand where I'm coming from. No woman will ever be cut out for this business."

I blink a few times, trying to refocus my eyes, expecting myself to be in some kind of time warp where I land back in the 1840s. But no. I'm still seated in the office with modern decor and an out-of-date CEO. "No, I'm afraid I don't understand."

Henry leans forward, drawing the tips of his fingers together in front of his face. "I've seen successful companies fold under the control of women. They're emotional and not cut out for this world."

Again, I'm stunned silent. I want to remind him of some of the most epic business failures of all time. Blockbuster, Pan Am, and Compaq all suffered catastrophic losses because they refused to innovate or keep pace with their competitors. Their out-dated and profit-focused mentality was the cause of their demise. I'd say *McNamara Enterprises* ticks both of those boxes. In contrast, companies like Nasdaq, General Motors, and Best Buy have all thrived under a female CEO. Not to mention, in my brief encounters with Sophie, I didn't get the impression she was incapable of anything.

I finally find my voice just to say, "Thank you for the offer, but I don't think I'm who you're looking for."

Henry's jaw tightens and his eyes narrow at me.

"I don't believe in stringing anyone along, so I appreciate your time, Mr. McNamara, but I'm going to pass."

Through gritted teeth, he replies, "That would be a mistake."

A mistake would be staying here to discuss this any further. "I'll see myself out."

I exit the office just as a growl that rivals a grizzly sounds from behind me. The polite receptionist's eyes widen.

I send him an apologetic look. "Could you tell me where Sophie McNamara's office is?"

He gives me a kind smile and instructions to head down the hall.

When I reach my destination, a young brunette man is seated in the receptionist area, wearing a headset, typing furiously.

"Excuse me." I wait for him to make eye contact. "Would it be possible to take a few minutes of Soph—Miss McNamara's time?"

He studies me from behind his computer screen. "Who should I say wants *to take a few minutes of her time?*" He smirks, lowering the mouthpiece on his headset.

"Boyd." My voice cracks speaking one syllable because the skinny receptionist makes me more nervous than Henry McNamara ever did. I didn't realize coming down here, I'd have to face Sophie's real guard dog. I try again, "Boyd Edwards."

"Okay, Boyd Edwards. Take a seat there. I'll see if she has a few minutes for you." He winks at me and gestures to the chairs against the opposite wall. They're the same as the ones outside of Henry's office, but these feel far more intimidating.

I lean back in the chair, scanning the area. It's devoid of much character, with a few fake potted plants and abstract art on the walls. The chair rail is painted a pristine white, with the bottom of the walls a medium grey and the top half a subtle damask-patterned wallpaper. I question their design choices for a brief second before I question my own decision to be here. My immediate urge to warn Sophie she's wasting her time here, slaving for a man who is never going to value her dissipates, and I lose all confidence in doing what I thought was the right thing.

A clearing throat draws my attention to the reception area.

"She has five minutes for you." The man gestures to the door that sits slightly ajar.

There goes my opportunity to take off before he returned. I stand, brushing my sweaty palms on the knees of my pants. "Thanks. I'll be quick."

"Not too quick, I hope." He winks again, which propels me forward faster than necessary.

I enter the comfortable office, adorned with soft grey chairs, a heavy black desk, and shelves of books and framed diplomas lining the wall behind Sophie.

She looks up as I walk in, tugging off her black cat-eye glasses and setting them on the papers in front of her. "Mr.

Edwards. What can I do for you?" Her tone is abrupt and cold. All business.

"Sorry to stop in unannounced but—"

"Andy announced you. Should I congratulate you on your new job?"

After speaking with her father, I understand her demeanour a little better, so I let the snark in her voice slide without acknowledging it.

"Why did you want me to take this job?"

She inhales a deep breath and takes her time releasing it. "If I'm being honest, I didn't."

I'm still standing on the far side of her office, but I choose to keep my distance. Her presence is also more intimidating than her father's.

"Why?"

Apparently she doesn't want to maintain the wide gap, because she gets up and walks around her desk. She looks as stunning in her royal blue skirt suit as she did in her gown. The white blouse she wears underneath the fitted jacket is buttoned all the way to the top. It looks conservative, but there's no hiding her feminine curves. She sits on the front edge of her desk, crossing her arms and ankles. "I have my reasons. So when do you start?"

If I were in a joking mood, I'd tease her or try to get her worked up before I confessed, but I'm not. "Never. I told your father I'm not the right fit."

She uncrosses her arms and places one hand on each side of her hips, pushing herself upright. The movement strains the buttons keeping her chest contained. "Why did you say that?"

I'm torn whether to confess what her father said or play off my decision as my choice. The part of me that understands complicated family dynamics doesn't want to sully Sophie's view of her father. "I want to focus on finishing my JD, then I'll re-evaluate."

Her shoulders drop a couple of inches as her arms bend, relaxing her rigid posture. Her facial expression also softens, so she's no longer glaring. "That makes sense, but Henry McNamara is unlikely to give you a second chance."

"I know."

The door opens behind me, and the receptionist pops his head in. "Miss McNamara, you're needed in your next meeting." He studies me with a tilted grin, undeterred when I make eye contact. "Do you need a few more minutes?"

I glance back at Sophie, who looks indifferent.

"Thanks, Andy. I think—"

"No. I was just leaving," I interrupt. "Thank you for your time, Miss McNamara. And for considering me for the job." I attempt to keep my tone professional so Andy will stop looking at me like I'm a gourmet meal he wants to devour.

I send Sophie a nod before I exit the room and traverse the hallway back to the elevator, filled with regret. Henry McNamara didn't deserve my time, but my bigger concern is that he doesn't deserve Sophie's. And it's not my place to tell her.

She's *just* a customer.

15

SOPHIE

Alpha Dog

Not only am I confused why Boyd really turned down a job offer, but baffled why he came to my office. After how we left things yesterday, I assumed he'd never speak to me again. Not unless he took a job here and Henry granted him more authority just because of a box he ticks on medical forms.

But it doesn't look like that's happening. I should feel some relief knowing that. Instead, I feel trepidation and anxiousness over who Henry will set his eye on in the future. I'm on board with hiring new people who can usher *McNamara Enterprises* into the next fiscal year and push us to make changes to keep pace with competitors. More than just on board, I'll encourage it. But I won't sit back and watch as someone slips in here and takes my job. Family business or not, I deserve this position based on work ethic and qualifications. Very few other people can claim they've been learning this business since before they lost their first tooth.

Andy pokes his head in my door again after leaving a moment ago. "Mr. McNamara would like to see you."

Judging by the look on his face, it's not a social visit. Not that I'd expect it to be, because not once in my life has my father ever asked how I was doing.

"Thanks, Andy. I'll go now." I straighten my blazer when I stand, suddenly feeling like it's strangling me.

The walk to his office is a repeat of the apprehension-fuelled trek from this morning.

Joel's face only catapults my unease into full-fledged anxiety. The deepened wrinkles on his forehead are pronounced by the upturn of his eyebrows. "Go on in, ma'am."

I take a steadying breath and march through the door with as much confidence as I can muster. It's hard to hold on to when I see Henry's scowl.

"Are you proud of yourself for wasting my time?"

I bite my tongue, holding in the testy retort I'd rather reply with. Instead, I ask, "How did I waste your time?"

"You arranged to have Boyd Edwards come in to meet with me, and he wasn't even interested in the job."

What I wouldn't give to have been a fly on the wall for their conversation. I'm assuming Boyd wasn't forthcoming with the full reason he said he didn't want to take the job. "I didn't know he was coming to meet with you. Yes, I spoke to him like you asked, but when I left him yesterday, I didn't think he was interested."

"So you didn't win him over."

Of course this is my fault. It can't ever be because someone has a mind or opinions of their own. It can't possibly be because Henry's reputation has left a wake no one wants to be caught in.

Before I can reply, Henry bites out, "No wonder why. You walk around looking like a nun, buttoned up to your neck. No self-respecting man wants to look at that. If you're going to keep your place here, you need to learn to use your strengths."

His words hit me like a slap to the face.

"Are you suggesting I convince people to work here with my cleavage?" Saying the word "cleavage" in my father's presence would be uncomfortable if I wasn't already at my max.

"When you don't have much else to offer, you have to use whatever assets you can. No wonder he didn't want to work here." He slaps a file folder down on his desk and presses himself to stand. "The only reason I haven't married you off is so clients see you as available. Don't make me regret my decision."

Sometimes, it takes every ounce of self-preservation for me not to shout "I quit" and walk out. With my entire life being spent guiding me to this job, I haven't taken a moment to think about any other options. This is it for me. My purpose. So, as much as I want to scream at my father that I have more to offer than my boobs or that Boyd made the decision for his own benefit, not because of my lack of sex appeal, I don't. "Maybe once he finishes his JD, he'll reconsider."

"Do whatever it takes to get him back in here." He wafts me away like a bothersome fly, and I'd be lying if I said it didn't make me feel like one.

I exit his office, feeling sick to my stomach. Joel flashes me a sympathetic smile and asks if there's anything he can do for me. He's such a genuinely kind person, I often feel guilty that he spends more time with my father than anyone. Henry hasn't even taken the time to learn Joel's name in the past eighteen months since he started here. It's *one* syllable. In this situation, there's nothing he can do, though. The expectation is on me to solve the perceived problem, even at the cost of my self-respect.

A day in the life of a narcissist's daughter.

I return home and amble toward Celeste's door. Twenty seconds after I knock, she opens it and greets me, followed by an exuberant Wilson. I'm so happy to see them both after this disaster day.

"Come in. I'll make dinner." Celeste takes my hand and pulls me inside. She doesn't give me the opportunity to argue.

It surprises me that I don't want to. Ashlyn has left for her competition in Montreal, and if I told her what transpired with my father today, she'd either tell me to shake what my momma gave me or she'd march down to the office, put Henry in a figure-four leg lock, and make him scream 'uncle.'

"I know no one kicked your dog, so take a seat here and tell me whatever is going on in that pretty head of yours." Celeste pats a stool at her counter, then walks over to the fridge and pulls out a bottle of chilled rosé.

Over too much wine, I confide in the woman who has seen it all when it comes to men like my father. I explain my previous interactions with Boyd, the lie I told him, my reason for doing so, and the resulting fallout with Henry.

"He said what?" Celeste gapes over her plate of chicken breast and Greek salad.

"I know. He's made comments in the past that have implied using my body to get my way, but this time was different. Henry missed out on every protective father instinct when they were being handed out. He skipped right over that line and headed for a healthy helping of misogyny."

"If I ever see that man, so help me, I'll slap him with a frying pan. Does he treat your mother the same way?"

Celeste and I have talked about my working relationship with my father at length because she's asked me on countless occasions why I stay at my job. Family dynamics have come up less often, and I'm certain that's because her situation is as uncomfortable as mine.

"Not as far as I know. I mean, he's no Prince Charming, but he's not whoring her out to close a business deal." I cringe at the harshness of that statement. The sad thing is, it's accurate, which fills me with an overwhelming sadness. So much so, tears prick my eyes once again. This is becoming a frequent occurrence, but I don't cry. I haven't cried since Caleb got on a plane to cross the Atlantic to pursue *his* dreams. Now I'm wishing I felt some kind of calling elsewhere that could land me thousands of miles away.

"Oh, my darling. You don't deserve this. I don't care if you have to sell your place and bunk with me for the next five years. I'll walk in there with you—and my frying pan—so you can tell your father you're quitting."

I sniffle a laugh, but her words make me pause. "It's not that easy. I can't quit. This job has been my goal since I was a kid."

Celeste reaches across, placing her hand over mine. "Was it your goal or his?"

The saddest thing about that question: I don't know the answer.

Expensive Mistakes

My meeting with Henry keeps replaying in my mind. How he was so convinced that a female at the helm of his beloved company would ensure its failure. Any business-minded person—scratch that, any reasonable person—knows that's not true. A CEO's gender has no bearing on the success of a company. It also makes me furious for Sophie, because she's dedicating her life to a company where her work may never pay off. The more I think about it, the angrier I get. That anger is seeping into my current job, which causes me to snap off the steam pipe on our expensive espresso machine, creating an unmistakable hissing sound.

"Dammit." I scramble to unplug the machine behind all the other equipment on the counter. After a few seconds, the steam slows and stops.

"Whoops," Tessa comments from behind me. "I'm glad that was you and not me."

That's less than helpful. This machine cost nearly six thousand dollars. Not to mention, it's required for a lot of our orders. The only saving grace is that it's almost closing time, so espresso isn't popular right now.

I turn around to face the customer who was waiting for the Americano I can't deliver. At least, not without busting out the French press and taking at least fifteen minutes to heat the water and brew the espresso. The woman is disappointed, but seems understanding after seeing the near disaster.

The good news is, I have a friend who does small appliance repair, so I send him a quick text, hoping for a rapid reply. We'll need this machine in the morning.

"Excuse me," a soft voice calls from the pickup counter. "Are you Boyd?"

I study the elderly woman for a moment, finding nothing familiar about her. "I am. Can I help you?"

Her kind smile reassures me she's not here to complain about a past order, but also leaves me wondering why she is here, asking for me.

"I'm a friend of Sophie's. I was hoping you wouldn't mind speaking with me for a moment. If you're not too busy."

This woman couldn't be more opposite to Ashlyn, but mention of being friends with Sophie piques my interest. I glance over at the lack of a lineup and gesture to Tessa that I'm taking a few minutes.

I turn back to Sophie's friend. "Sure. Can I get you anything first? An Earl Grey or peppermint tea? Anything other than espresso."

"Oh, thank you, darling. A tea would be lovely. Whichever you suggest. I'll find a seat over here."

I quickly make a peppermint tea for the woman whose name I still don't know and stroll over to where she's seated in the back corner of the café, farthest from the door. I drop into the seat across from her and set her drink on the table.

"Thank you for seeing me. I'm sure you're busy. And thank you for the tea." She smiles, but her face turns sombre. "Oh, where are my manners? I'm Celeste Miles."

"Boyd Edwards. Nice to meet you, Celeste. You came at a good time, actually. I was in need of a break."

"Yes, I've heard you're a hard worker."

That surprises me. Not that she's heard I'm a hard worker, but that she's heard of me at all. I assume if she was Sophie's grandmother, she wouldn't have introduced herself as a friend. Her characterization of herself has me curious. "How do you know Sophie?"

"Oh, she's my neighbour, but we've become good friends. My husband died two years ago, not long after Sophie moved next door, and she was my saving grace. When she's at work, I dog-sit for her, and she comes over for dinner a few nights a week."

So much of that surprises me, too. Sophie's claim that she barely had time for a social life seems to be true. I never would have guessed she spends most of her evenings with an elderly widow. Looks like we've both made assumptions that were wrong. "I'm sorry to hear about your husband. It's nice you have Wilson to keep you company."

Her forlorn expression disappears in an instant. "Oh, have you met my dear Wilson? He's just the sweetest thing. Sophie doesn't know I know this, but she got that dog to keep me company because she knew I couldn't handle one on my own all the time. She's an angel, that girl."

More surprises.

"I don't know a lot about dogs, but my few minutes around Wilson, I'm sure he's the friendliest one around."

Celeste's smile fades as she takes the spoon out of her cup, setting it on the saucer. "I came to speak with you about Sophie. I'm quite worried about her, and I wasn't sure who to turn to. Her brother is difficult to get a hold of."

For some unknown reason, a pit forms in my stomach. Whatever Celeste is going to say is not good, because she looks genuinely distressed.

"I'm not sure how I can help, but I'll try."

"Thank you. I understand you met with her father on Friday."

I nod.

"After speaking with you, Henry called Sophie into his office and made some disgraceful comments to that poor, sweet girl. She came home on the verge of tears. I had half a mind to march down to his office and confront him, but I don't want to make things worse."

The pit in my stomach turns into a churning crater. "What disgraceful comments?"

Celeste takes a sip of her tea, delaying her answer. "I don't know how much to tell you, because I don't want to upset Sophie." She exhales a deep breath, and each ticking second is amplifying my level of concern.

As Celeste continues to fill me in on the vitriol Henry McNamara spewed at his own daughter, I come to two conclusions. One, I was right not taking that job. Two, Celeste might not want to walk into his office to confront him, but I do.

It was easy to make my way into the building again by contacting Joel and asking if I could see Henry for a few moments. After the way he treated his own daughter, I hope he doesn't lash out at his assistant for allowing me in, but I'll be sure to take the full brunt of his anger.

The elevator doors open on the eleventh floor, and I turn right toward Henry's office. Intention is evident in the tempo of my steps as I march down the corridor. That tempo is disrupted when I see Sophie ten feet ahead, walking with her head down.

"Sophie?" I step to the left so I can block her path, forcing her to look up at me.

She's not crying, but she looks like she's fighting not to. "What are you doing here again?"

I'm not about to admit Celeste came to talk to me because I won't rat out an old lady. "What's wrong?"

She sniffles and straightens her posture. "Nothing. You didn't answer my question."

I scan the area and see a few gawkers looking at us. "Not here. Can we go to your office?"

She leads me to the opposite end of the corridor, where we pass an exuberant Andy and walk into her office. She calls out, "Hold my calls a bit longer, please, Andy," as she closes the door behind her. "Okay, why are you here?"

I'm farther inside her office than I was last time, and it feels weird having her closer to the exit. This is her space, but from this viewpoint, she looks like the visitor. I wait until she rounds her desk before I speak. "Something your father said on Friday really bothered me. I was coming to give him a piece of my mind."

"Ha! Don't be ridiculous. People don't give Henry McNamara a piece of their mind. A piece of their business, their real estate holdings, their first-born child, sure. Never their mind." She stares at me for a long pause.

I don't flinch under her gaze. "Maybe that's why he is how he is. *Because* no one does."

"No, people give in to him because he's ruthless. Why do you think you've never heard of anyone who has gone toe to toe with him, hmm? Anyone who has, has been buried. Punted straight into a life of obscurity, lucky to find a job as a septic tank scrubber." There's not a hint of doubt in her words. She's had a front-row seat to Henry's dealings her entire life. I don't doubt she's witnessed that exact thing happen.

"Why do you stay here? Keep this job?"

"It's my legacy. There are people here counting on me to run this company one day." There's a lot less conviction in those words.

I war with myself, whether I should tell her what he told me. It's possible he'll change his mind down the road and everything she's hoping for will be handed to her. It's also possible he'll string her along for the next decade and she'll lose the opportunity to achieve her full potential. I may not know her well, but I can tell she has the ability to succeed. So, what I was convinced was not my place to share, I feel compelled to now, because I don't like being strung along, either. "He told me he's not going to pass down the business to you."

Sophie doesn't look the least bit surprised. "I know."

I Don't Care

This isn't a surprise to me. It hurts to hear the words, but I'm not shocked. Boyd knowing that floods me with embarrassment, though.

He stares at me for way longer than what's comfortable, looking like he's trying to redirect this conversation down a line of questioning that suits him. Something he's very skilled at. "I don't understand why you'd stay where the ceiling is capped where you're at."

Now I'm the one searching for the right words. It takes considerable effort to decide how much to divulge to a man I barely know. But after lying to him before, and having that backfire spectacularly, I owe him the truth. "If I stay, the women under me stand a chance. Without me at the top, it becomes a testosterone zone, and the women here won't have a voice. Every man in the upper echelons of the payroll follows my father's lead. None of them have the guts to stand up to him. So the women here are counting on me, whether they realize it or not. If I can stick it out and break the cycle, you're darn right I will."

"So you've known that he wasn't going to leave you in charge, but you stay in hopes he'll what? Change his mind someday? Like he'll have an epiphany and his distorted view of gender roles will leap ahead several decades." Boyd seats himself in the chair opposite my desk, resting his elbows on his knees, though nothing about his posture is relaxed.

To match his level, I drop into my desk chair, placing my palms on each armrest and leaning back. "I hope that one day, he'll see that my work speaks for itself, yes. And that there's no one better suited to run *McNamara Enterprises* than a McNamara."

"What if I go talk to him? I'm not his employee, so he can't fire me. What if I'm the person to stand up to him and tell him he's being a misogynistic schmuck, and try to make him see what a mistake he's making?"

I blink at Boyd, who looks handsome in his casual suit, and try to rationalize why he's so invested in my future. There's no logical reason. "I don't need you to save me from him. You're not exactly high on his list of valued opinions. Though I'm pretty sure that list is one person long."

"You need someone to come save you from *you*." He leans back in his chair and closes his eyes for a brief pause. "I'm sorry, but this isn't how a company is supposed to operate. I don't know if you just don't realize it because you've spent your life under his thumb, but this place is toxic. I don't care what the revenue reports say. You deserve better than this."

His assessment of the situation makes me a little angry, because he's making broad assumptions. "It's not about revenue. It's about not giving up on something I care about. I know it's majorly flawed, and I want to have the chance to fix it. So no matter what you say to me, I'm not walking away. Did you think you could just come in here, tell me something I already know, and I'd ride out on your white horse so you could shout to everyone what a gallant man you are?"

He releases a tortured sigh, but doesn't reply.

Since I ran into him in the hallway, I've been trying to figure out his motivation. It has occurred to me that he's trying to convince me to quit, so he'll have an easier time sliding into my job—though Henry made it pretty clear that was no longer on the table. It has also occurred to me that he's telling the truth and Henry did inform him of his plans for the future of this company. Nevertheless, I can't unravel this mystery myself.

"Why do you even care?"

"I don't know." He shrugs. "But I do. It didn't take me more than five minutes to figure out that you deserve better than this. Celeste said..." His eyes light with alarm.

"I'm sorry. Celeste said what?" I stand, placing my palms on my desk and leaning forward. The second I register that's one of my father's intimidation tactics, I straighten.

Boyd utters a PG curse word before standing to meet my gaze. "She's worried about you. She told me what he said to you... after I left on Friday."

I sink into my chair again. This time, when I lean back, it's not a casual pose intended to evoke a powerful persona. Now it's a mixture of upset, rage, and embarrassment. The rage is squashed almost immediately when I consider Celeste and don't question her intentions. She's hardly the type to sabotage my career or personal life. If she spoke with Boyd, I'm sure it's because she thought that was the best thing to do. That doesn't ease the embarrassment, though.

I can't make eye contact with him now.

"She's worried about you."

"I know. But I can handle it." Normally, I wouldn't give details of something a friend told me in confidence, but Celeste has never tried to hide her complicated family dynamic. Still looking down, I continue, "She's a little sensitive to domineering men. Her stepson is like Henry. Maybe even worse. He hasn't spoken to her for more than a decade because she's 'just a woman.' He showed up at his father's funeral, but didn't even acknowledge Celeste. So each time I tell her about a situation at work, I think she puts herself in my shoes." I really should stop confiding in her so she doesn't worry, but she's so good at reading me, she knows as soon as something is wrong.

"From where I'm sitting, her concern is justified."

Finally, I look up. "Like I said, I can handle it."

My intercom buzzes before I can continue, and Andy informs me I have an important call waiting.

"I appreciate your concern, but right now, I'm going to focus on the work I need to get done."

Boyd adjusts his suit jacket. "Take care of yourself, Sophie." With that, he turns and leaves, quietly opening and closing the door.

Twenty seconds pass and Andy still hasn't transferred this important call through, so I pick up the receiver to question him about it. Then my door flies open and he pops through like Cosmo Kramer.

"What did he say?" he asks, closing the door behind him in a rush.

I glance up at him as he stops in front of my desk and I notice his scheming smile. "There's no phone call, is there?"

"No. I figured if you didn't want an out, you'd tell me to take a message." He adjusts the chair Boyd just vacated and drops into it. "So, what did you guys talk about?"

Andy is privy to certain aspects of my relationship with my father. Considering he's not just my employee, but a friend. Some things I'm not willing to share, though. I don't want my role or people's perception of me compromised. I have to maintain some professional dignity, and explaining that my father views me as nothing more than a harlot will not do me any favours.

"He was asking me about the company culture and what kind of work he'd be doing." I close my eyes and exhale a long, silent breath. Now I'm lying to Andy too.

"And what did you tell him?"

This guy is way too invested in the seven-minute conversation Boyd and I had. Any other time someone has left my office, he's never asked anything more than pertinent details he'd need to record.

"Why are you so interested? He asked *me* out, so I don't think he'll be—"

"Woah. Back up. He asked you out? Today?"

I level him with a stare that asks, *are you serious right now?* "You know I'm your boss, right?"

"Pssh. Insignificant detail. So he came here to ask you out? I knew it." Andy performs an obnoxious golf clap with his hands near his face.

This is an awkward conversation to have at work, but I should at least be honest in this. I proceed to tell him about our strange encounter, me turning him down—though I leave out the part about the fake boyfriend and the Chad disaster— running into him again at the gala, and our failed meeting at the coffee shop.

"I knew I should have rearranged my schedule. Girl, you withheld the tea. I may never forgive you." The right side of his mouth lifts a fraction of an inch. "Unless you make it up to me."

"And how should I do that?" I shouldn't have asked. "Keep signing your paycheques? Maintain your employment?"

"Those are bonuses, but no. You need to ask him on a date."

I love Andy, but sometimes, he lives in a fantasy world.

"That's not happening. Maybe you missed the part about me shooting him down or the fact my dad is trying to hire him?"

"Ooh, a workplace romance. This is getting even better." Andy leans forward, placing his hands on the arms of the chair as if he's going to get up, but pauses instead. "So, yes. Ask him on a date."

"Why are you so invested in this?"

He settles back into the chair, holding eye contact. "Because my skill-set includes answering phone calls and reading people. And that man is as good as it gets."

I shouldn't ask. I really shouldn't ask. "How do you know that?" My people-reading skills leave a lot to be desired.

"Ah, sweet Sophie. A magician never reveals their tricks. Just ask him out."

"But—"

"I've got to get back to work." He jumps up and speed walks to the door. "Boss is a real ball-buster." With a backward wave, he exits my office.

I lean back in my chair and blow out a long breath. My assistant is very good at his job, but good grief, he's weird. So why don't I hate the thought of what he's asking?

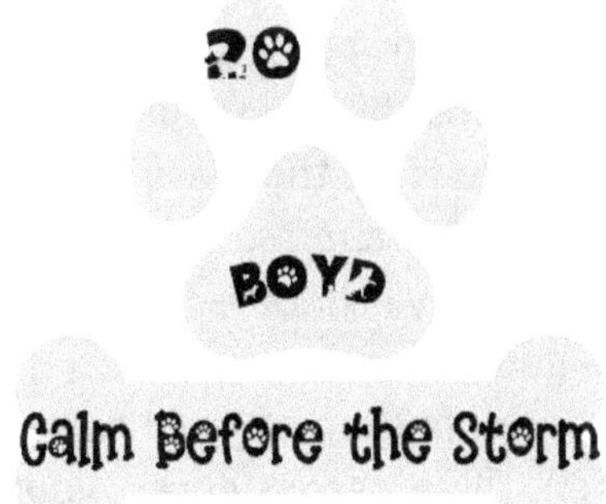

Calm Before the Storm

Joel eyes me as I approach his desk, then lifts his arm to check his watch. I'm ten minutes later than I agreed to. My stop in Sophie's office was unplanned, but now my actual plan has changed.

"Good afternoon, Joel. Sorry I'm late. I had to take a detour." Not a lie.

"Mr. McNamara will be a moment. He had to take a phone call. I'll let you know when he's ready for you."

After thanking him, I turn toward the waiting area. I pull out my phone to check my emails, clicking on a few spam messages to delete, then scrolling social media, looking at lawyer memes and photos Phoebe has posted of Grace.

"He'll see you now."

Henry McNamara made me wait for twelve minutes, and I can't help but wonder if that was intentional. A man like him probably doesn't take well to waiting. It wouldn't surprise me if he was trying to regain the upper hand. But I don't care how much power and money he has, he's not playing me.

I walk into his office and stop short inside the door. "Mr. McNamara, thank you for seeing me."

He doesn't look up from his spot under the massive *McNamara Enterprises* sign. After one real conversation with the man, even the size of his office signage comes across as an intentional choice to boost his own inflated ego. Like he needs a reminder whose name is on the lease for the three floors of this building his company occupies.

"You've thrown off my schedule for the day, Mr. Edwards, so I hope you have good news for me."

Depends on your definition of good news… but I keep that comment to myself. "I've reconsidered your offer," I reply, moving farther into the unwelcoming space. I imagine entering this office feels a lot like my father described walking in for a prostate exam. A moderately vulnerable feeling and wishing you were anywhere else.

He glances at me from behind a pair of angry, narrowed eyes. "My offer no longer stands."

That doesn't shock me like I'm assuming he hoped it would, but it doesn't make sense why he'd agree to meet with me again.

"Can I ask why you allowed me to come all the way down here just to tell me that? You could have declined my request for a meeting."

Henry stands, leaning over his desk, much like how his daughter did moments earlier. It would probably infuriate Henry to know that Sophie is ten times more intimidating. With him, I don't even flinch.

"Because I wanted to waste your time like you wasted mine. And I wanted to see the look on your face when you realized your grades can only get you so far in this world, *boy*. You needed to learn a lesson, and I'm happy to be the one to teach you."

Once upon a time, I had a flicker of respect for the CEO of *McNamara Enterprises* because I know he started this company from scratch and turned it into an empire. But he will not rule over me.

"I hate to disappoint you, *Henry*."

His piercing gaze radiates even more hatred when I use his first name in the same way he called me "boy".

"I actually came here to tell you off. For no other reason than because you're a misogynistic prick who sees his daughter as a prop to win over perverts and impotent morons foolish enough to keep themselves under your thumb."

His jaw clenches as tight as his fists, and part of me hopes he'll punch me so I can really dismantle him, but that would be too easy. He knows it. No one gets to the position he's in by doing their dirty work themselves.

He grates out through gritted teeth, "Boy, I can crush every opportunity for you in this town before you even pass the bar. Don't come in here and tell me how to run my business. And certainly do not tell me how to parent my daughter."

I almost laugh at his use of the word "parent". "You may think you have the power to destroy me, *Henry*, but along with building your business, you've built a reputation. Not a single person I'd be interested in working for would take your ego-induced tantrum seriously." With zero desire to drag this conversation out, I turn to leave and repeat, "I'll see myself out."

"You have no idea what kind of enemy you've made. In twenty-four hours, you won't be able to find a job on Desolation Island."

I turn my head over my shoulder to look at the reddening face of the worst malignant narcissist I've ever had the displeasure of meeting. "I'd be more concerned about the glaciers surrounding that island you call a heart, Henry." With great satisfaction, I exit his office to the sound of him slamming something on his desk.

Again, I'm met by Joel's startled expression, so I stop to apologize. I feel bad for the man, but it's not like I can ride through the office like Paul Revere, warning of the impending danger. I can't make people quit just to sabotage Henry. As much as I value right and wrong, I understand that it's not a cut and dry situation for everyone who relies on this job to survive.

I can't push Sophie to, either. I respect what she's doing to protect the other women who work here, but if they collectively stood up to Henry, they could make more waves than any one person would on their own. But this isn't my job. It's not my decision. The futures of Sophie, the other employees, and *McNamara Enterprises* are out of my hands.

So I do the only thing I can do and descend in the elevator, exit the building, and head to the one job that rarely gets more complicated than balancing three cups with two hands.

Four days have passed since my confrontation with Henry. The one thing he was right about is that grades can only get me so far, but I've got plenty to keep me busy between now and my call to the bar in June. Once that is over, I'll take job searching seriously. Right now, I have to focus on my training and doing the job that actually pays my bills.

Fulfilling orders is automatic. I'm so familiar with our menu, as soon as an order comes up, I know exactly which caffeine source to grab, which cup, and which equipment I'll need. My mind flies through each request on auto-pilot, never giving anyone a second glance after passing them their drinks.

Until one flashes on the screen: *10oz flat white – Sophie.*

I can't help but look up after seeing her name. It is a common name and a popular order. But that's definitely

Sophie McNamara giving me a shy smile from the other side of the pastry display.

The weather has turned, so it's a bit cooler and windy today. She's wearing a trench coat that's the same colour as the drink I'm making her. Beyond that, I can only see her windswept hair falling in loose waves around her face.

Not for the first time, I realize I thought a lot about her over the past few days. Wondered if she had decided to cut ties with her father and strike out on her own, or if she was still suffering under his command. As angry as I was with her for lying to me before, now that I've been in Henry's company for more than ten seconds, I get it. A lowly barista would never hold up to his impossible standards and, for some reason, Sophie values his opinion even when he doesn't value her existence.

Instead of passing her the piping hot cup, making a joke at her expense about its temperature, and continuing on with my day, I signal to Tessa that I'm going to take a break. Her questioning smirk tells me she's got the wrong impression and I probably have Monica to thank for that.

I walk around the counter, stopping three feet in front of Sophie. "Hey. Do you have a minute to sit?"

She pulls her phone from her coat pocket and checks the screen before replying, "Sure. I have about ten."

We both appear unsure when deciding on a table. She moves for the one she sat at with her brother, and I head toward the one I sat at with Celeste. We settle on one halfway between.

"How's my buddy Wilson?" I ask as Sophie sets her drink down and unbuttons her coat, revealing a burgundy two-piece skirt suit.

Her lips tilt into a grin as she sits. "He's good. My neighbour spoils him rotten when I'm not home."

"Celeste? Yeah, she seems to really love him."

Sophie leans back on her stool, spinning her cup on the table. "Right. You've met."

I grimace, noting her annoyed tone. It doesn't sound like she's angry, but she isn't pleased about Celeste coming to speak with me.

"She really loves you, too. Just so you know. That's the only reason she came to me." I hope the sincerity I'm trying to portray with my eyes is getting the message across. "Besides, if someone had to go toe to toe with Henry McNamara, I'm glad I can say it was me."

Sophie's already uncomfortable demeanour turns sombre. The corners of her lips droop, her shoulders slump, and her eyes refocus on her coffee cup. "He didn't tell me what you said, but I figured it wasn't good. You shouldn't have done that."

For the first time since my verbal sparring with Henry, I consider the ramifications of my words reaching beyond me. I wonder if he took it out on Sophie, since my first meeting with him was the catalyst for his initial comments Celeste told me about.

That thought, in turn, makes me question Sophie's presence here. "Are you here for retribution? Or to make me apologize? Because I wo—"

"No." Her eyes flick up to me as she exhales a long breath. "I don't know why I'm here, actually."

21

SOPHIE

The Kids Aren't Alright

Work life has been miserable for the past few days. More than normal. It's reached a point where even Andy is begging me to apply at different places and bring him along. The level of tension surrounding my office in particular is palpable. Like an invisible toxin surrounding you, but you won't escape before it's too late. My office is Chernobyl. It's draining the life out of me, and learning that the toxicity is affecting Andy added a new stress to the dynamic.

So when I had the option to eat in the office or take a drive to clear my head, I chose the drive. I found myself driving to *Just Add Coffee* as if on autopilot, but beyond that, I don't know why I'm here.

Andy's words keep replaying in my head, that I should ask Boyd out. That can't happen, though. Especially not after he declared war with my father. With Boyd across from me, nausea swirls in my stomach. Again, I don't know if that's because I'm anxious about what lengths Henry will go to in order to destroy Boyd's professional life, or if it's because I've realized he's the first person Andy has suggested I date, and I didn't hate the idea of it.

That's some sort of cruel cosmic joke.

"I guess I just wanted to warn you. If you're on Henry's radar, he won't stop until he wins. And he's the only one who knows the rules of the game." Somehow, I feel responsible for Boyd being in this position.

"It's fine, Sophie."

His blasé attitude is shocking. It's like he learned nothing in his years of schooling. At least, not about the real world. Textbooks and essays don't cover vindictive businessmen with fragile egos.

"It's not *fine*, Boyd. Not even a little. Confronting him could derail your career before it even gets started. You have no idea how—"

He cuts me off by placing his hand overtop of mine. The weight of it feels oddly comforting, and his skin radiates a heat that travels through my hand, up my arm, and across my chest. He doesn't look away when I make eye contact. "Don't worry about me, okay? I can handle it. I know he's your father, so I mean no offence, but I'm not bothered by men like him. Trust me, my mother is a much tougher adversary."

Why am I worried? Why do I even care? It's not like he's a lifelong friend or someone I have a vested interest in. He's the man who makes me coffee on occasion and inadvertently became a rival for my job. But he's not a threat to my position now. I should just wash my hands of him and carry on with my life. It's easier that way. A clean break and a renewed focus on my work.

So why can't I just feed him to the wolves and walk away?

Because I'm so used to dealing with men who view me as a commodity, it's nice to be treated like a person for once. One with skills and value and feelings. Except, Boyd Edwards can never be anything more than my favourite barista.

"I don't want your hard work to be for nothing."

He leans back in his seat, removing his hand from mine. My eyes track his hand as it retreats and mine is cloaked in a chilliness that makes me miss his touch.

"You don't need to worry about me. By June, the whole thing will blow over. He'll have a new victim to pick on by then. That's how people like him work."

I take a sip of my coffee, which is now a reasonable temperature, and allow the warm liquid to soothe my throat. Boyd gives me a satisfied nod when I look up from my cup. His naivety would be endearing if I wasn't so concerned about his future.

"You're underestimating him. He's perfectly capable of picking a new victim and still keeping his old ones."

Boyd leans forward, close enough to whisper across the table, "I'm not afraid of Henry McNamara."

My evening is occupied by dinner with Celeste, where I speak little of my day at work, and don't mention seeing Boyd. I'm still mortified she went to speak with him, but I can't be mad at her.

My thoughts drift off during dinner, realizing Boyd has now met all of the most important people in my life, short of my grandparents.

"That young man is quite a looker. He seems like such a nice fella, too." Celeste winks at me, making me pause to question if I said my thoughts out loud.

I'm sure I didn't. I glance down at Wilson to avoid direct eye contact with the woman can read my mind, apparently. He's curled up at my feet, doubling as a foot warmer and a grounding object. I focus on how he feels against my aching toes, and the comfort he gives without even trying. I wiggle my toes to give him a little tummy tickle. Then I take a deep breath to acknowledge Celeste's observation. "He is nice. And, I'll admit, he's not bad to look at."

"He makes a great cup of tea, too," Celeste adds with wide, smiling eyes.

"His coffee skills are beyond reproach. I've never had tea there, but I'll take your word for it."

"Well, feel free to invite him over. That boy can make me tea any time. If you know what I mean." She winks again before abruptly standing to clear our dishes.

No, I don't know what she means. Is "make me tea" a euphemism the elderly are using these days? Did she learn about this on *Jeopardy!*? I'm afraid to ask. But she's rushed off to the kitchen and dropped our dishes in the sink. Wilson is hot on her tail, leaving my feet cold and questions unanswered.

No answers come to light between the end of our meal and when I prepare to leave. I give Celeste a hug and make my exit, confused by these flip-flopping feelings. Like why I've spent my life catering to my father's every whim, and now I want to defy him.

Wilson still needs a walk, so, when we return home, I trade my skirt suit for joggers and my heels for sneakers, then we set off down a walkway through Craigleigh Gardens.

Midway through one of my favourite tunes, my music pauses for a phone call. I glance down at the screen, but the annoyance I felt over the interruption quickly disappears.

"Hey, girl."

"Hello, gorgeous," Ashlyn says in a deep voice. Her goofiness draws a laugh out of me that feels good to release.

"How did your competition go?"

"Meh. Eighth place. I need to work on handstand push-ups, but I killed DT."

I rack my brain for any mention of what DT is, but come up short. "Speak English for me. What's DT?"

"Deadlifts, hang power cleans, and push jerks."

I could go for some jerk pushing right about now. "Gotcha. Eighth is still amazing for your first competition. So you're back in town?"

"Yeah. Jim and I got back last night, but I didn't get a chance to call. I was exhausted and had to work today."

Wilson and I approach the off-leash dog area, so I decide I'll let him go in there and tire himself out so I can talk to Ashlyn uninterrupted. Win-win.

"Don't worry about it. The past few days have been crazy for me, too."

"Did the barista ever call you?"

The mention of Boyd brings all the uncertainty and embarrassment I've felt in his presence back to the surface. "No, he hasn't. But I'm not impressed you left him my number."

Ashlyn laughs, but stops abruptly. "Wait. If he hasn't called, how did you know I left your number?"

Oops.

"I've seen him a few times. He just hasn't called. One of those encounters, he said he wanted to call you and he was happy you left him *your* number. Imagine my surprise when he showed me a photo of a coffee cup with *your* handwriting and *my* number. If you had any thoughts that he was interested in me, you were mistaken."

I find a large stick along the perimeter of the park and get Wilson's attention with it. Then I do my best to toss it, but I'm so terrible at throwing, he arrives to the stick's destination before it does, snatches it out of mid-air, then flops on the ground to chew it.

"Lies. I saw the way you two looked at each other. And he seemed to like your slobbery beast, so that's got to count for something."

"You and my father are the only two people on Earth who don't like Wilson. That's not a selling point." I pat my thigh, trying to get Wilson to return the stick, but he's determined to demolish it.

"Please don't group me in any category with that man. I beg you. How is the ol' Scrooge, anyway?"

"Worse than ever." The words spill out automatically, but I wasn't planning to say them. My brain took over to share the words I needed to disclose to my best friend.

"What's he done now?"

"Besides telling me I need to unbutton my blouse to win over clients, he said the only reason he hasn't married me off is so I appear 'available'."

Ashlyn sucks in a sharp breath. "Please, can you leave that place now? He's an abusive megalomaniac. Enough is enough. I hate seeing you waste your life there."

The same sense of despair I was feeling at Celeste's falls over me like a weighted cloak again. "He's not always abus—"

"A relationship that is ninety-eight percent fine and two percent abusive is still abusive. And I know he's more than two percent. Don't do this to yourself. It will never be worth it."

Wilson walks up beside me, carrying his mangled stick, and sits at my feet. He's either bored of being the lone dog in the park, or he notices I could use some emotional support. I lean down to scratch the top of his head and thank him for his thoughtfulness.

"If I don't have that, I don't know who I am anymore."

BOYD

Start Today

Sophie hasn't returned to the coffee shop for the past eight days. My shifts are shorter and in the evenings during the week to accommodate my training, so maybe that's why I keep missing her. Or maybe she's stopped coming in altogether. *Maybe* she finally quit her job, and she's working somewhere else that isn't close by. I certainly hope that's the case.

Whatever the reason is, I've opened and closed the gallery on my phone at least fifteen times today. Not to look at photos of Grace or funny memes I've collected. I keep swiping until I get to the photo of an empty coffee cup with a loopy scroll across it. It's begging: *Call me*. I've gone so far as to write down the number on the corner of a napkin. Would Ashlyn take it the wrong way if I called her to ask for Sophie's number? She seemed like an easy-going person and, from what Sophie said, she's in a committed relationship. Though, to be fair, she said that about herself too.

There's only one way to find out. With a lull in customers and no sign of anyone coming in the next few moments, I dial Ashlyn's number. I take a deep breath as I press the green phone to connect the call.

It rings four times through my earbuds. Finally, I hear a click and heavy breathing in the background. I'm just now realizing this will be incredibly awkward.

"Hello?"

My eyes dart left to right, scanning the café while my brain processes what's happening. "Sophie?"

She pauses for an equal amount of time before she replies, "Boyd?"

"Ashlyn left me your number?"

"She did. But honestly, I didn't think you'd ever use it. If you want me to give you her num—"

"I don't. No, I thought I was calling her so I could get *your* number. It uh… it didn't feel right to call your office, but I haven't seen you at the café." I lean back against the counter in front of the recently repaired espresso machine.

Sophie says some muffled words not into the phone before addressing me again. "Don't take this as a blowoff, but can I call you back later? Wilson and I are out for a walk."

That sort of explains the heavy breathing, but it would have to be a pretty intense walk. I'm about to reply when she interrupts again.

"Actually, we're out for more of a jog because there were these two guys lingering at the park who gave me a weird vibe. I… Would you… Ugh, never mind."

My instincts force me to jolt into action, standing straight and reaching around to untie my apron. "No, what is it? Is something wrong?"

"No, nothing is really *wrong*, but they made me nervous. I was just going to ask if you can stay on the line for a minute."

There's a vulnerable note in her voice. Something tells me Sophie McNamara isn't used to asking anyone for favours. Even more so, given the interactions I've had with her father, she's probably not too keen on being a damsel in distress. So if she's asking, there's a reason.

"Of course. Where are you?" I pause after asking, realizing how I sound demanding. Really, I just want to be able to call 911 should the need arise. I'll make a lousy rescuer considering I'd have to take a ride-share or a bus.

Before I can clarify, she blurts, "Beaumont Park. Just on the trail that runs alongside the creek. There's another trail up ahead that cuts through Craigleigh Park back to my place."

I scratch down the information on the same napkin with her phone number.

"This is ridiculous. I'm sure you have more important things to do. I can't even see them anymore. You don't have to—"

"Sophie, it's fine. I'm not doing anything else. My experience with Wilson says he won't be much of a guard dog."

She chuckles, alleviating some of the tension in her voice. "Not at all. This big goof befriends everyone."

"My brother got attacked by a chihuahua outside of the library. So I guess it's not the size of the dog in the fight that matters."

She laughs again, harder this time. "Wilson is afraid of recycling bins and pylons. I kid you not, I can't walk him on garbage day or through construction zones."

A hand-holding couple walks in the door, making the bell chime.

"Stay on the line, okay? I'm just at work and some people walked in."

"Oh… you can—"

"Just give me a second." I press the mute button so she can't hear me, but I can still hear her if she has any issues.

The customers ask for a doppio and a café latte. I can't say I get a lot of orders for a double shot of espresso at 8:30pm, but I'm not going to comment on the caffeine consumption of the first customers I've had in thirty minutes. While I'm preparing the espresso, Sophie starts muttering into the phone and it puts me on high alert. I crank up my volume so I can hear clearly.

"I should just listen to Andy and ask him out, right? I mean, he'll probably say no because I lied to him." She pauses a few seconds and says something else I can't understand. "But I want to redeem myself and prove to him that's not who I am. Plus, he's hot. Like steaming milk hot."

I cough into my elbow to mask the laugh that wants to erupt. Then I clear my throat, realizing my customers would prefer a laughing barista over a coughing one. I turn to look back at the young couple, but they're too caught up in each other to be bothered by anything I'm doing.

"Should I just go for it? He called... but I don't know why. Maybe he was calling about work..." She trails on, rambling to Wilson, but I can't make out what she's saying.

I feel a little bad for not telling her I was muting myself, but the selfish need to continue listening overshadows that guilt. The part of me that swore I wouldn't get involved with another woman like Sophie is warring with the part that can't get her out of my head. The logical part of me says to ignore her date talk, make sure she gets home safely, and move on with my life. But that *logical* part has sent me down some miserable paths. The only times I've been truly happy are when I acted on instinct.

I rush to finish the couple's orders, clear my throat to draw their attention, and pass them two piping hot takeout cups. They seem to understand my subtle gesture to take their drinks and leave, because seconds later, the young red-headed guy is holding the door for his blonde-haired companion.

Finally, I'm able to unmute myself. Sophie has been silent since her monologue trailed off.

"Are you there?"

She clears her throat. "Mm, yeah. Yeah, all good. No sign of those guys and I'm almost home."

"Do you always walk Wilson so late?"

"Boyd?" Her stern voice makes my name sound like something you'd shout when you stub your toe.

"Yeah?"

"Why did you call?"

I don't know why I called. Curiosity, I guess. I wanted to know if she had changed her mind about her loyalty to her job. Beyond that, I *needed* to know if she was okay. It shouldn't matter to me either way, but it does. Yet, my main concern right now is knowing she gets home safely. "I just wanted to check in."

"Why?"

I take a deep breath and distract myself by spraying the countertop with disinfectant. "Because you deserve better."

"You don't even know me. I lied to you. Clearly I'm not an upstanding citizen."

Under normal circumstances, I'd say yes. Lawyers have an old Latin saying, *Falsus in uno, falsus in omnibus.* Generally, it refers to people on the stand and a jury or judge's perception of them. If they're caught in a lie once, they're more likely to be perceived as a liar in all things. But after my interaction with Henry, I see Sophie's perspective. "That was different. You're also the person who bought a dog to keep her widowed neighbour company and refuses to leave a job so she can protect the women below her."

She doesn't reply for several seconds, but it sounds like she's unlocking a door. "How did you know that?"

"You told me that's why you were staying at—"

"No, about my dog. I've never told anyone that."

I wipe the counter again, trying to formulate an explanation. Before I can, she answers her own question.

"Celeste told you, didn't she?" She blows out a breath, and it sounds like she turns the shower on.

I glance up at the clock and see that it's two minutes to nine. The distraction of performing my closing duties is just what I need to pull my thoughts from whatever it is Sophie is doing on the other end of the phone. "In all fairness, she was just singing your praises."

"She's a perceptive old bird, I'll give her that. Anyway, I'm inside now and about to jump in the shower. Thanks for walking me home."

This phone call hasn't resulted in answers that I was initially looking for, but it was nice to chat without work being the focus. "You're welcome. Have a—"

"Do you want to go out with me?"

The silence is killing me. Actually, it's not silent; the shower is pounding on the ceramic tile in spurts because my water-pressure is unsteady. Specifically, Boyd's silence is killing me. So here I am, standing with my track pants pooled at my ankles, waiting for an answer to a question I blurted out before all of my courage left. Something I've been in short supply of tonight.

There's something about Boyd that makes me feel like I don't have to be power-suit Sophie, determined to control a boardroom. I can just be regular Sophie with flaws and fears and dreams that exist outside of my job. A woman, instead of someone striving to be a boss someday. He cares, and that's not something I take for granted.

"Boyd?"

"Sorry. I... It's just... you didn't want to go out with me before because of what your dad might think... and now—"

"He hates you," I clarify. I know what he's getting at, but for once, I want to make a decision that isn't based on Henry's demands. "But I don't, and what I do outside of work shouldn't be his business."

"Sophie, he's your father. His involvement in your life doesn't stop after work hours."

This sounds a lot like a shutdown. I should have known this was coming; I deserve it. "You don't know Henry McNamara very well. But it's fine. I'm a big girl. I can take no for an answer." Though I've never been rejected before; I can't say I'm enjoying it. This is exactly why I made up an excuse to spare Boyd's feelings.

"Well enough to know it could make life more miserable for you. That's the last thing I want."

I'm so embarrassed by this obvious snuff, I just want to hang up and let the shower wash away my shame. "It's fine. Thanks again for making sure I got home safely." I end the call, pull my ear buds out, get undressed, and step inside the shower. The lack of steady water pressure makes washing my hair a nightmare, but on the bright side, it almost feels like a massage. It alleviates some of the tension in my shoulders and upper back.

Twenty minutes later, I add *call superintendent* to my to-do list to address this water issue once and for all, then drop on the couch with a cup of chamomile tea and Wilson.

"Why didn't you warn me it was a stupid idea to ask him out? I confided in you and you let me look like an idiot."

The poor guy looks sad at my half-hearted chastisement. In his defence, a dog's way of showing a fellow canine he's interested isn't the best course of action here. He curls up beside me and lays his head on my lap. I realize I forgot my phone after he's already comfortable, but at least I can reach the remote. My plan for the rest of the evening is watching a few episodes of *The Wire* and wallowing in self-pity.

Lately I've been feeling increasingly lonely, despite Wilson's company. Despite my job, Ashlyn, Celeste, and Caleb. Everyone has their own lives and I feel like a bystander watching everyone go for what they want without being held back.

Is that what made me misread the signals with Boyd? Loneliness making me see things that aren't there?

He's right; if Henry found out I had gone on a date with Boyd, he'd blow a gasket, but there's something about Boyd that makes me want to risk it. I guess some risks just aren't worth taking, so for tonight, I'll settle for snuggling my dog.

I wake up to my alarm at 6am, as usual. When I finally dragged myself to bed last night, my phone was dead, so I plugged it in across the room, knowing I'd be forced to leave my warm cocoon to shut it off. Wilson grumbles from his perch at the end of the bed when I remove my foot from under his head. Early morning wake-ups are the only time he's ever cranky.

Once I shut off the incessant beeping, I look at the multiple notifications on my home screen. Seventeen emails, one voicemail, three text messages, and various social media alerts. I start by opening my personal email and clearing out the junk mail. Then I move on to my business account and forward some to Andy to deal with and mark others for further review once I get to the office. Then I move to the text messages. Ashlyn is checking in, letting me know she signed up for another CrossFit competition in Boston in February, asking if I'll come watch. The second is my brother, replying to my earlier message checking if he's still alive. He is. The last one is from an unsaved number.

416-555-2793: *You didn't let me answer your question.*

I scrunch my nose at the cryptic message, suddenly realizing that's Boyd's number when I compare it to my call log from last night.

What do I even say to that? I'm pretty sure he said all he needed to. He asked me out. I lied. I asked him out. He shot me down. The circle of non-dating life.

Sophie: *I think you answered it fine.*

I drop onto the mattress beside Wilson, burying my face into his curly brown fur. He needs a bath and my olfactory system recognizes that fact, but there's no way I'm wrangling him in my malfunctioning shower. I love him anyway. Stink and all. My phone chimes again, so I try to hold it up from my sideways position. Thanks to modern technology, the screen rotates, so it's harder to access my text messages. It's a battle and requires extra thumb stretchability, but I get it open to find Boyd replied.

Boyd: *I said I didn't want to make things harder for you. You didn't let me say I'd like to take you out.*

I pause and restart typing a few times, but a message interrupts my reply.

Boyd: *I wouldn't have asked you the first time if I didn't mean it.*

That stings a little. The reminder of me shooting him down for no reason other than I judged him the same way my father does. They way I *hate* how he judges people. That's what upsets me more than anything about the situation. I don't want to be like my father in any capacity.

This is my chance to rectify the situation.

Sophie: *You misunderstood.*

Boyd: *I'm confused.*

Sophie: *I didn't ask you to take me out. I asked you to go out with me.*

Boyd: *What does that even mean? What's the difference?*

I chuckle to myself.

Sophie: *Oh, Boyd. Semantics matter. I'd think as "the greatest legal-minded business student" at Montgomery, you'd know that by now.*

It's silly how much his reply has changed my mood. My injured pride rejuvenates a bit more with each of his messages.

Boyd: *So…?*
You want to take me out?
Sophie: *Bingo.*

24

BOYD

Where Is Your Boy?

It's been a long time since I picked a woman up for a date. Since my last relationship went down in flames, I swore I wouldn't do this to myself again. Especially not when it's as complicated as things are with Sophie McNamara. Throw in a narcissist father/boss and professional lives that could intersect or be in direct competition with one another, and you have a recipe for disaster.

Yet, here I am, standing at her door, trying to build up the courage to knock. My knuckles finally cooperate and make contact with her cookie-cutter door that has a small six-panel window across the top. It's just high enough, I can only see the top of Sophie's head as she approaches.

She pulls the door open, revealing her simple black turtleneck sweater and fitted black pants that conform to her curves like a lucky second skin. I've seen Sophie in several different styles of dress, but this one—knowing she got dressed to go out with me—is my favourite.

"Hi." A light blush appears on her cheeks that has happened during several of our interactions. The lawyer in me has deemed that her tell.

"Hey." I lean in to kiss her cheek before thinking through the implications. My lips connect with her flush skin and send a surge of electricity through my veins. A mixture of anticipation and reservation. "Where's Wilson?" I ask, not wanting to analyze that reaction.

Sophie tucks a strand of straightened hair behind her ear and touches her cheek where my lips just did. "I took him over to Celeste's a while ago. She insisted." She tugs the door open a little wider. "Come inside for a minute."

I respond like an obedient dog, not questioning her command. "Wow. Uh... nice place." I scan the room and take in the light pink velvet sofa, gold and glass shelf with matching decor, abstract art on the wall opposite the one large window, and more elaborate throw pillows than I can count at first glance.

She's digging through her foyer closet, pushing an irrational number of jackets to the side before settling on a long wool grey coat that ties at the waist. "Don't judge me. I spent my life in the shadow of my twin brother, watching my mother capitulate to every one of my father's demands, and spend my work days being treated as inferior. So here, I wanted it to be the one place it's okay to embrace being female."

Her response makes me a combination of sad and angry. I'm the big brother in my family, but still have spent plenty of time feeling inferior to my academic superstar brother. At least I've had the opportunity to outgrow that and find my own path. For Sophie, it seems to get worse as the years go by.

She pulls her coat tight, enhancing her hour-glass shape. There is nothing inferior about this woman.

"Anyone who makes you feel that way is intimidated by everything you offer, Sophie. No one who is secure in what they bring to the table wastes time belittling anyone." A strong urge to wrap my arms around her nearly wins out over rational thought. I have a deep desire to absorb every feminine part of her. How she smells. The suppleness of her skin. How her curves feel against me.

But the look she's giving me in return is one of appreciation and respect—mutual respect—and I won't discount that by making her feel like an object here to satisfy my impulses.

"Ready?"

She looks down at her sock-clad feet and turns back to her closet. "Almost." With an elegant confidence, she slips on a tall black leather boot with a small heel. The way she trails the zipper up on the inside of her calf makes me wish I was the intricate plastic pieces, allowing her to pull me together. "Ready."

"You look beautiful." I run my hand through my roguish hair, stopping myself short of what I want to say. It's hardly Shakespearean to tell her *Oh, that I were a zipper upon your calf, so I may touch your calf.* That's a solid way to start this date off on a weird note. Instead, I ask, "Where are you taking me?"

Since Sophie was the one who asked me out, she insisted on planning everything. One thing I know from our time together is that traditional gender roles hold little appeal to her, so it was an easy concession to make.

"You'll probably think it's lame, but I've been wanting to go to *Casa Mesa* since we moved to the city, and I haven't had the chance. I figured it was a smart choice because it's heated."

"Would you believe I've lived in the city my entire life and I've never been?"

Sophie's eyes light up, and a soft smile brightens her face. "Perfect." She saunters out the door with me trailing close behind, only stopping to lock her door, then she leads me to her SUV. Not only has she planned the evening, but she's driving.

The trip takes less than fifteen minutes from Sophie's condo to the parking area at the elaborate estate. Our conversation is free-flowing and easy as we walk to the entry gates, where Sophie flashes her phone to show pre-paid tickets for a tour of the castle in the city.

The grounds are immaculate, even well into the fall when things are typically dormant and dull. The gardens are well kept and neatly trimmed back for the impending winter. The exterior of the main house is ornate and gothic, like a genuine castle.

"Wow." Sophie marvels at the immensity of the ninety-room home that has stood since the early twentieth century.

We take a guided tour, during which we learn about the history of Sir Henry Fernsby, along with his financial rise and fall. The estate itself is fascinating, with a room for every occasion, secret tunnels, and features that were cutting-edge technology at the time it was built. I enjoy watching Sophie appreciate each curved detail carved into furniture and comment on how ostentatious some things are. Our guide, Rick, ties up the tour by directing us to the restaurants and gift shop.

"Hardly seems fair, does it?" Sophie chimes as we browse the souvenirs on offer.

"What's that?"

"This Henry left school at seventeen to work for his father and, by twenty-two, he was made partner. I know it was a different time, but I've worked my butt off, gotten my degree, learned the ropes of the business, *never* stopped working, and I barely get acknowledged."

We spent the entire evening talking without ever having a lull in our conversation, and work hasn't come up since she mentioned her choice of house decor. I wish it had stayed that way. If I'm being honest, any mention of *McNamara Enterprises* or its current CEO turns my mood sour.

Before our face-to-face interaction, I admired him to an extent. From a business perspective, he has done well for himself. I'm just not the type of person to idolize someone because of their profit margins—especially not when they treat their own child so poorly. He won't be getting a souvenir.

Sophie picks up a single printed photo of the estate, and I grab a onesie for Grace that says "Queen of the castle".

"Ready for dinner? I made reservations at *Don Giovanni*."

I glance across the great hall at the Italian restaurant that now occupies what was once a ballroom. There is probably an extensive history of "important" people enjoying a meal within those walls. I've never been a fan of high-end dining, but this is Sophie's night to plan, so I go along with it.

The hostess directs us to our seats at a secluded table near a stone-faced fireplace. As far as ambiance goes, this place has it in spades. But I sit down at the table, open the menu, and struggle to read the contents. I settle on a rib-eye because it's recognizable and I can pronounce it without making a fool of myself.

"I don't even know what half of this stuff is. What is *bagna cauda*?" Sophie groans as she closes her menu in front of her.

Her exasperation makes me a little relieved that she isn't the type to frequent elaborate Italian restaurants and is as uncomfortable as I am. That relief disappears as soon as she continues speaking.

"I should have made reservations at a French restaurant. At least I can read the menu."

On one hand, I'm impressed she can read French because I gave it up the minute it was no longer mandatory in school. On the other hand, I keep getting glimpses of the woman my first impression told me she was—the one I want to stay away from—and that floods me with disappointment.

For the rest of dinner, we eat in relative silence. Sophie attempts to direct conversation, but I'm lost in my thoughts.

Trying to reconcile the Sophie who buys her dog a designer collar and drives a seventy thousand dollar SUV with the woman I've been slowly getting to know. The one who lied to brush me off and the one who asked me out. Which one is the genuine Sophie?

When our server comes to clear our plates and asks about dessert, Sophie blurts "no" with a level of enthusiasm that tells me she's eager to get this night over with. The young woman returns with our cheque, which Sophie insists on paying. I was fine with her planning our evening, but she already paid for tickets to get into *Casa Mesa*. Conceding to her demands in this case is tough to swallow. She picks up the near $300 tab without batting an eye. Another hint that she's used to this level of extravagance.

We walk outside without another word and head toward Sophie's car. She asks if I want a ride home, but as much as I'm trying to accommodate her hatred of traditional gender roles, that feels a bit demoralizing. Not to mention, my mother is basically a secret agent and she'll notice a woman dropping me off from two doors down. I'm not prepared for those questions.

"It's fine. It's in the opposite direction. I can just catch a ride-share from your place."

She stutters before finding her voice again. "Oh, you don't have to come all the way back to my place, then. You can just order a car from here. Save a few bucks."

The twelve or so dollars I'll save isn't enough motivation to abandon making sure she gets home safely. My father ingrained some things in me as a child about what it means to be a gentleman. Ensuring a lady arrives home safely is one of those things. Before I can express my determination to do so, Sophie pulls her key from her small purse, assures me she had a nice time, and starts speed walking down the path to the parking lot.

"Sophie, wait." I jog a few steps to draw even with her. "At least let me walk you to your car."

She nods, and a second later, we stroll along the empty walkway to the well-lit parking area, stopping beside her rear bumper.

"Thank you for tonight. It was… extravagant." I bite the inside of my cheek to resist grimacing at my summary of the evening. As awkward as this moment is, there is an intense tension between us that's begging to be cut by a kiss.

Sophie licks her lips and tilts her head back. Her body inches closer to mine, but at the same time, her eyes portray the same degree of confusion I'm feeling. I want nothing more than to end this night on a good note, but figuring out where we stand is a lot like trying to predict which way a jury is going to swing.

"Good night, Boyd." She blinks her usual confident mask back on and takes one step back.

"Good night, Sophie."

And with that, she's ducking into her car and driving off into the night.

25

SOPHIE

Growing Up

I've been on a lot of dud dates in my day. I've had guys take me out, only concerned with their anatomy and not with forming a connection. There have been a select few who made it through an entire evening without letting me get a word in because they were too self-absorbed to stop speaking about themselves. I've even experienced a couple of painfully shy guys who just blushed and stammered over their words. Throw in the rest, who viewed me as a career move instead of a person, and that's the history of my dating life.

Conversation with Boyd was effortless and comfortable. We didn't talk much about work, and mostly touched on childhood antics with our siblings and university escapades. I talked about funny stories with Ashlyn and Celeste, and how opposite they are—minus their united front when it comes to my job.

But once we sat down for dinner, things went sideways. Boyd all but shut down and did little more than give short answers to my questions. What bothers me is that I don't know why. Is it because I paid and he got bent out of shape about it? If that's the case, good riddance to him. I'm not interested in dating an insecure man-child who takes issue with a woman being independent and striving for a world of equal opportunity.

It's been three days since we parted ways at *Casa Mesa*, though, and the lack of an answer is eating away at me. I need a man's perspective to tell me where this went wrong.

I ask Andy to hold my calls, then dial Caleb's number, knowing he has Tuesday mornings off.

"How did you know I was just going to call you?" he answers.

"Twin intuition. My ears were burning."

He laughs, which is muffled by rustling on his end.

"Caleb McNamara, are you still in bed? At 10:40?"

"I got home late. Not all of us operate on banker's hours."

That sounds intriguing. I dig for some details on his late evening, but he brushes me off and claims it was just "work stuff." In an effort to encourage him to spill his guts to me, I offer a tidbit of my own complicated life. "You know the barista?"

"Yes." There's a note of amusement in my brother's voice. "Don't tell me. You went on a date with him and he got you to pay, then he called to say he was in a tough spot and needed you to loan him two grand so he can get his car fixed."

I scoff at that assumption. "That happened once. The other time the guy's dog was sick and you know I have a soft spot for animals."

"Soph."

"I know, I know. No, that's not what happened. I mean, we went on a date and I paid, but now I haven't heard from him at all. He doesn't have his own car, though."

"Sounds like another deadbeat."

"But he's not. Remember that gala I asked you to go to?"

"Yeah." Caleb grunts like he's finally getting out of bed and taking a good stretch.

"He was there, and they presented him with the Medal for Academic Excellence. He's finishing his MBA/JD and Dad was champing at the bit to have him come work for us."

"So, is this guy using you for a job? If he's not a deadbeat, why did you have to pay?"

"This is the twenty-first century, thank you. I paid because *I* asked *him* out." I don't want to get into the details of why I insisted on paying. That's beside the point. I explain the events that transpired between the gala and our date, hoping Caleb can make sense of it.

Instead, he only focuses on the vitriol I received from our father. "Geeze, Soph. Why do you put up with that?"

"One of us has to!" I snap, annoyed he's missing the point of this conversation.

"That's not fair. Don't put your decisions on me. I made the best choice for me and there's nothing stopping you from doing the same, except this undeserved sense of loyalty. Like you've been controlled by a narcissist your entire life and can't see a way out."

Everyone thinks I stay because I can't see it, but that couldn't be further from the truth. I'm well aware of how toxic the work environment is in this building, which is why I'm determined to fix it. It's a lot harder to fix things when you're on the outside looking in.

"Right now, I just need you to support me in my choice, even if you don't agree. I constantly have people chirping in my ear that I need to quit and find a new job, but I need you to trust that I'm doing what I think is best. Not just for me."

Caleb blows out a long sigh. "I do. You know I'll always have your back. That's why it makes me so angry when I hear how he treats you. It has nothing to do with him being your boss; it's because he's your father."

A small part of me misses the days when Caleb and I were ushered around from cross-country track meets, to violin and piano practice, to weekends at our grandparents because our parents were going away on a business trip. I miss the years of learning to ride bikes with our Grandpa Fred because our dad was too busy to teach us. I miss the days of having a glimmer of hope that things would be different as an adult. Because now I'm here, and it's not easy at all. Life was less complicated when Henry was too busy to remember we existed.

I click out of an email from a client who is having a sale at her designer purse boutique and roll my eyes. I literally arrange your shipments, Adeline. No way am I paying your ridiculous markups. "Just tell me what to do about Boyd."

"I don't know what to tell you, Soph. If you want answers, just talk to the guy."

"Ugh. What good is having to share a womb with someone if they can't just miraculously solve your problems later in life?"

"I'm not sure that's a thing. As much as I wish I could, I can't… and it's only a problem if you make it one. Would you rather I call to talk to hi—"

"No."

Caleb chuckles. "I thought so. Doesn't sound like it went too well when he talked to Dad, but kudos to him for standing up to the old jerk."

Andy pokes his head in the door, gesturing wildly in some kind of interpretive dance I can't figure out.

"Sorry. I have to go. Andy is… malfunctioning. Let's make plans for your next day off, okay?"

Caleb snorts a "ha!" and we both know a day off is not in his immediate future. "Sure thing. Let me know how things go with the barista, okay? Maybe you can bring him into the restaurant for a date."

I return my own "ha!" and assure Caleb I'll send him an update, then end our call. "What is it, Andy?"

"Boyd is down at security. He asked if you have a minute." Andy is beaming at me, but schools his expression when I glare back. "Or I can tell him to get lost. Your call."

"You can let him in. But please, if you appreciate your job at all, don't be weird."

"I make no promises," he retorts as he leaves with an exaggerated sway of his hips, demonstrating the salsa lessons he claims to be taking.

My mind races for the several moments it takes until there's a knock at my door. Boyd flashes a tentative smile—if you can call the straight line his lips form a smile—as he squeezes inside. "He is a very… enthusiastic assistant."

"That's one word for it." I return his almost smile, waving for him to come in.

He only steps inside a few feet, then stops. "I'm sorry I haven't called."

That sounds like a precursor for a pre-emptive breakup. The start of an "It's not you, it's me" speech. I wait patiently for the "but…" It doesn't come.

"Do you like Mexican food?"

My eyebrows collapse together as I study Boyd, trying to get a read on where this is going. I doubt he's asking me out for Mexican food at 11am. "Sure. Who doesn't?"

"What about street food… not like food off the street, but food trucks? Barbeque?"

Now I'm even more confused. "Yeah. All of the above. As long as it's cooked, I like it. Don't get me started on how much I hate sushi."

"As much as you hate pumpkin spice?" He stares straight ahead, still not changing expressions.

I restrain my giggle, recalling my comments when he suggested that as a drink. "More."

"Wow, okay. Noted." He takes a step forward, reaching down to the back of a chair to lean on. "What about French food?"

"Well, my brother studied in French culinary schools for several years. I went over to visit on every school break and spent a full summer in Paris. So I guess you could say I'm familiar with it. Is it my preference? Not necessarily."

I'm not sure what my answer satisfied for Boyd, but he finally takes a seat.

"Can we try again?" He looks at me expectantly. "I guess what I'm asking is, will you go out with me?"

His choice of words is intentional. He's gone through law school. Words matter, and he's asking the same thing I did. Since he's here now, obviously he wasn't put off by my insistence on paying and planning our last attempt. Maybe it was just a terrible plan. The only fair thing to do is hand over control for a night and see what happens.

"Okay."

'm more nervous to knock on her door now than I was on our first date. My knuckles graze the door and make a faint sound. No answer. That only serves to increase my heart rate. I knock again, louder this time.

"One second!" Sophie shouts from inside. She sounds panicked.

Crank up the speed of my heart a little more.

My foot taps on the concrete stoop of its own accord as I wait. At least sixty seconds pass before Sophie comes to the door. She pulls it open wide, and she looks like she's been caught in a deluge. She's sopping wet, with her drenched hair matted to her head. "Help."

I duck inside and close the door behind me. "What happened?"

"Shower…" She makes an exploding sound and a matching gesture with both hands.

"Utility closet?"

She points to a door beside the kitchen, so I run in and find her small furnace, washer and dryer, and fuse panel. I search along the water pipes to find the shut-off valve. The sound on the other side of the wall eases and stops by the time I walk through her bedroom, into the ensuite. Her bathroom is soaked from top to bottom, with water pouring out onto the hardwood in her bedroom. The stand-up shower only has a door covering half of its width, so there was no chance of containing the spray.

"How did this happen?" I try not to chuckle at Sophie when she walks into the room behind me, looking defeated. Even Wilson is wet, but he looks thrilled. I bend down to give him a scratch behind the ear and he responds by doubling the speed of his wagging tail. "Hey, buddy."

"I called the super to fix the issue with my water pressure. He came and told me it was just my shower head, but that's not his job to change it. Direct quote: 'It's not a building problem; it's a *you* problem.'" She mimics the super's voice, making it even harder not to laugh. "I looked online, watched a few tutorials, and felt confident I could handle it. Pete the Plumber's YouTube channel made it look easy, so I followed along and all was fine. But the problem was *not* my shower head. I turned it on to get ready, but a surge of water blew off the shower head and well... all hell broke loose."

There's no stopping my laugh now. She looks incensed over the situation, and I can't blame her, but the way she explains it is hilarious. "Pete the Plumber? Why didn't you call an actual plumber?"

She places both hands on her hips, drawing my attention to how her dripping wet tank top and yoga pants cling to her curves. "I'll have you know, I'm capable of doing things on my own. This was not my fault."

I straighten my expression to match her serious one. "No doubt it wasn't. Why don't we get what we can cleaned up, then I'll take a look at it?"

The tentative smile she offers sends mixed signals. Like she appreciates my offer to help, but hates accepting it. The same protective instinct I had the first night I called her consumes me again. She doesn't *need* me to come in and fix things, but I want to.

"I'll be right back." She exits the bathroom and returns a minute later with a mop and bucket to start soaking up water that has pooled on her bedroom floor.

For the first time, I look at her space. She has a pink upholstered king-size bed in the same shade as her sofa, topped with a crisp white duvet and floral throw pillows. Wilson has his own bed under the window, but I suspect the furry grey blanket spread across the foot of the bed is for him. The art above the headboard is a woman's silhouette, but somewhat abstract in strokes of pink and grey. I stare at it for a moment before Sophie interrupts.

"I had that painted in France. You know… 'paint me like one of your French girls'?" She winks at me, and I realize what she's implying. That painting isn't just a woman… It's her.

Now my urge to study it is even stronger, but I need to distract myself. "Do you have some towels I can use to clean this up? Then we can just throw them in the washer? Otherwise, this will take hours."

She turns to face a tall, narrow shelf behind the door, then bursts out laughing.

I poke my head around to see what's so funny and discover all the towels are already wet. The two of us have a good laugh as I pull them off of the shelf one by one, mopping up what I can from the floor with any remaining dry spots, then haul them to the laundry room. Sophie walks in behind me, now wearing dry clothes, carrying her wet ones. Her hair is pulled back into a tight ponytail, exposing the delicate column of her neck. She's stunning. Even when she's flustered, soaked, and defeated.

"Guess I can't wash these until we turn the water back on." She tosses her clothes into the washing machine and shuts the door.

"Let me see what I can do."

We take forty-five minutes just to get the room dry, then another hour for me to take off the stop valve, clear out the debris that has collected in it, and reattach it with new Teflon tape. I reinstall the shower head and when I'm confident it's not going to flood Sophie's house again, I return to the shut-off valve in the laundry room.

Sophie is in the bathroom when I re-enter, standing in the centre of the patterned black and white ceramic tile floor. She's facing me, not the shower. "Thank you for this. You didn't have to—"

"I wanted to. It was really no trouble." I step forward, stopping a few inches in front of her. This wasn't what I had planned for the evening. We were supposed to go skating and then see where the night took us. I thought we'd be debating which food trucks to try. I wasn't expecting a busted shower to bring me within five inches of Sophie in her bathroom.

"Thank you," she repeats. Her eyes trail up my face without her moving her head, so she's looking at me through her thick lashes.

The racing heart I was dealing with when I knocked on her door was nothing compared to how fast it's beating now. I breathe out her name, "Sophie."

She doesn't hesitate to reach her arms around the back of my neck and close the gap between our lips. The tingling sensation is automatic, shooting from my mouth, right down to my knees. I could turn into a puddle if I wasn't convinced she had mopped enough already for one evening. Everywhere her hands graze along my skin and through my hair leaves a new sensation, intensifying the feeling of her soft lips caressing mine.

Too few seconds later, she pulls her head back, but doesn't release her grip on my neck. "This would have been so much more romantic if I was soaked because it was raining."

She smirks with her glistening lips. "I've always wanted to kiss someone in the rain."

I lose all sense.

With my arms around her waist, I tug her into the shower and turn the water back on. It flows from the faucet at a steady pace, but the initial jolt is cold. Sophie yelps, so I turn her back against the far wall and shield her by leaning forward, placing one hand on either side of her head. My pants and back are soaked, but I hardly notice because I'm distracted by the hungry look in Sophie's eyes.

She grabs at the loops on my pants and pulls me against her. "Kiss me."

I don't waste a second before I comply. I'm convinced even without the water, we'd steam up the entire room. The way she keeps her hold on me, clutching me close, is a level of hot that tap water could never compete with. She whimpers into my mouth when my teeth graze her lips, granting me permission to take this up another notch. I spin her around so the warm water rushes over us both, drowning me in a mix of water and Sophie.

We finally pull our lips apart, standing under the shower like a low-budget version of *The Notebook*. Sophie's brown eyes stare into mine, blinking away the dripping water.

"I hope it rains every day." My voice is hoarse. Raspy. Laced with wanton desire.

She chuckles at my lame line, but it quickly morphs into a full on laugh. An unencumbered belly laugh. It leaves me confused what she finds so funny about what I thought was an intense few moments. I may be out of practice with jokes, but it wasn't *that* bad. I turn to shut the water off so I can figure out what's so hilarious.

"We…" She takes a deep breath, easing her laugh. "We don't have any towels."

Whoops. That was an oversight in the heat of the moment. If we used the towels in the washer, we'd be worse off. I really didn't think through my own situation, because it's hovering around freezing and I have to get home in wet clothes.

We both stand in the shower with dripping clothes, laughing and sneaking glances. At least, I know I am. This woman is an enigma. She's shown me so many facets of her personality and I'm not sure which is the dominant one that defines who Sophie is. But that's part of her intrigue. She can't be boiled down to one adjective.

"How did you get so good at plumbing?" she asks, clutching her arms around me and shivering.

I wrap my arms around her, pulling her into my chest. "I do a lot of repairs at the café."

"You're a very dedicated worker, Boyd Edwards. Your boss is lucky to have you." She tilts her head up to look me in the eyes once again.

"It's my café, Sophie. I am the boss."

27

Irresistible

He's not a barista. He's an entrepreneur. A business owner. Not just *a* business owner, but one who owns a thriving café in downtown Toronto. One who rolls up his sleeves to do the work instead of sitting in the back office ordering people around for minimum wage. He did all that while pursuing a double degree and getting top marks in his graduating year? Despite our conflicting encounters, my level of respect for Boyd has increased tenfold.

"Your café? How did you...?"

He keeps his arms wrapped around me—which I appreciate because it's freezing in here after shutting the water off—and rests his chin on top of my head. "Why don't you get changed into something dry?"

If most other men suggested that, I'd probably stand here in my soaking wet clothes just to prove a point that I don't have to listen to them. The exception being a select few men in my family. But I don't get the impression Boyd is trying to boss me. He's showing concern—something Henry hasn't done a day in my life.

I agree and carefully slink out of the bathroom into my bedroom closet. My clothes sound like a pile of slop when I drop them to the floor because they're saturated. But wow. Totally worth it. That was, hands down, the most passionate kiss of my life. I always thought people who said, "It took my breath away," were either asthmatic or dramatic, but it is very much a real thing. Boyd stole my breath and performed mouth-to-mouth to give it back.

Quickly, I use a spare T-shirt to dry off my damp skin, pull on some dry pyjamas, then use the shirt to wrap my hair so it doesn't get me wet all over again. I grab some extra clothes I've had stashed in my closet and rush back to the bathroom. When I fling the door open, I'm caught a little off guard. Boyd is standing in front of the sink, topless, wringing out his shirt.

"Oh. Sorry, I..."

"Sorry, I..."

We talk over each other, but he doesn't look affected at all. My cheeks are burning, and it's not because I'm embarrassed. It's because I'm flustered, staring at this man who is so much more than a barista, but has a torso like a fit lumberjack. I mean, probably one who cuts down small trees, but still. Now his deep, rumbly voice seems to match.

"Caleb's clothes." I hold the T-shirt and joggers out to him. "I thought you might want to..."

"Yeah, that'd be great. Thanks." He takes the two items from my hands and I rush out the door into my kitchen.

While he's changing, I go turn on the load of laundry to clean all of my soaking wet linens so I can have a proper shower tomorrow. I don't think I'll ever be able to stand in that shower without that very memorable kiss replaying in my head. What's the opposite of an amnesiac? Because that's what I'm going to be.

"Hey." Boyd interrupts my daydreaming as I turn the washing machine on.

I'm going to have to write Caleb a thank-you card for leaving his clothes here. His *Ecole de Cuisine* shirt was from his early years in France and fits about half a size too small on Boyd. The grey track pants and no socks beats a tux any day.

"Do you want to put your stuff in the dryer?"

He walks forward with his damp clothes that he's folded into a neat pile. "That will make getting home a lot more comfortable. If you don't mind."

He's not implying he is in a rush to leave, but the reminder he will be makes me sad already. Having him in my space that is supposed to be my female sanctuary has been a nice short-term reprieve from the silence I normally have here.

I take his clothes and set them for a twenty-minute cycle. When I spin back around, he's standing only a foot away. The biologically motivated part of me that is still reeling from his kiss wants to make a memory to implant in this room too.

He leans forward, placing one hand on the top of the dryer. Just when I think he's going to kiss me, there's a loud knock at the interior door to the hallway.

He smiles with one side of his lips, not looking nearly as disappointed as I am. "You should get that."

Seconds later, I open the back door and find Celeste. Wilson comes to greet her with a wagging wet tail. Between my wet dog, the T-shirt on my head, and the chaos that has consumed my condo, Celeste looks a little confused.

"What happened? I thought I heard some noise, but I assumed it was your pipes acting up again."

"That's one way to put it." I laugh at her wide-eyed expression. "My shower exploded and flooded my whole place."

Before I can explain that Boyd helped me, Celeste peeks her head around me and spots him exiting the laundry room. "Oh dear. Look at you poor kids. Have you eaten?" The smile on Celeste's face is so transparent, it's laughable.

I'm about to tell her we'll order in, but Boyd beats me to a reply.

"No, we haven't. Have you?"

Him asking if she's eaten catches me by surprise. I should have learned by now that I can't assume when it comes to Boyd Edwards. He's not eager to shoo away my elderly friend like I thought. It sounds like he's welcoming her into our date. And I appreciate that so much more than a candlelit dinner for two.

"No, but I made paella. Sophie's favourite. I was coming over to invite her for some." She sends Boyd an exaggerated half-face wink. "It'll be ready in ten." Then she's headed back next door with haste.

Boyd is scratching Wilson's ears when I turn around. "Paella, huh?"

"My cousin Isla makes it all the time. I had it once and was hooked." I watch as Boyd further bonds with my dog—who I'm convinced could bond with anyone—but it still means something. "That was Celeste's way of ordering us over for dinner if you didn't catch that."

He steps forward, my Velcro dog close behind. "I figured." He stops two feet away.

"You're not disappointed we got interrupted?" I raise my eyebrows, issuing a silent challenge.

Boyd closes the gap between us. "Very." He teases my lips with a breath, but doesn't make contact. It's torture. "But I hope I'll have other chances to kiss you."

Celeste could dump ghost chilis in this paella and it wouldn't compare to the heat Boyd is bringing. I need a glass of ice water. Or a cold shower. Except the thought of my shower does the opposite of cool me down.

We walk the short distance to Celeste's door, which she's left open a crack. True to her word, dinner is served a few minutes later and we chat over Spanish cuisine and rosé until Celeste convinces Boyd to make tea for everyone. The number of times I tried to help with anything in this woman's kitchen and she used actual violence, but Boyd shows up, and she insists we could both "use some tea." I'm still so confused about this—especially when she gives me the same dramatic wink she gave Boyd earlier.

Celeste continues, asking Boyd questions about himself that I didn't know answers to. She also asks me questions I *know* she knows the answers to, but asks for Boyd's benefit. My favourite place in France—easy, French Riviera. My most cherished childhood memory—the day I found out Aunt Zara adopted two daughters and our grandparents took us to meet them. Where I see myself in twenty years—running *McNamara Enterprises*.

I learn that Boyd's parents came from England decades ago, but have held onto their British roots. He was on the tennis team in high school, but gave it up before he started University. He's never owned a pet, but you wouldn't know that the way Wilson has become obsessed with him. And he hasn't been in a relationship for seven years, but he sidestepped subsequent questions about that topic.

After we help Celeste clean up, we excuse ourselves and return to my place. Wilson needs a walk, and since it's dark, Boyd offers to come with us. A likely side effect from our first phone call. He changes back into his clothes and leaves Caleb's old stuff neatly folded on my dresser.

We stick to the well-lit sidewalks and tour my neighbourhood, commenting on holiday decor and curb appeal. There's such a level of comfort and familiarity between us, it's almost suffocating. Only because of my own fears of what could come from life after a second date. Things have never ended well for me beyond this point. His presence is a promise of inevitable heartbreak. Not to mention what will happen if Henry finds out.

Boyd stops walking. "What happened?"

I've lost count of how many times he's asked that tonight. "Nothing. Just thinking."

"Care to enlighten me?" he asks, continuing his steps forward at Wilson's command.

"No. Let's just enjoy tonight."

He accepts that response, and that's exactly what we do. Less than an hour later, Boyd leaves and I fall asleep wearing the shirt that smells like him, hoping I'm not setting myself up for heartache.

28

BOYD

Sugar, We're Goin Down

Once bitten, twice shy no longer applies to me. Not in this case. Then again, it's unfair to lump Sophie into the same category as the woman who bit me and left me to bleed out without a second thought. Clearly we both made snap judgements about each other based on first impressions, but each moment I spend with her, I peel back another layer of the complex fabric that makes up Sophie McNamara.

And I like what I see. A lot.

She's invading my thoughts when I'm not around her and consuming me when I am. I'm nearing the end of my LPP training and will transition into the work placement in the new year. That will place new demands on my schedule, but Sophie has been nothing but supportive. She even pored over resumes with me to find someone suitable to help in the evenings and weekends at the café. Once I'm in my work placement, I can't guarantee I'll be able to get here before the day shift ends, so it's necessary to have someone reliable. The college student I hired, Donnie, seems to be catching on well after two weeks of training.

Tonight is his first shift closing on his own. It's been years since I wasn't in this café to either open or close—sometimes both. But it's time to start transitioning into my new career and trust my staff to keep *Just Add Coffee* afloat without my daily presence.

I hand Donnie a key for the front door. "If you have any questions, just call me, or send me a text if it's not urgent. I'll talk you through whatever you need to know."

"Got it. I think I have everything under control." The tall, redheaded college student nods.

"Don't forget to put the cash in the safe and lock the back door before you go. And lock the front door as soon as it hits 9 o'clock. Not a minute before."

Donnie smiles, but it grows twice as wide when he spots something behind me. "Excuse me. I've got a customer to serve."

I spin around to see what's got him so happy and the sight has the same effect on me. "I've got this one, Donnie."

"But I thought—"

I interrupt him by walking around the counter and greeting Sophie with a searing kiss. Not marking my territory. Just happy to see her after four days.

"Hey." I soak in the faint smile adorning her soft lips.

"Hi." She leans around me to look behind the counter. "This is the new guy?"

I spin myself so I'm standing beside Sophie and put my arm around her back. "Sophie, this is Donnie. Donnie, this is"—I pause for a second, unsure how to introduce her—"Sophie." Safe bet.

"Nice catch, Boss."

I tighten my grip around her waist. "I didn't catch her. She hunted me like a hungry lioness and I was just a helpless gazelle."

She smirks and raises one dark eyebrow. "Really?"

"Give me this one. It will give me some cool points," I whisper. "Do you want a coffee before we go?" It's a perfect opportunity to judge Donnie's flat white skills.

"No thanks. I'm trying to limit my caffeine intake."

I mock gasp and clutch my chest. "Why would you say such a horrible thing?"

"Giving me free coffee every time I come in isn't going to keep your business afloat. This is my way of widening your profit margins." She makes the statement with a note of humour, but something is off.

"Always the wise business woman." I kiss her temple. "Ready?"

"Absolutely."

We make our way down the street to where Sophie's vehicle is parked. She's quiet as we walk, and because it's out of character for the Sophie I've become familiar with, it's unnerving.

"Everything okay?"

"Hmm?" She tilts her head to glance at me, then turns her focus back to the sidewalk. "Yeah, sorry."

"Are you sure? If you're too tired…"

"No, I'm fine." She straightens her posture, walking around to the driver's side. Before she climbs in, she pauses. "Do… uh… do you want to drive?"

Something is wrong. Besides the fact she's relinquishing control of her vehicle, since we stepped outside, she just hasn't appeared excited about tonight.

We both round her SUV, coming to a pause at the front.

"What's wrong?"

"Nothing. I…" She blows a long breath that turns to fog and dissipates in the cool air. "Just had a rough day. You don't want to hear about it." She attempts to walk past me toward the passenger side, but I stop her by sweeping my arm out to grab her waist.

"Soph, of course I do."

Her shoulders slump, and she leans into me. "Can we have a quiet night somewhere? I don't know what you had planned, but—"

"A quiet night sounds great."

A soft smile spreads her lips. "Thanks."

We settle on grabbing takeout and going back to her place. She has been missing Wilson with the long hours she's been working and feels guilty about the burden that places on Celeste. As we stand at the edge of the Thai restaurant, waiting for our order, I try to reassure her it's not a hardship for Celeste to watch him. Despite my efforts, it doesn't seem to alleviate the distress she feels about it. As our order gets called, I realize that her not being home for Wilson may not entirely be the long hours she's working, but partly to do with her coming to visit me at the café after work several nights a week.

That makes me feel some of the measure of guilt she must be. It also makes me pause. For as pragmatic as I try to be, when it comes to my romantic life, my history says I'm reckless. Blind to obvious faults and afflicted with rose-coloured glasses. Things between us are moving too fast.

When we pull into her parking spot, she seems lighter. Happier. Like all she wanted was to just be at home. Whereas, I feel the opposite. Heavier, sombre. But just because I think it might be a good idea to pump the brakes, doesn't mean I'll flake on our plans or abandon her after I said I wanted to hear what's bothering her. My word means something.

We pick up Wilson from Celeste before going to Sophie's and his presence lightens her mood even more. He's bouncing around both of us, making Sophie gush over him just for existing. As we dish our food, he keeps gifting me with a slobbery plush toy. After the third time, I pick it up to look at it and realize it's a stuffed California roll. I toss it into the living room, so Wilson goes skittering after it.

"Sushi?"

Sophie looks up from placing a spring roll on her plate. "Caleb thought he was funny. Figures Wilson would love it. He also bought him that obnoxious collar and leash set that cost as much as a car payment."

That makes me feel like more of a jerk for assuming she bought it as some pretentious way to show off. Based on how her face brightens whenever she mentions her brother, it's not the designer things she appreciates. Their interaction at the café all those weeks ago was a stark contrast to me and my siblings, and is surprising for a pair of kids raised by a man as unaffectionate as Henry McNamara. I'd never wish Henry's parenting on anyone, but I'm glad Sophie didn't have to face it alone. It's also promising that Caleb got out of Henry's grip, so I hope Sophie realizes she can do the same. Some day.

We finally sit down to eat, crowded at the two stools along her kitchen peninsula.

"So, you going to tell me about your day?"

She quickly stuffs a bite of green curry in her mouth, as if she's trying to buy some time before responding.

I wait… and wait for her to chew.

"I swear, the longer I'm in this job, the less clients listen to me."

"What do you mean? All clients or specific ones?"

She stuffs her mouth… again. I wait… again.

"Just the ones Henry is friendly with. Ones who subscribe to his mentality. I swear, he sends them to me first, knowing they won't listen, just so they can complain to him and tell him I've failed. I don't understand why someone so focused on building a successful business puts so much effort into sabotaging it."

I have a few choice words I could use to describe Henry and explain why he does what he does. None are suitable terms to use on a date or to describe your date's father. No matter how true they may be.

"You can't understand it because it doesn't make sense to anyone but him. He caters to his ego, not to business sense. Not even common sense."

"Yeah. I guess. Do you know how humiliating it is when these men request specific obscure products for an impossible price point, and I spend weeks tracking down someone else in the country interested in the same product to condense costs, only for person A to back out on the deal? Then I have to call person B, or sometimes persons B, C, D, and E, to tell them it's not happening. Not only do I waste days or weeks of my time negotiating a deal that falls through, I end up with ticked off potential clients who take their business elsewhere."

It requires a lot of restraint not to go on a tangent about how she should find somewhere that appreciates her and her tenacity in making clients' demands happen. That she doesn't deserve to have her time or skills wasted. That her job should be a point of pride, not a source of endless stress.

But I know that's not what she needs to hear right now—thanks to life with an outspoken sister and years with an opinionated best friend—so I tell her what she does. "I see your value, Sophie. I'm not trying to feed you a line, but I do. I see you and everything you offer."

And the second her lips land on mine, I'm not sure I want to pump the brakes at all.

Saturday

Things are moving fast. Faster than I expected when I first asked Boyd out. But in the five weeks since our first date, he's leapfrogged other people in my life as the person I want to confide in. I love my brother, but he's not understanding when it comes to my tolerance for our father. Caleb doesn't know how much his leaving to pursue his dreams impacted our family. Impacted me. And I'd never tell him, because I don't want him to regret his choice. I'm proud of him for everything he's accomplished, but that doesn't mean I can pursue the same path—not culinary school, but the path to a different dream. Running *McNamara Enterprises* has always *been* my dream. I have a different threshold for when I'm ready to walk away, and I haven't reached it.

When Boyd left here on Tuesday, I felt like I had suffered a loss. My feminine sanctuary turned into an emotional prison once he was gone. A transformation from a place where I could bare my soul to one where my walls keep my secrets and don't confess to anyone that the Sophie I show to the outside world isn't the one present here.

Sophie behind these doors is lost. Conflicted. Defeated.

But I'm also determined and focused. I just don't know if my focus is in the right place.

Like I said: conflicted.

I do my best to shove down my flip-flopping thoughts and focus on getting ready. I haven't seen Boyd since Tuesday, and the pathetic part of me that doesn't prioritize a social life is sitting home alone on a Saturday, desperate to see him. He's working tonight, so I'm going to surprise him.

The drive takes nearly twenty-five minutes to go six kilometres. Moments like this, I miss life in the small town I grew up in. You could drive from one end of town to the other in ten minutes. Not to mention, before Henry relocated *McNamara Enterprises* to Toronto, he was often gone on work trips, which made life more peaceful. That might be the real reason for my feelings on the matter.

Regardless of my thoughts on my current postal code, walking up to the front door of *Just Add Coffee* gives me a new feeling of home. I swing the door open and spot Boyd and Monica standing behind the counter, having an animated conversation. There's one teenage boy at a table toward the back, but the café is otherwise empty.

Boyd turns my way, smiling as soon as his eyes land on me. "Hey! I didn't know you were coming." He walks over to the edge of the pickup counter, pulling me in for a tight hug.

Admittedly, his friendship with Monica makes me a little insecure, but part of that is because I've never taken the time to get to know her. Boyd eases that insecurity when he kisses just above my ear, then grabs my hand to pull me toward the young guy sitting at the table with his headphones on.

"Captain." Boyd taps his shoulder, waiting to continue until the kid acknowledges him. "This is Sophie. Sophie, this is Phoenix, Monica's son."

A pair of grey eyes focus on me, then light up with a bright smile. "Hi." Phoenix stands to an impressive height that surpasses me by an inch or two, and reaches out a hand to shake mine.

Again, my insecurities ease a bit more, because that doesn't seem like the reaction of a young kid whose mother is being two-timed.

"Hi, Phoenix. Nice to meet you." I offer him a smile—partly because I am happy to meet him, and partly because I'm grateful he helped the fist around my heart relax.

Boyd elaborates on his introductions, telling us each a little about the other. It's obvious Phoenix is important to him. "Do you mind keeping Sophie company for a bit, Captain? I've got a bit of work to do and need to finish chatting with your mom." He waits for a nod from Phoenix, sends me a wink and a promise to bring me a non-caffeinated drink, then disappears back behind the counter.

I take a seat across the table from Phoenix. "What are you listening to?"

"Old stuff." He turns his phone to face me so I can look at his playlist.

"Fall Out Boy? You listen to them?"

"Yeah, the coach on my soccer team says he's a reformed emo kid, but can't let the music go. Whatever that means."

I chuckle at the accuracy of that statement. There's never been anything outwardly "emo" about me, but my musical preferences are another story. "Fall Out Boy is my favourite band ever. I'm not one to gush over celebrities, but I'd spontaneously combust if I ever ran into Patrick Stump." I lean forward to whisper, "Don't tell Boyd."

Phoenix laughs as he fiddles with something on his phone. Suddenly, *Dance, Dance* is playing through the speakers. "My mom hates when I do that."

Sure enough, Monica's head peeks around the corner that leads into the employees-only area of the café. "Child, what have I told you?"

Before Phoenix can open his mouth—and likely dig himself a deeper hole—I reply, "Sorry, Monica. I love Fall Out Boy. I asked him to."

She looks at her son with a skeptical stare. "Well, good. Next time they play a concert, you have a new chaperone." Then she disappears back behind the wall.

I'm surprised by how easily she let it go… and how willing she is to trust me with her kid. Whether it would happen is a different story, but it eases my insecurities a bit more, to the point they no longer exist.

"So, soccer, hmm? What position do you play?"

"Centre forward. I was the captain of the middle school team this year, but next year I'll have to try out for the high school team… start at the bottom again. I play in a league, too."

Boyd's nickname for him makes sense now.

"Sounds like you're a busy guy."

He shrugs. "I guess. You should come watch sometime. We don't start again until April, but Boyd sponsors the team, so he tries to come when he can."

Two things about that surprise me. One being that Phoenix must be more familiar with me than I am with him if he is comfortable enough to invite me to an event nearly five months down the road. Two, Boyd never ceases to amaze me with the secrets he keeps. Not illicit drugs or illegal vices, but things he should be proud of—brag about—and he doesn't say a word.

"Want to hear a cool story?" I ask, veering away from my internal gushing. "Well, it's kind of tragic, but cool."

Phoenix's eyes widen as he leans closer. "Okay."

"My family is Irish… well, my dad's family. My mom's family is mostly Greek. But anyway, my great-great-grandfather lived in Belfast in the early 1900s and was part of the crew who worked on the Titanic."

"Well, that doesn't sound like a claim to fame. No offence."

I laugh at his bluntness. I like this kid. "That's not the cool part. After they were done building the ship, everyone was so excited about it because it was cutting edge at the time, right? My great-great-grandfather, Thomas, bought a ticket on the Titanic, wanting to come to America for greater opportunities."

"Oh no." Phoenix's lips tilt downward and all excitement in his eyes disappears.

"You have to hear the whole story. Patience. So he bought the ticket, made all his arrangements to make the move, quit his job as a shipbuilder—but who could blame him, because the conditions were terrible? Everything. He was set to sail across the Atlantic."

"What happened? Please don't tell me he was one of the guys who left women and kids behind and made off with a lifeboat." He glances over at the opening to the employee area. "My mom and I watched the movie."

"Oh." I pause for a moment, recalling how old Caleb and I were when we watched it behind our parents' backs. I distinctly remember having just turned thirteen. Feels like forever ago. "Well, no. He never even got on the boat. His mom got sick two days before he was set to leave, and since he was her only son and he knew he'd likely never see her again, he stayed to take care of her."

"Wow."

"I know. Lucky. But that's not even the end of It. He missed the boat. Obviously it sank, but his mom passed away a few months later, and he still wanted to come to America. So almost two years later, he bought a ticket on the Lusitania and left Europe only weeks before the First World War. Then a year after that, the Lusitania sank too."

"Luck of the Irish, eh? So what did he do when he finally got to America? Win the lottery or something?"

I hear a deep chuckle behind me and turn to find Boyd leaning against the wall, apparently listening to our conversation.

"No, he moved to Detroit, where he stayed for a while, then, for some reason, decided that wasn't quite cold enough. So he packed up and headed north until he made it to Muskoka. Have you been there?"

"Yeah, my friend has a cottage in Port Carling. I went there for a week last summer."

"Nice. That's where I'm from… well, from Bala. My grandparents and aunts still live there, but I don't get to visit them much."

He smiles, but it's marked with a sadness in his eyes. "You should. Family's important."

I stare at the young sandy-haired kid, soaking in his wise words. "Yeah. It is." With a deep breath, I refocus to finish my story. "Anyway, Thomas got married to a woman from the area, then they moved down to Toronto. And you'll never guess what he did once he got here."

"This is going one of two ways. His luck continued, or it ran out."

"He was recruited to play for Canada's professional soccer team, and spent the next ten years as a footballer. After that, he was a team manager until he retired."

His bright eyes and upturned lips return at the mention of soccer. "That's so cool. That's my dream. Minus the sinking ships and dying mom part."

I figured. "It's important to have dreams." I just hope his dream works out better than mine has, because all too often, the dream is a lot better than reality.

30

BOYD

The Last of the Real Ones

One thing time with Sophie has taught me is that I should always trust my gut. My head reminded me of my past—the heartache and rejection that were so prevalent. It reminded me of failures and lessons I'd committed to, forever swearing I'd be smarter. But this woman who, on the surface, represented everything I promised myself I'd stay away from, couldn't be more different.

She's real. Easy-going. Vulnerable—though she doesn't like to be.

Watching her bond with Phoenix, seeing how he's fully engaged in her story, makes me appreciate her even more. Monica walks up behind me, squeezing my arm when she sees it too. I've only recently confided in her how deep I'm in with Sophie, and, despite our years' long commitment to staying single, she's been very supportive. She may have even uttered the words, "Told you so."

"Are you ready to go, kiddo?" Monica asks.

Before Phoenix can respond, Sophie speaks up. "Oh, please stay and hang out for a bit. I mean, if you don't have somewhere else to be." She smiles at Monica, and there are no words to describe how much that one sentence solidifies everything I'm feeling.

Monica looks at me as if she's asking permission. It's so out of character for her, because she's the first person to tell me what to do, even though I've been her boss for years.

"Yeah, Mon. Stay. I've got to lock up in twenty minutes. Order some late-night food and we can hang out for a bit."

In a move that chases away some more of the rain cloud that's been surrounding my heart for years, Monica pulls out the third stool at the table and drops in between Sophie and Phoenix. "If you insist. You're paying, right?" she asks me.

"Anything but sushi," I reply, smirking at Sophie.

"I'd rather eat yesterday's Danishes off the floor of the dumpster." She pulls up her phone and starts scrolling through something.

"You two are going to get along great." I leave them to their food-ordering decisions and walk into the back to finish my evening tasks.

No more customers come in before closing, so I'm done with the important stuff by the time our food arrives. I lock the front door after our delivery driver leaves and move a stool over between Sophie and Monica.

I was so tired when I started my shift today, but now I'm wide awake and it has nothing to do with caffeine consumption. The animated conversation flowing between three important people in my life energizes me. A meeting between Sophie and Monica didn't worry me, but I was trying to work out the perfect setting for them to be able to talk that also provided a distraction if they couldn't find common ground. It didn't occur to me to let them meet in the place I met them both. The place that feels more like home to me than my actual address. All along, the answer was right in front of me.

We all talk for almost two hours until Monica and Phoenix prepare to leave. Sophie insists on driving them home since it's cold and dark, but Monica assures her they're fine. They live less than a ten-minute walk from here. Like she's been part of our little unit all along, Sophie leans in to hug them both before they walk out the door.

And finally, we're alone.

"Hi," I say as I flick off the lights, leaving us under the dim security lighting. She leans closer and I smell her sweet, floral shampoo. In one swift move, I taste her lips. Sophie mixed with sweet and sour sauce and MSG; she tastes like the remnants of the Chinese food we gorged on, which catapults it to the top of my favourite cuisines.

"Hi," she replies when we pull apart. "Sorry for dropping in unannounced."

"Did I give you the impression I was upset about it?" I offer a smile, but with the light behind me, she probably can't see it.

"No, but you were busy... with Monica. I didn't mean to interrupt."

I clasp my hands around her back, pulling her tight to my body. "I had to do inventory, and normally I'm here until the middle of the night getting it done. She just came to help so I could get some sleep."

Sophie tenses in my arms. Her soft body turns rigid against mine. "Oh. If you want to g—"

"I'm glad you're here, Soph. Sleep is overrated." I continue to explain to her how I was trying to come up with a plan so they could meet, and I'm glad they hit it off. Monica and Phoenix are an important part of my life, and now Sophie is too. Two more puzzle pieces fit together.

The major remaining one is my family, but they're wild cards. Holden is preoccupied and indifferent about my personal life. Phoebe is a busy new mom, and she gets attach-ed to people quickly—I learned that the hard way last time. My parents... well, Sophie would have a better chance of winning over a pride of hungry lions on the Serengeti. At least my mother.

So that's a subject for another day. Not only is my family a little precarious, but Sophie's actually makes me *want* to win over a pride of lions. During a drought. After I've fattened up and covered myself in bacon grease. I'd prefer that scenario over meeting with Henry McNamara again.

"I want you to meet my brother," Sophie blurts. "I mean... I know you've already kind of met him, but I want you to really meet him."

I blink a few times, wondering how she knew where my train of thought was going, and ended up at the same station. "What is required to 'really meet' someone? Do we need to come up with a secret bro handshake? I'm not sure I've had to 'really meet' someone before."

She slaps my chest. "I'm serious. Last time was... weird. But he knew from the minute he saw you that I liked you."

That statement surprises me. "You liked me, hmm?"

Silence.

Once again, I pull her in close, letting my lips find hers. She immediately responds, wrapping her hands around my head, greedily pulling me in closer. Somehow, we traverse the room and end up with Sophie backed against a table for two set along the far wall. She twists and shifts until she's seated on the table, giving me a better angle to ravage her mouth. Her neck. Her collarbone. It's too much and not enough all at once. Her breathy moans and sharp inhales. I don't stop until her legs are wrapped around my waist and I'm out of breath.

"And... how do you like me now?"

She giggles and throws her head back. "Would have been better if it was raining... but you, Boyd Edwards, I really, really like you."

"I really, really like you too, Sophie McNamara. If meeting Caleb is that important to you, count me in."

She doesn't reply for a few seconds, and when she does, it's through a fit of laughter. "Good. Is it weird we went from talking about my brother to me being backed up on a table with your tongue down my throat? I think that's weird."

"Shh. We won't tell him that. Trust me, I wasn't thinking about Caleb at all."

Sophie hops down from the table while straightening her V-neck sweater. "Well, come on. Let's get your to-do list finished so you can get some sleep. What's next?"

"You don't have to—"

"I'll disinfect this table first. No one wants to eat a croissant off a table that my butt was on. Well… maybe some people do. Not gonna judge." She starts walking toward the opening in the counter. "Where's your disinfectant?"

"Soph, it's fine. I can handle it."

"I know you *can* handle it. You can handle anything apparently, and do it flawlessly. But my point is, you don't *need* to do it alone. Let me help." She pauses her search for the cleaner to look straight at me. "Please."

She's not just offering to help. She's asking. Borderline begging, and I'm not sure if it's because she wants to stay longer or she feels like she owes me after her shower broke— even though she more than made up for that small repair. But I'm not about to refuse her.

"Inside the cupboard over the blender. Rags are under the sink."

"Thank you."

Minutes later, Sophie is disinfecting tables and chairs while I count the money in the register so I can finish the day's accounting. I'm in the midst of tallying the five-dollar bills when Sophie interrupts.

"So what's the deal with you and Monica, anyway?"

31

BOYD

Moving Pictures

figured this question was coming. It would be different if Monica was named Maurice and was a single dad. Our relationship has always raised questions and eyebrows.

"We've never been romantically involved, if that's what you're wondering. Just friends. Only ever friends."

"I–I wasn't asking that," she stammers from across the room. "I just meant… okay, yes, that is what I meant."

"Figured. Our friendship came about from repeated exposure, I guess."

She stands, grabbing the bottle of cleaner and flinging the rag overtop. "How sweet."

I laugh at her obvious sarcasm as I bundle the last of the bills. "She'd say the same thing. When we met, I was in a serious relationship, actually. We just became… work friends."

"Do you want to tell me about it? Your relationship?"

No. If I had it my way, it would never come up again. If I could help it, I'd never think about it again. But that hasn't worked for the past seven years. "Her name was Maggie."

Sophie nods as she walks closer to clean the display case.

"We met in our first year of university. I was doing my undergrad in biology with intentions of going to med school."

She scoffs. "Seriously? What even are you? Med school. Law School. Business owner. Am I cutting into the time you spend moonlighting as the city's secret superhero or something?"

"Now that you mention it, an elderly woman on Front Street got mugged on Tuesday night because I was tied up at your place." I give her a sly smile as I finish my current task. "Let me run this to the safe. Two seconds."

"Yeah, yeah. Go save a cat in a tree or whatever."

I laugh all the way to my office and realize that's the first time Maggie's name has left my lips in years and I was able to do anything more than scowl or mope. That alone is enough to have me walking super-speed back to Sophie.

When I come back out, she's emptying the garbage can near the front door. "Soph, you don't have to—"

"Ah. I want to. Keep talking." She waves one hand at me to continue after she grunts to pull the bag out.

I won't tell her now that it actually opens at the front so you can just slide it out. Minor detail. "I had this whole plan I thought I had to fulfil. My parents gave my siblings and me every opportunity to succeed, and the obvious choice was becoming a doctor. Right? That's the immigrant parent's dream. You work hard, scrape the barrel, build your life from nothing so your kids can be something."

Sophie nods again, carrying the garbage toward me with her nose scrunched. "I can relate to the parental pressure."

"It's a heavy load to carry. Let me take this." I slip the garbage from her hand and place it in the back. "Anyway, Maggie and I ended up being assigned as lab partners in a chemistry class. Things... progressed quickly. By the end of our first semester, I was convinced I was ready to propose. I knew we were young, so I didn't."

Sophie's shoulders droop. "That serious, huh?"

"That blind, really. I'd been working as a barista since my junior year of high school and enjoyed doing it. I was working thirty hours a week while going to school full time and trying to balance a relationship. She resented me for working so much and complained that she was getting the 'scraps'."

"That's kind of unfair. You were working when you started dating. Did she think you'd trade your job for her?"

So much of that question hits hard. With Maggie, I didn't even consider taking fewer shifts to appease her. I tried to make her feel important, but enough was never enough. With Sophie, I hired another staff member to clear up my schedule so I can spend more time with her and her dog. She never asked. She's here dealing with trash bags and cleaning butt marks off of tables. Never once has she made me feel like I had to choose. Yet, I despise her job. I hate everything about how she's treated and how small that company—or rather, Henry—makes her feel. How can I ask her to choose?

I swallow down the disappointment over Sophie's career choice and continue, "Maggie was the type of girl who had to have the best of the best. She'd say she wanted to enjoy the finer things in life and felt she worked hard to deserve them, but she was the only student walking around with an *Hermes* purse."

"Yikes. Did she come from money?" Sophie asks, dragging the mop and bucket from the utility closet. Looks like she's finding her way around just fine.

"No. She had a single mother who was on disability and they lived in geared-to-income housing. She received some scholarships and a lot of student loans just to afford university." At the time, I felt bad for the tough hand life had given her, so I complied with her demands... for a while. "I certainly didn't come from money, either. My parents saved by working hard and being financially smart. Once I reached university, they gave me a nest egg with stipulations. It had to be put to use to benefit me somehow. I couldn't just waste it on frivolous nonsense. With Maggie's obsession with designer things that was apparently my job to supply her with, I was afraid to tell her no. So I bought a failing coffee shop and tied up every dime I had."

I look at Sophie, expecting to see a little judgement or anger. Maybe look at me like I'm a hypocrite because I couldn't just tell Maggie the truth, so I lied because I didn't want to anger my parents. But none of that is there.

Instead, she smiles and concludes, *"Just Add Coffee."*

"Yeah, only it was called *Brown Water* at the time."

She laughs, sloshing some mop water across the floor. "That's a terrible name."

"Now you know why they were failing. I spent a good chunk on rebranding and making it look more professional. It was a mess from top to bottom."

"It is a much better name. I thought it was cute when I first went past. That's why I stopped."

Remind me to send a thank-you card to *Harbour Campaigns* for helping me with the relaunch. "I'm glad you did." I smile at the woman who walked into my café and changed my entire life. Maggie may have changed it too, and I can be grateful for her selfishness pushing me into an opportunity that ended up being a blessing, but that doesn't mean I forget the lessons I learned from her, either. "Toward the end of my third year, my dad was diagnosed with stomach cancer and the prognosis wasn't good. I was drowning in coursework I didn't understand, failing, hating every minute of it, and afraid for my parents to find out." I laugh, understanding how silly it might seem to be twenty-two years old and afraid of passing your parents a report card with failing grades. I'm confident Sophie understands the implications, though. "So I dropped out. I used the excuse that I wanted to work more to support my family since my dad wasn't able to anymore. Really, it was the coward's way out because I couldn't hack it in the biology program, let alone med school. Worst-case scenario would have been failing *and* losing the business I had sunk all of my money into."

She moves a little closer, pausing her task. "And how did that go over?"

"My dad was still disappointed. Mum was too distraught over my dad's condition to express her opinion. And if you knew my mother, you'd understand how out of character that is. She has no issues sharing her opinions, even when she's been proven wrong."

"Sounds like someone I know." She rolls her eyes, biting into her bottom lip. "So, how did Maggie take all of this?"

"As soon as I dropped out, she kept harassing me about my plans and asking what I wanted to do with my life. She made it clear that she dated me because she thought I was going to be a doctor someday, but there was no way she would stay with a barista. And that was it. While I thought my father was dying and my entire life had been turned on its head, she walked away."

"Wow. What a—"

"It was for the best," I interrupt. I spent enough time wallowing after we broke up; I don't need Sophie to waste time being angry over it. "All the signs pointing to her being selfish and spoiled were there all along. I just chose to ignore them, hoping things would change." With the espresso machine dismantled and clean, I start reassembling the pieces. "That wasn't even the worst of it, though."

Sophie pauses, dropping the handle of the mop to her waist and staring at me from her spot on the other side of the counter. "How did she get worse?"

"I guess that's where Monica comes in. When I first bought this place, it took two months for renovations, so all of *Brown Water*'s staff quit and moved on. Monica sent in her resume, and I almost skipped over her because she didn't have a ton of experience, but something told me to call her for an interview. She came in and immediately sold me on hiring her. She was so determined and willing to learn, I decided to give her a chance."

"Done," Sophie declares after reaching the door with the mop. "Let me guess. Maggie hated Monica."

"Despised her. She was convinced something was going on between us and nothing could change her mind. Even after we broke up, she'd show up here and hurl insults at both of us in front of customers. Long story short, it ended with a restraining order." And it is a very long story, indeed.

"Wow. So, Maggie never had any real reason to be jealous, did she?"

I know what she's really asking. Did I cheat on Maggie? "Never. I may not have picked the right person to be loyal to, but I can promise you one thing: I am loyal. Always."

32

SOPHIE

Champion

pparently, to spend time with my brother, I have to show up at his door at 7:30am on a Sunday before he goes to work. At least, that's the lengths I go to so I can interact with him in person. We text each other every day, but he's in the same country now; there's no reason why we have to communicate like he's still in France. I have a lot to tell— and ask—him, which needs to happen face to face.

He swings open his front door, wearing a scowl and sweatpants.

"I brought coffee." I hold up the tray of *Just Add Coffee* cups, grateful Tessa provided me with options.

"Soph. I just got home five hours ago and I have to be back at the restaurant at eleven." He answers like he's mad, but he pulls me in for a hug when I step inside.

"Sorry. I missed you and knew I had to take extreme measures to have some actual face time." But really, he's just being a whiner, because I didn't get home until after one and I was out the door by 6:30 to make a coffee stop on my way here. "If you want to go back to be—"

"Get in here." He pads his way into the open living area in his two-storey condo. "Want something to eat? I'll whip up breakfast."

I can hardly contain my excitement as an exuberant "yes" spills out.

My brother laughs, coming to a stop in his kitchen. "Don't get your hopes up. I haven't bought groceries for over a week."

That does sound less appetizing, but I'm pretty confident Caleb could strip bark from a tree, season it with crushed earwigs, and it would still be amazing. "I'll take whatever I can get."

Caleb twists the cups in the takeout tray before settling on one and taking a sip. "*Just Add Coffee*, huh?" He's perceptive... and insufferable as he smirks at me from behind his cup.

"Best coffee in the city, if you ask me."

"Right." He draws out the word like he doubts my declaration. It's the truth, though. "So, tell me about the barista slash lawyer guy. I can tell you're about to burst." He tugs open his fridge, then rummages through the contents.

I try to steady my bouncing leg that must have given me away. "He's... I don't know."

"That doesn't inspire a lot of confidence, Soph. Don't tell me he's another Darren or Draven... whatever his name was."

Not even close. "Drew. And no, he's not. I told you that already."

Caleb pulls out a paper bag, eggs, some kind of cheese, and a shallot. "So, what's the problem?"

I blow a long breath and take a sip of my flat white. "With him? Nothing. It's almost... scary how perfect he is. He's smart, ambitious, kind. He's everything."

"But?"

I hate admitting this. Partly because I know how Caleb will reply. "Henry hates him. Boyd stood up to him, and we both know that won't be forgiven. Ever."

"You knew that when you first asked him out, no?" he asks casually while thinly slicing the shallot.

"Yeah." I stare at my coffee, begging it to give me answers. "I've never done anything major to defy Henry. Sure, we stayed up late when we were at Grandma and Grandpa's, or watched movies he told us not to, but I've never gone against him. Part of me just wanted to do something behind his back because *I* wanted to do it. I wasn't expecting it to turn out this way."

"So," he starts while cracking an egg into the hollow of a portobello mushroom, "why is it that you can defy Henry when it comes to who you date, but not with your job?"

I knew that was coming. "Did you miss the part where I said 'behind his back'? Because it's one thing to keep my personal life personal, but it's another to cut ties with every professional and family link I have. I'm not as strong as you, Caleb. I can't just walk away."

"You're a lot stronger than me—than you give yourself credit for. What do you really lose by walking away?"

"My job, for one. My legacy. My future. Everything I've worked toward for over twenty years. Not to mention, if I quit, Mom will choose him. She *always* chooses him." I take a sip of my coffee, trying to chase away the bitterness of the words spilling from my mouth, but it's no use.

"Is any of that really a loss? You know your future isn't tied to him, right? So what if you don't inherit the company? Ol' Henry will probably sell it off before he retires anyway, and bury himself with the fortune he's accumulated before he leaves either of us anything. And who cares? Let him have it. It's the only thing he's ever loved." Caleb bends down to slide whatever concoction he's created into the oven. "If you stay there, the only legacy you're carrying is misery. Don't get bogged down by that." He walks around the end of the counter with his coffee in hand. "Come on. That'll take fifteen minutes."

I follow him into his living room, where we sit and talk about him until the oven timer beeps. It's nice to catch up, even if his words are hard to swallow.

The frustrating part is, I've heard these sentiments a thousand times. Caleb, Celeste, Ashlyn, Boyd, my Aunt Zara. They've all tried to convince me. But they also haven't seen the lengths Henry will go to destroy someone who has wronged him. His son pursuing a different dream? That was embarrassing enough. His daughter walking away from his company to work somewhere else? He'd never let that slide. And I learned when I was a lot younger that it's easier not to anger the beast. Placate him and don't give him a reason to attack. It's safer that way.

So, as much as I understand what everyone is telling me, I'm not convinced I can go to battle with Henry and come out on the other side. Certainly not unscathed.

"Food's ready," Caleb calls from the kitchen.

Instead of dwelling any more on the logistics of my job and relationship—or whatever I should be calling it—I seat myself at the table and let my brother present the fruits of his passion. The result of his years defying our father in search of his dream.

And let me just say, for the record, it is divine.

"I'd like you to meet him," I blurt around a mouthful of eggy goodness.

"Me? Why? I already met him."

I roll my eyes. Of course he'd be content with their twelve-second meeting from nearly three months ago.

"That doesn't count. We were still strangers then."

"And what are you now?" He lifts one brow, levelling me with his intense little brother eyes.

"I... We... I'm not sure." I grab my coffee cup, draining the last of the room temperature espresso. "It would mean a lot to me."

"As long as you promise he's not another Darren."

"Drew," I grumble. "But thank you. So, back to you and your predicament. Let me offer some big sister advice."

Caleb laughs, and we spend the next hour reconnecting. For a short while, it feels like we didn't lose the better part of a decade to the 6,000 kilometres that separated us. Things may have changed since we were both on this side of the Atlantic, but my love for my brother will always be the same.

I leave Caleb's around 9:30 so he can relax before going to work.

Now, my plan for the day is to spend time with the other top guy in my life. I stop at home long enough to pick him up, and he greets me with a wagging butt that would make anyone think I've been gone for four years. I treat him to a day at the groomers, where they give him the bath he desperately needed and a handsome bowtie. After that, he struts around the pet store like he owns the place, picking up toys from the display. Once he's selected four new toys to take home, we pay a visit to *The Barkery* to get him some pupcakes. He's a happy guy by the time we get home.

Celeste went out of town today and Boyd is at his family dinner, so I settle in for an evening alone to unpack everything Caleb said today. I know he doesn't understand—no one understands who isn't standing in my shoes—but I hope he respects my decision.

Everything is easy when you only see the surface. The Titanic wasn't sunk by the iceberg visible above the water. And all it took was one square metre of damage to change history.

He'll just have to accept that I'm being cautious of the unseen dangers of Iceberg Henry.

33

BOYD

The Mighty Fall

I haven't had to meet the family of someone I've been dating for a long time, and even then, Maggie only had her mom, who was too high to comprehend anything. And my meeting with Henry doesn't count. Whether he deserves the title of Sophie's family is something she and I disagree on, but I'm not going to bring that up today. My last interaction with Caleb was a little strange, but I hope he didn't pick up on that.

Apparently, Caleb's schedule is insanely busy, and he only takes Tuesday mornings off. Today is the only day that will work since I have a gap week between my training and when my work placement begins in the new year. Sophie has a short lunch break, so Caleb and I both agreed to meet at this new-age, healthy eating joint that is close to her work. She was stressing over meeting at a restaurant where Caleb would complain about the food, or a café where I'd complain about the coffee. This is the compromise she came to.

Sophie and Caleb walk into the restaurant arm in arm, looking like the picture of sibling loyalty that has been forged over years of living with an emotionally abusive father. Sophie looks at Caleb with so much adoration, it's obvious from fifteen feet away how much he means to her. It's weird how they've maintained their bond after years apart, separated by thousands of miles; yet I live in the same house as my brother and next door to my sister, but we're so distant. Watching Caleb and Sophie makes me determined to repair my sibling relationships—since the deterioration of our bond falls solely on my shoulders.

Caleb reaches out a hand when they approach. "Boyd. Nice to officially meet you."

He's already shown me more kindness and respect than Henry did, and he wanted me to come work for him.

"Likewise. Sophie has told me a lot about you."

He glances down at his blushing sister. "Likewise," he repeats.

We both laugh, and Sophie seems to take offence.

"Ha-ha. You're both so funny," she deadpans. "Let's at least order, so I can stuff my face with something and tune you both out while you poke fun at me." She steps forward to the order area, leaving Caleb and me behind.

"You didn't happen to smuggle any coffee in, did you?" Caleb asks as we join Sophie.

I pause for a second, considering that possibility in the future. "No, it didn't cross my mind. I'll buy a few flasks for next time."

Caleb claps me on the back. "Good man. I like your thinking. I guess we'll just have to choke something down today." He steps forward to place his order, and I follow right behind.

After we've all ordered, Caleb grabs our fares and walks toward a table in the corner. Finally, I have a second to stop Sophie for a proper hello. I grab her hand, leaning down to kiss her cheek. "Hi."

She gifts me with an enthusiastic smile. "Hi. Thanks for doing this."

"Soph, it's not a hardship. You don't need to thank me."

"That doesn't mean I don't want to. This just... it means a lot."

Knowing how much she loves and respects her brother, the fact this is so important to her gives me a clue that I'm important to her, too. She's repeated the same sentiment at least twenty times since she first asked me to have a proper introduction to Caleb, so I have no doubt that this is a big deal to her. Again, it makes me regret the state of my sibling relationships, because I can't reciprocate and say it means the same to me.

She drags me to the table, not releasing my hand, and takes the chair to the right, so I'm left with the chair between the McNamara twins.

Caleb has already set out everyone's food, which, judging by his turned-up nose, I'd say was more to inspect it than be hospitable. "Soph, remind me not to let you choose a place to eat again, yeah?"

"Oh, hush. We only have forty-five minutes left, and this was the fastest option. You don't need five-star cuisine every day."

Caleb scoffs, dropping his plastic fork. "No, I don't, but I can't afford to get food poisoning, either."

"Then don't eat." Sophie reaches across and pulls Caleb's quinoa bowl toward her. "I'll take it for dinner."

"You're better off feeding that to Wilson."

I watch as the twins bicker back and forth, neither one missing a beat, dishing out snarky retorts. It's entertaining and makes this meeting a lot less stressful.

"So I hear Henry isn't a big fan of yours," Caleb states out of nowhere.

I choke on an errant grain of rice I inhaled instead of chewed. Once I clear my throat and swallow my food properly, I reply, "The feeling is mutual." My eyes widen as I process what I said, and immediately try to backpedal. "Sorry, I know he's your dad. I shouldn't say that."

Caleb chuckles, staring down at the paper napkin he's shredding. "I haven't called him Dad for a decade. If someone wants to be a father, they act like one. Safe to say, I agree with you."

Relief? No… that's not what I'm feeling. It's sadness. Also, a little hatred toward Henry. I have no sympathy for a man who disowns his child for pursuing their dreams. Not that I would have had any sympathy to spare on account of his treatment of Sophie, anyway.

Sophie has gone silent, chewing her kale salad concoction. I reach my hand over to cover hers. She doesn't look up to acknowledge me, which has me worried I've offended her. My feelings toward her father have never been a secret, though.

"So tell me about your life in France," I prompt Caleb, trying to redirect our conversation.

He glances at Sophie, seeming to understand Henry isn't a topic she wants to broach today. "That's a better question for Sophie. My life in France was mostly spent inside a kitchen or at the culinary school. I didn't explore as much of it as she did."

That subject perks her mood back up. She spends a solid fifteen minutes discussing the sights and sounds of France, once again gushing over her love for the French Riviera. I've been to England several times, but I've never been to France. The expression on Sophie's face makes me want to take her, though.

The rest of our brief meetup goes well. Caleb seems like a good guy. Passionate, clearly, in all things. His career, his sister, his hatred for his father. I get the impression Caleb doesn't do anything halfway. Much like his twin.

Caleb is the first to take off, telling me he'll see me again soon. I guess that means I have his seal of approval. That leaves me and Sophie alone, but we both have tight schedules today, too.

"Let me walk you back to the office?"

She freezes in the midst of searching for something in her purse. "Uhh… no, that's okay."

Does she not want me to because that's something considered old-fashioned? Is she trying to save me the trouble? Does she not want to spend more time with me? None of the above.

I know exactly what her concern is. "You don't want to be seen with me, do you?"

"Boyd." Her shoulders drop and her arm falls out of her purse. "It's not like that. I'm just—"

"It's fine. I have to go anyway." I huff past her toward the door. It's stupid to be annoyed by it. One of the reasons I hesitated when she asked me out was because I didn't want to cause more issues for her. But I thought that one day down the road, I'd come to matter enough, she wouldn't be bogged down by Henry's opinion. It doesn't look like today is that day.

Sophie doesn't attempt to stop me. She lets me go, and I walk away with the exact feeling I was trying to save myself from.

34

SOPHIE

One and Only

Things with Boyd have gotten more serious than I ever expected. I assumed, like everyone else I've dated, we'd either come to the mutual conclusion that we weren't right for each other, or I'd discover some glaring flaw in his personality or intentions. Neither of those things have happened. It has been weighing so heavily on me that, at some point, I'm going to have to break the news to Henry.

Ever since meeting with Caleb nearly a month ago, it feels as though Boyd has erected some tall walls, and I'm afraid I've done the same. We see each other a few times a week. We talk every day. I go by the café often, and I've spent more time with Monica and Phoenix.

On the surface, things appear fine. But in my gut, I have a nagging feeling that things have shifted. I keep trying to tell myself it's just because he's doing his work placement now, and he's mentally drained.

I need some girl talk. No offence to Celeste, but she's been out of the dating scene for a long time, and I'm not sure she's the right person for the job. So I text Ashlyn an S.O.S. message, which she responds to immediately. She's just finishing her morning training session, then she'll be right over.

The fact she needs to specify morning, afternoon, and evening training sessions is enough to make me want to take a nap.

Thirty minutes later, Ashlyn walks in carrying a massive *Starbucks* tumbler—which feels like sacrilege—and a paper bag. Wilson jumps up to greet her, but quickly takes a detour to my bedroom when he realizes who it is.

I raise an eyebrow at my muscular friend. "You realize that my dog, who loves everyone, high-tailed it out of here the second he saw you?"

"Listen, if I'm rubbing anyone's butt, it better be someone who can repay the favour."

I laugh as I take the bag from her hands to let her remove her shoes. "How was training?"

"Meh." She slips off her sneakers and walks with me to the kitchen. "Jim had me doing burpees to muscle-ups, and I thought I was going to die."

I have no idea what that means, but I pretend I do by giving her a sympathetic smile. "Well, you've earned sustenance." I take the Styrofoam takeout containers out of the bag, opening all three, realizing they're from the same place I took Caleb and Boyd to.

"We can go grab you something else. I just thought—"

"No." I spin to grab plates from the cupboard. "The food is fine." I explain to her about Caleb and Boyd meeting at the small bistro and the subsequent change in mine and Boyd's relationship.

"Well, first of all, I'm offended. Hot brother made time to go out with Boyd, but he hasn't made the same effort with me. Rude." She scoops a healthy portion of some sweet potato chickpea medley, chicken breast, and mixed vegetables before she continues. "Second, you know I don't conform to typical gender roles, either, so I'm all for your independent ways, but what was the big deal about him walking you back to work?"

Yeah, I skipped the real reason why I didn't want him to walk me. So I decide to fully confide in my best friend, hoping she won't judge me for my choices. "He's made a mortal enemy out of Henry. Before we ever went on a date, Boyd told Henry off, and you know that's never being forgiven."

Ashlyn's lips turn up into a mischievous grin. "And you're just telling me this *now*? You and your brother are both withholding the goods from me." She takes a hardy bite of veggies and starts speaking around her food. "So he told the old bastard off. It's about time someone did." She swallows, then asks, "So what now?"

What now? I have no idea. "I thought he'd be like everyone else. That we'd fizzle out before it got serious. But I lied to him and he was angry about it... then I wanted to redeem myself. It never occurred to me I'd end up this deep." I take a bite of my food, coughing at the cardboard flavour of it.

Caleb may have had a valid point. He has a lot of them, honestly.

"I am in deep, though. He's so different from anyone I've ever met before. Sounds weird, but he kind of reminds me of my grandpa."

"Yes, that *is* weird. That will be our little secret. Don't tell Boyd that."

I chuckle, not wanting to explain *how* he reminds me of my grandpa. The man who spent his career as a firefighter, running into danger when everyone else ran out. A man who values right and wrong and won't compromise on that for anything. A man who loves with his whole heart and treats people with respect.

They say women usually choose men like their fathers, but for my mother, she couldn't have been more off the mark. I hope the same will be true for me.

Ashlyn starts clapping out of nowhere. "Here's the plan. You're coming to my competition in Boston."

I try to argue, but she holds her hand up and gives me her best *this is non-negotiable* look.

"You're coming. And you're going to bring Boyd. A weekend away will help you two decide if you want to pursue things or call it off. Somewhere away from Henry. He clouds your judgement and you can't make a decision with him lingering in the background."

It's actually a good idea. Whether I can convince Boyd to take time off is a different story. But it's worth a try. Plus, I'd like to see Ashlyn in action and see what the fuss is all about. She's worked so hard, I want to support her.

"Okay. I'll ask him."

She resumes clapping and adds on a few whooping cheers, drawing Wilson out of my bedroom. He walks up to me and nudges my leg dangling from the stool. It's almost like he understands I said I'd make arrangements to leave for a weekend, knowing he can't come along. I feed him a piece of chicken to ease both of our sad expressions. It works for him, but it doesn't have the same effect on me.

What if our decision by the end of the weekend is to end things? How will I recover from that? Because like it or not, Boyd has burrowed himself into my heart and if he leaves, there will be nothing but a gaping hole.

I checked with Celeste to make sure she'd be okay watching Wilson for the weekend if I go away. Of course, she said yes. She actually seemed excited about it because Wilson has never slept over before. It's nearly three weeks from now, but I already feel guilty. I know people leave their pets to go on vacation all the time, but with my work schedule and the time I've been spending with Boyd, I feel like a terrible dog mom.

But Ashlyn is right. This opportunity could be good for Boyd and me to see where we stand. His world has been marked by drama and strained family relationships the past few weeks. Not to mention his work schedule that makes mine seem like a cakewalk. He deserves some time away. The more I think about it, the more I find the potential positives. Even though I'll be absolutely heartbroken if things go south, at least I'll know. Right? That's the better option than stringing each other along and ending on a note of resentment and hatred like he did with Maggie. I don't want him to associate my name with misery and betrayal. Ever.

So I'll brace myself for whatever comes from our time together.

First, I need to convince him to come with me.

35

BOYD

Young and Menace

This day has been less enjoyable than a convenience store coffee and has resulted in twice as much crap. My work placement was a disaster, start to finish. We were scheduled to sit in on a deposition, but it ended in more of a yelling match than anything productive. For eight straight hours.

My mother has called me no less than fifteen times to insist I speak to Holden and convince him to "see her side of things," but she won't even tell me what that side is. Like my legal expertise allows me to sway people's opinions without even knowing what I'm swaying it to.

On top of that, I got a message on my social media from none other than Maggie. Rather than reply, I creeped her profile and discovered she's on her third marriage. An impressive feat for someone not quite thirty. It appears her mother passed away two years ago, so I have some sympathy for her, but not enough to open that door again.

Instead of replying, I blocked her.

Now, because people couldn't behave like rational adults and answer the direct questions being asked of them, I'm running late for my shift at the café. I barrel in the door forty-six minutes after I should have. I speed walk behind the counter toward my office. "Hey, Mon. Sorry I'm…"

My words halt when I spot Sophie seated at a table with Phoenix. She lifts her eyes to look at me, but she doesn't smile. She looks… nervous.

"Go talk to her. I can stay another fifteen minutes." Monica gives me an understanding smile, paired with a gentle hand on my arm.

My stomach flip-flops as I walk toward Sophie. I rustle Phoenix's hair when I approach. "G'day, Captain. You good?"

"Yeah, man. Just talking to Sophie." He smirks and winks.

I rustle his hair a little rougher. "Easy now, Casanova."

Sophie laughs, and a little of the tension on her face dissipates.

"Come to my office?" My timeframe for this conversation is shrinking, and whatever she wants to say looks like we could use privacy for.

She speaks to Phoenix as she stands, "Back in a bit. Don't touch the playlist."

As we round the corner into my office, I ask, "Am I going to have to worry about this kid? I've always loved him like a son, but I'm not opposed to discipline."

"Don't be ridiculous." She giggles again, alleviating the rest of my lingering concern.

I close the door behind me as we walk into my office. I know there are people on all four sides of this room, but being in here alone with Sophie fuels me with a primitive urge to kiss her. *Really* kiss her. Whatever her reason for coming here— whatever caused her to look as stressed as she did—I want to make her forget.

As soon as she spins to face me, I close the distance between us, snake my arm around her lower back, and pull her close. "Do you know how happy I am to walk in here and see you?"

She tilts her head down, catching my heated gaze through her lashes. Her mouth turns up into a coy smile. The second she sucks her bottom lip between her teeth, I don't want to wait for a response to my rhetorical question. I'll make sure she has a clear answer.

She whimpers into my mouth and puts both arms around my neck, pulling me closer. She sets a frantic pace, taking what I give and begging for more. Before I know it, she's backed up against my cluttered desk, and I'm undoing the top button on her blouse so I can continue my journey down her neck. She utters my name, leaning her head back to give me better access to the soft skin I'm craving.

"If you give me a hickey, I'll give you a black eye."

Her threat stops my trail of kisses.

I pull my head back to look at her. "Deal." That's not enough of a deterrent to stop, so I carry on my way down to the hollow of her collarbone.

"Boyd," she moans. "I have to ask you something."

I groan as I pull away. "Now?"

Her tentative smile makes every ounce of euphoria drip through me like a percolator.

"Well, I know Monica has to leave in a few minutes, so yes."

Oh, shoot. I forgot about Monica. I forgot I was at work for a few minutes. Now is not the time to get sidetracked by a make-out session. "Okay. What do you need to ask? Please ask if I want to make out."

She relaxes a little, but can't seem to get her words out. I lean closer, wanting to kiss her again, but she blurts, "Will you come to Boston with me on the tenth?"

Not what I was expecting. "For... a work thing? Or..."

"Ashlyn has a CrossFit competition in Boston. It's three days, but I know you have your work placement. We could go Friday evening and be back Sunday."

A weekend away with the woman I'm crazy about? Sounds like a no-brainer. "I'll have to sort a few things, but tentatively, yes."

There's a pounding knock at the door, tearing my attention from Sophie.

"Boyd! A little help out here, please?" Monica's panicked voice calls through the door. Monica is known for her level-headedness. She doesn't panic.

"Yeah, Mon." I turn back to give Sophie a quick peck. "There's a mirror over there." I nod toward the left side of my desk. "Someone messed up your hair," I say as I head to the door and swing it open.

"*She*'s here," Monica declares. "And she demanded to see you."

My blood runs cold. *She* hasn't been an issue since we got the restraining order, but that expired long ago. There's nothing stopping her from being here now. I shuffle past Monica, telling her and Sophie to stay in my office. The last thing I want is Maggie targeting either of them. The other concern is Phoenix.

I walk out behind the counter and spot him seated on a stool with his headphones on, fully immersed in something on his phone. Now that I know he's okay, I scan the near empty room until my eyes land on *her*. Maggie. The woman who broke my heart in a way I thought it couldn't be repaired until recently. Her dull auburn hair is tucked in a cashmere hat, and she has more makeup on than I've ever seen. Time has not been kind to her, because she looks at least fifteen years older than the last time I saw her.

"Maggie," I greet as I walk past Donnie, toward her. "What are you doing here?"

"That's no way to welcome your first love, Boyd," she purrs, and it turns my stomach.

"Why are you here?" I slip past the countertop and walk toward the farthest corner from Phoenix. There's no way I'm taking this woman somewhere private. More eyes on her antics mean a better chance of getting another restraining order if necessary.

She follows me to the corner, sashaying the eight feet. I seriously want to puke.

"I miss yo—"

"Stop." I shake my head and hold up a hand. "Stop right there. I'm not wasting my time on any of that. If you couldn't take a hint from me blocking your message, the feeling is *not* mutual."

The woman I spent more than three years loving starts to sob in front of me. And I feel nothing. Not a hint of anger, compassion, regret. There isn't even any resentment left.

"Maggie, I don't know what possessed you to show up here, but you need to leave. There's nothing for you."

"I need help. My husband kicked me out, and I need a place to stay. I have nowhere to go." She blubbers out a few more fake tears, but my sympathy is gone.

"There's a saying for situations like this, Maggie. You make your bed, you lie in it. I'd say this is your comeuppance."

She steps forward, twirling a lock of her hair around one finger. "Don't you—"

"Let me be very clear. The *only* thing you will get here is coffee." I'm tempted to tell her I'm seeing someone, but since she already saw Monica, I don't want her assuming it's her and restarting that stress in my friend's life.

Donnie peeks around the corner, so I give him a subtle wave.

"We're fine. Maggie was just leaving." I glare at her, hoping to make it clear I'm not the pushover twenty-two-year-old boyfriend I once was.

She scoffs and turns toward the door. Her crocodile tears evaporating as fast as our relationship. I almost celebrate too soon, because she spins on the heel of her leather boot.

"You never deserved me, anyway. And this"—she waves her hand around—"is never going to get you anywhere. You've hit your peak, Boyd. How does it feel to be at the bottom of the social hierarchy?"

Yep. There's the woman who broke up with me. The true Maggie who hides under her cloak of fake smiles and exaggerated compliments until she's ready to strike.

Sure, I could defend myself. Tell her I'm mere months away from my call to the bar. Or that I've found the woman of my dreams who isn't *her*. But I don't care what she thinks, so I step forward and let her know I'm not intimidated. Not affected at all. "I'd rather be at the bottom than be at the top with you. Come back here again, and you'll be slapped with another restraining order. Don't test me."

She clenches her fists and jaw simultaneously, releasing a shriek. Phoenix finally looks up from his phone, just in time to see Maggie storm out the door.

"You okay, Boss?" Donnie asks from behind the cash register.

"All good. Thanks, man," I reply, rushing toward Phoenix.

He was six years old the last time he saw Maggie, but it's hard to forget a woman who tried to kidnap you. Judging by his face, he remembers her. "Was that...?"

"It was. She was here for me. I set her straight, and she's gone now. You okay?" I place a hand on his shoulder as he exhales a slow breath.

Monica comes running out of the office, around the counter, and wraps Phoenix in a hug. "I'm so sorry. I hoped if I stayed out of her way, she wouldn't recognize you. Are you okay?"

Phoenix looks at both of us and nods. His head starts slow and picks up speed, so he looks like he's bopping to music. Then I realize Fall Out Boy's *Immortal* is playing through the café speakers.

Sophie steps out from the doorway behind the counter, holding her phone. "We made a joint playlist on Spotify. Thought it was about time to liven up this joint." She makes her way around the end of the counter, coming to a stop beside me. "Monica told me about what happened. Is everyone all right?"

"We're good. I'll dig out the old paperwork and report her showing up today. Just in case."

I can tell Monica and Phoenix are both rattled. After Maggie and I broke up, she was still so convinced there was something going on with me and Monica, she showed up at Phoenix's school, pretending to be his mom's friend. Since she was familiar with Monica, Phoenix fell for her ploy. Thankfully, his teacher suspected something strange and refused to let him leave until she got confirmation from Monica.

None of us have any idea what Maggie's plans or motives were, but that was the last straw before getting a restraining order. It was also a main catalyst for me swearing off dating ever since.

I wrap an arm around Sophie's waist, tugging her close to me, watching Monica cling to her son.

With so many distractions, negative memories, and intrusions, a trip to Boston is exactly what we need.

36

SOPHIE

America's Suitehearts

Since adopting Wilson, I haven't taken a single weekend away. Aside from my trips to visit Caleb in Europe, I've never officially taken a vacation. As our plane descends into Boston's Logan Airport, I wonder to myself if a forty-eight hour jaunt to watch a women's CrossFit competition counts as a vacation. With Boyd at my side, it feels like one. I squeeze his hand when the wheels touch the runway and the plane bounces before it slows to a stop and the passengers applaud.

"Welcome to Boston," he offers and kisses the back of my hand. There's a note of familiarity in his greeting.

"Have you been here before?"

He hesitates to reply, making me assume he came here previously with his witch of an ex.

"Oh, did you come here with Mag—"

"No." He stops speaking while the flight attendant instructs the passengers when and where to disembark the plane. "I came here five years ago for a barista championship."

I drop his hand, needing my own to cover my face and contain my laughter. "I'm sorry. Did you say barista championship?"

"Don't laugh. It's serious business." His deadpan expression is disrupted by a smirk, making me laugh more.

"I need to hear all about this."

We gather our carry-ons from the overhead compartment as he tells me what the competition comprises, the purpose of it, and what's at stake. I revel in the new information because this may now be my newest favourite kind of competition. Coffee. No sweating. Travelling the world, tasting world-class espresso. Yes, please.

"So how did you fare in this international coffee spectacle?"

He exhales a long breath. "I finished third as an individual. Our team finished ninth."

"Wow. So you're the third-best coffee maker in the entire world? I believe it."

He chuckles, but I'm dead serious.

"Just the third-best competitor on that day."

I hook my arm through his as we tug our wheeled baggage through the terminal, bypassing the luggage carousel. "Forget about international recognition. You'll always be the best coffee maker in my world. That's all that really matters."

He glances down at my smiling face, making me oblivious to the hoards of people crowding the airport. "Agreed."

Our car drops us off in front of the upscale hotel I booked because it looked like it had a lot of things within walking distance. We approach the checkout counter, where I present our reservation number. The front desk clerk works efficiently to get things sorted until it comes to authorizing my credit card. For some reason, it won't go through.

"There's no way it's maxed out. I always pay it. What if someone... hacked it or whatever they do? Oh, my—"

"Relax. It's fine. We can use mine. I've got you covered." Boyd kisses my forehead before pulling his credit card and passport from his pocket and handing them over.

The startling realization that I like when he has my back sends a rush of butterflies through my chest. I make a second realization and can't help but laugh. "I'm sorry, but is your name actually Boyd Oliver Nicholas Edwards?"

He closes his passport quickly and tucks it away. "I'm not sure my passport would be legal if it wasn't. I've heard all the jokes before. Go ahead; get it out of your system."

"When you've worked a long shift, are you B.O.N.E. tired?" I laugh at my own stupid joke, but Boyd does show signs of breaking his stoic expression. "Oh, oh. When you get out of the shower and wrap yourself in a towel, are you B.O.N.E. dry?"

Even the clerk flashes a smile at that one.

"Maybe don't bring up showers when we're going to be sharing a room all weekend," he breathes in my ear.

That's enough to cause a hitch in my breathing and I lose all ability to be cool.

"Ready?" Boyd holds up the keys the employee passed him, sporting a wicked grin.

"Absolutely."

After we get settled into our hotel room and grab a quick bite to eat, we head to the event space where Ashlyn is competing. Jim is doubling as her coach and fiancé this weekend, but he helps us find good seats based on Ashlyn's lane assignment and tells us he'll check in later.

The competition is intense. This event is women only, running as a fundraiser for women's cancers. Just because it's a fundraiser doesn't mean anyone takes it easy. I learn that EMOM stands for 'every minute on the minute' and AMRAP stands for 'as many reps as possible.' I also learn that I have no interest in trying CrossFit. The way these girls are collapsing at the finish line is a hard no from me.

Ashlyn finishes the day in second place. We try to invite the couple on a double date for dinner, but Ashlyn insists she has a date with 'gym' because neither workout in the competition actually counted as her workout for today. Another hard no from me.

Regardless, that suits me fine, because I get Boyd to myself for an evening in Boston.

Unfortunately, by the time we get outside, temperatures are well below freezing, so we don't make it too far from the arena before tucking into an old Irish pub.

"I wonder if there's anyone here from 'The Office'. You know?" I scan the room, looking for anyone who screams mobster, but everyone just looks like a misplaced college student or single middle-aged person hoping to make a love connection.

"The Office? Like the TV show or the Irish mafia?"

"The mob, obviously."

"What do you plan on doing if you run into someone?" Boyd's face is a textbook depiction of concern, but I'm enjoying this.

"Depends if it's a street soldier or an underboss. The conversation will be different depending."

"Sophie, wha—"

I erupt with laughter as we take two empty seats at the bar. "Your face. Priceless."

He scrubs his hand over his stubble, running his finger and thumb along the sharp line of his jaw. "I thought you were going to try to make connections or something."

"It's not what you know, it's who you know." I wink and smile, hoping to make it clear I'm kidding. "I wouldn't be surprised if my father has mobster connections in Toronto. Isn't importing and exporting a big part of their operation?"

Mention of my father immediately changes the entire mood of our evening. We came here to get away from him.

"Henry has such a superiority complex, he's not taking orders from a capo. It's more likely he thinks he's The Godfather, and you're his territory to control."

I stiffen at Boyd's words. Gape at him. Want to fight back, but I can't dispute his assessment.

"Soph... I'm sorry. I didn't mean..." He trails off, searching the room like he's waiting for someone to rescue him. "I'm going to run to the washroom. Try not to befriend any Irishmen while I'm gone." Boyd kisses my temple and walks toward the back of the narrow space.

The dark wood interior, dim stained-glass lighting, and hunter green vinyl upholstery make it feel small in here, but it's cozy. That coziness doesn't combat the lingering upset over Boyd's comments, though. Seems like a job for liquor.

I flag down the bartender, who acknowledges me, but his hands are full with a tray of stout that he's delivering to a booth at the far end of the room. While I wait, I feel a body press up against my back.

"Hello, beautiful. What brings you here?" A man who tops out at 5'3", smells like cigars, and has no concept of personal space, stands entirely too close to my stool.

I shift sideways, creating distance between us. "My feet."

"Ha! Clever. Can I have your name?"

Again, I inch back, creating more space. "Oh, you poor thing. Did your mother not give you your own?"

The nameless smoker is not taking the hint. "You're funny. What do you do for work?"

I lean forward just enough to act like I'm telling a scandalous secret. "I'm a slaughterhouse worker." For fun, I paste on my best serial-killer smile and waggle my eyebrows.

Unsurprisingly, he takes a few steps back, then leaves without another word.

The bartender arrives seconds later and takes my order. I request two glasses of Knappogue and wait for Boyd to return.

He arrives back to his seat at the same time as our drinks. "Make any shady connections?"

"Funny you should ask." I giggle, trying to let the earlier tension from his comments dissipate. "A guy hit on me, so I may have implied that I had a career killing innocent animals."

His face transforms from indifference to annoyance. Eyebrows pulled together. Lips slanted downward at the corners. He looks like he'd prefer I made friends with an underboss. "You really can't shoot anyone down straight, can you?"

My jaw clenches at the same time my fingers do around my glass. I down my drink in one go, slam it on the counter and stand. "And you really can't let that go, can you?" I shake my head as I walk to the door.

Boyd comes running up behind me. "Sophie, wait. It was a joke." He turns me so our shoulders are square. "I just see you as this ultra-confident, fierce, intelligent woman, and I wish you'd just tell it like it is sometimes. You could have told *him* you were seeing someone."

My rage level decreases slightly, but not enough to relax my scowl. I can see why that would come across the wrong way, like I don't value our relationship enough to claim it. But I'm stuck on him being so upset about my lie to him. "Sue me. I don't *enjoy* hurting people's feelings. I couldn't tell a virtual stranger that I didn't want to go out with him because I've been taken advantage of so many times, I've lost count, and I was tired of being used as a stepping stone. I couldn't just blurt out that my father has expectations for who I date and I didn't want to give him more reason to be disappointed in me. I'm sorry if I hurt your ego, but I thought we were past that."

"I am past it, and believe me, after one meeting with Henry, I understood." He reaches out to take both of my hands and pulls them behind him until they connect. "Why don't we go back to the hotel and get room service? Rent an overpriced movie on Pay-Per-View?"

It may have taken some prompting, but I clutch my hands behind Boyd and rest my head against his chest. "As long as it's not sushi."

He chuckles, so I feel the rumble, and that alone starts to melt away the fury I felt seconds ago. Not for the first time, I recognize how hard I'm falling for him. With every instance of push and pull, I get reeled back in tighter. With that, I'm also getting tired of resisting. Tired of putting up the fight and trying to stop myself from falling. Because he may be the first man who has shown romantic interest in me *for* me.

And that feels good. Really good.

"Ready?" he asks, tugging my hand.

"Absolutely."

We settle into our hotel room, changing into pyjamas and curling up on the stiff sofa together. I almost forget that this is a temporary weekend away. I miss Wilson, but it's nice to ignore pressing responsibilities that come from work and bills and narcissists.

Though, Boyd's words from earlier linger in my mind as we watch a comedy that pre-dates both of us. The classic one liners result in a few belly laughs, but my mind is never far from the truth in what he said. The worst part is, I know staying at this company makes me look nepotistic or weak—both which are terms I don't want to be associated with—but it's not an easy decision to abandon a position that means abandoning my parents, too. It's not easy to walk out on the women in that building who I made a promise to myself I'd protect. And it's certainly not easy to walk away, knowing I'll have the wrath of Henry to contend with.

"Hey, what's wrong?" Boyd leans down to kiss my bare shoulder. "You didn't even laugh at that one."

I blink several times until the TV comes back into focus. "Nothing." I tilt and turn my head so it's resting against his chest and I'm looking up at him. "Just thinking how nice it is to get away for a bit."

"Yeah. It is." He doesn't look convinced that I'm telling the full truth, but he doesn't press me on it, either. What he does is press his lips against mine, adjusting the angle with a soft finger under my chin.

My entire adult life, I've resisted doing what most men tell me. I've fought back when I felt like I had the power to do so, *just* for the sake of doing so.

But Boyd makes me want to concede.

To give in to him and let him lead.

To fall and trust that he'll be there to catch me.

37

BOYD

City In a Garden

While watching a CrossFit competition isn't my idea of a good time, I'm so glad Sophie invited me on this trip. Getting some time with her, away from family drama—on both sides—and the daily grind we're accustomed to, has been refreshing. I don't know if I'm supposed to ask her to be my girlfriend and make this official. Or maybe she'd resent that title because it represents a dynamic she wants no part of. Or maybe, like me, she feels like the natural progression of our relationship means that step is implied.

Whatever the case, I continue to stare at her sleeping form on the bed just a few feet from mine, wondering how my twenty-two-year-old self ever thought I was serious about Maggie. The best thing that woman ever did for me was respect what I said during her recent unwelcome visit to the café.

Sophie stirs and stretches, then rolls to face me. "How long have you been awake?" she asks, her voice heavy with sleep.

"Just a few minutes. I didn't want to wake you."

"Mm. You didn't." She sits up and stretches again, groaning as her white tank top lifts to expose the soft skin of her abdomen. "My bladder did." She pops up off of the plush bed and darts for the bathroom.

While she's doing whatever she needs to do in the bathroom, I check out the coffee maker left on the dresser. This may be a five-star hotel, but their coffee choice is sub par. I can't, in good conscience, consume this abomination. I pull up café options within walking distance on my phone and settle on the one I'll run to after I brush my teeth. We aren't supposed to be at Ashlyn's competition until 2pm, so we have time.

Sophie exits the bathroom, rubbing her eyes. "I need caffeine. ASAP."

I hold up the sachet of coffee grounds. "This coffee is awful. I'm going to run out to get some down the street."

"Oh. Just give me a minute. We can go together." She gifts me with a sleepy smile and something about her saying 'together' hits me right in the heart.

"Okay."

We dance around each other in the small room, darting in and out of the bathroom to get ourselves ready. Sophie slips on her boots while I zip up my jacket, and in what felt like a well-practiced routine, we're ready.

The streets are lined with multi-storey brick buildings, reminiscent of home. It's the first time we've been able to really see things in the daylight since we were so rushed yesterday before the competition, and afterward, it was dark. Like most cities, Boston is rich with history, and we stop to admire different statues and read about the people they were modelled after. The hunt for different statues leads us into Boston Common Park, so we follow the trail in search of caffeine.

We find a little souvenir shop a short way down the path, which we stop at to browse. I get myself a black sweater that says "Wicked Smaht" and Sophie a grey one with "Comfy

Clothes and Murdah Shows" emblazoned across the chest. She's giddy excited over it, and once again, I'm struck by how different she is than the woman I initially pegged her for. She's not just content with the simple things; she loves them. Even though there's nothing simple about her.

With our bag of sweaters in hand, we continue through the park until we reach a carousel. It looks magical behind the dusting of snow falling. Like the inside of a snow globe.

Sophie squeals, clutching my hand and dragging me toward it. "Come on. We need to take a ride." She doesn't give me the opportunity to argue, but I don't want to.

We pay for two tickets, then wait for the ride to stop and the current riders to vacate. I assume Sophie will go for one of the carriage seats that stays still and just goes along for the ride, but in another surprise, she chooses a frog wearing a saddle. She's near hysterics, looking at it as she climbs on its back. I try to stand beside her, because I can't bring myself to embrace a child's ride the same way she does.

"Mount your steed, Boyd!" Sophie insists.

I glance over at the weird creature that has been relegated to a life beside the strange frog. "This is a cat... with a fish in its mouth. It's not a st—"

"Hop on. You need to live a little."

A young girl on the back of a psychedelic butterfly behind us sends me a nod that is hard to argue with. Between her and Sophie glaring at me and the ride about to start, I give in to peer pressure. I mount my cat/steed and I've never felt so ridiculous. That is, until Sophie snaps a photo and starts laughing again.

Before I can get payback, the ride starts moving. Sophie has never looked so laid back and full of joy in all the time we've spent together. She's relaxed to a degree I didn't think was possible. I'm not sure if it's the change of location, the vision of me on the back of a pink cat, or the carousel ride itself, but I never want to stop seeing her this way. I slide my phone from my pocket and catch a series of candid photos of her. One arm out, catching the wind as we spin in circles. Both hands clutching the pole, leaning her head back. And gazing at me with an expression I'm so grateful I've captured.

Once we dismount and exit the fencing around the carousel, Sophie drags me to a food truck that sells coffee and pastries. Food trucks are notoriously overlooked as the true culinary delights they are. This one offers fresh ground espresso and pastries. We both order the same thing—flat white and a strawberry cream cheese Danish.

We walk over to the frog pond that is frozen over and used for skating. It's still early, so there aren't many people out on the ice.

"Remember the night your shower broke?" I ask around the last bite of my Danish.

"Pretty hard to forget," Sophie replies, shielding her smile behind her coffee cup.

I'm glad I'm not the only one who has reserved space in my memory for that night. "We were supposed to go skating."

"Oh! I would have loved to show you my moves."

Her irresistible grin makes me want to strap on a pair of skates right now and take her for a spin. Until she starts laughing and I realize she's teasing.

"Trust me, I liked the moves you showed me more than any triple axle you might have done."

She levels me with her sultry eyes that make me forget the rest of the world exists. "Good thing, because it would have been a miracle if I even stayed upright."

"I would have held you." I step closer, wrapping my arms around her, but I can't clasp my hands because of my coffee cup.

She licks her lips. Starts blinking rapidly. Leans in closer. All telltale signs that she's waiting for me to kiss her. Who am I to deny her? I press my lips to hers and she instantly collapses against me. Even though our bodies are pressed against each other, our lips are the point of contact that feels like the breath of life being blown into me. First her lips, then once she grazes her teeth along mine, our tongues meld together in a caffeine-fuelled fury. I have my own flat white, but I want to taste hers.

We stand here, lost in each other for several minutes, until a little boy, who was on the carousel with us, makes an exaggerated gagging sound and shouts, "Ew, Mommy, they're kissing." That's a rapid and complete buzzkill. Little Tommy couldn't just enjoy his ride on the back of his rooster and mind his own business.

The snow starts falling faster. Snowflakes have more staying power in greater numbers, so the ground turns white around us while we keep each other warm.

"Let's go be tourists." Sophie clutches my hand with a surprising intensity and tows me toward the park entrance.

"Can you squeeze a little tighter, Soph? I still have feeling in my fingers."

She releases my hand, dropping hers to her sides. "Sorry. I guess that's what you do when you find something worth holding on to." She shrugs, and she's off again.

And suddenly, I realize, even if it means losing circulation in my extremities, I never want her to let go again.

38

SOPHIE

Snitches and Talkers

Today marks the first time in history Henry called my office phone directly. I wasn't sure he knew how to dial a number other than Joel's. The fact he didn't pass off the task to him makes anxiety course through my veins as I walk down the corridor.

My trip to Boston with Boyd last month was magical. A perfect reprieve from the weight that crushes me within this city's limits. When we touched down at Pearson Airport, I could feel the pressure that comes along with being here. I used to feel it each time I returned from France. Almost enough to compress my lungs and make it hard to breathe. It has never had anything to do with changing cabin pressure.

The six weeks since we returned from Boston have been marked with more work stress, family drama, and time constraints, but Boyd and I are in a good place. I've been waiting for something to go wrong, and I have a sinking feeling this is the moment.

Joel isn't at his desk when I pass, so I continue to Henry's door and knock.

"Come in," he hollers from the other side.

I walk inside, expecting my father, but am surprised to see Gerard Knoll and his son, Derek.

"Sophie, sit," my father commands me with less affection than one would use with a misbehaving pet. Once I'm seated across from the father-son duo, he continues, "The paperwork is signed, so there's no point in drawing this out. You and Derek are getting married on May sixth."

If I wasn't sitting already, I'd drop to the floor. Even from a seated position, I'm struggling to stay upright. "I'm sorry. What?" I glance at Derek, who is the result of giving out participation ribbons to kids just for showing up. He has mousy brown hair, a smug expression, and a neck I have a distinct urge to wrap my hands around.

"You and Derek. Marriage. More of a business arrangement, but you will honour it." Henry rustles some papers on his desk as if this little meeting is inconveniencing his busy schedule.

"No." I attempt to stand, but my legs are not working. That makes my act of defiance lose all credibility.

Henry shoos Derek and Gerard with his left hand, assuring them he'll "get me in line," and the wedding date will proceed as planned. The second they've exited the room, his expression changes to the one I've grown to know and fear since I was a kid. "I don't know what kind of nonsense you think you're pulling here, Sophie, but you will do as you're told. This business arrangement is worth a lot of money, and more importantly, offers connections that we can't make otherwise. You will not screw it up with your tantrums."

Tantrums? Is this guy serious? He thinks not wanting to marry an entitled cretin, who has never spoken a decent word to me, is out of line? Maybe marriage hasn't meant anything to him, but it means something to me. At least, I want it to someday.

"And if I refuse? I'm seeing someone. I can't just go and marry someone else."

"I know. That's why we're here."

That declaration makes the coldness from Henry's heart chill the blood in my veins.

"Did you honestly think you could run around like a little harlot with that miscreant and I wouldn't know? Please, child. Give me more credit. If you had chosen anyone else, I may have let it slide, but I will *not* have you sleeping with the enemy." Henry stands to loom over me. "This is happening one way or another. I suggest you accept it, because if you don't, that loser you've been spending time with will feel the full force of my reach in this city. And don't think I'll forget about your brother—I know he's had a hand in this."

There are so many things in that one rant that bother me. For one, Boyd is the furthest thing from a miscreant a person could be. Our time together has been short, but he's been nothing but hardworking and doesn't have an immoral streak in him. Two, my father has been keeping tabs on me outside of work hours, which is a whole other issue. And three, he called me a harlot after trying to trade me as a commodity and encouraging me to unbutton my blouse to win over business deals. I've called Henry a lot of things before; now I can add hypocrite to the list.

But if I don't follow through with this, everything I've dealt with to date will be for nothing. The changes I've longed to make to usher this company into the future with a healthy, non-discriminatory culture will be lost. The women working here will be left to fend off the wolves. My father is evidence that people who pursue a life only to please themselves are never fulfilled. What I want isn't the priority here, and I'll do what I have to do to protect Boyd and Caleb.

"Fine." I stand to leave without being dismissed, but I refuse to let Henry see me cry. It's been a decade since I've shed a tear and he will not have a front-row seat to see it.

I return to my office, fending off the choking sobs begging to escape, but the second I walk through my door, the wave hits. I collapse in the chair facing my desk, refusing to acknowledge my position here right now.

A long stretch of time passes as I sit and stare into space, detached from reality, with tears trickling down my cheeks. My office phone rings a few times, but I ignore each one. It's not until a knock sounds at my door that I blink my eyes back into focus.

"Not now, Andy."

Against my wishes, the door opens. Andy drops into the chair beside me and sits in silence for close to a minute, which is a personal record for him.

"Okay, tell me what's going on," he prompts gently. There's no sign of sarcastic spitfire Andy.

But I can't find the words. Can't choke out anything more than a sob. Andy places his hand on my back and passes me a tissue. I'm mortified, heartbroken, and feeling utterly hopeless all at once.

Minutes pass before I utter, "I can't."

"Can't what? I need some insight here so I can help."

I shake my head again. "You can't."

There's nothing either of us can do. This is Henry's world, and we're just pawns in his sick game. Puppets to be directed as he sees fit. Consequences for anyone else be damned.

After several more minutes, I compose myself enough to say, "I'm taking the rest of the day off." I wipe my eyes with my tissue, toss it in the garbage as I stand, and walk around my desk to grab my coat and purse. "You can take the rest of the day off, too. If Henry is so convinced I'm no use around here for anything other than my anatomy, he can learn the hard way."

"Sophie, what the...? What do you mean—"

"I can't talk about it right now. Just set the voicemail that we're out of the office, don't check your emails, and take the rest of the day off. I'll pay you out of my pocket."

"What's going—"

"Andy, I can't say it out loud. I just... I'm not ready to explain yet, but once I am, I'll tell you everything, okay?"

He obviously wants answers, but it's going to be hard enough to get the words out once, and I need to reserve them for the one other person directly affected by Henry's orders.

I get in my car to drive to *Just Add Coffee*, knowing what I have to do. But part way there, I ask myself why I can't just tell Boyd the truth. See what he says. Ask if he's willing to go to battle with Henry, so things between us don't need to change.

I take a long detour and stop at a parkette about an hour east of the city. The parking lot allows me to stop close enough I can see Lake Ontario without getting out to stand in the cold. Water reminds me of home—even when it's frozen. It makes me recall the peace and love I felt when I spent time with my grandparents and my cousins on the shores of Lake Muskoka. Somehow, the presence of a body of water washes away the misery that Henry brings about with the force of hurricane winds. Except it doesn't today. I stare out at the water, crying, practicing different variations of the same conversation—each time with the same result.

Boyd is a good man. A great man. He'll say he can deal. That he's gone against Henry before and he's no worse off. That Henry's reach isn't as wide as he thinks it is, so it's not as much of a threat as he makes it seem. But I have a feeling

Henry has kept his fury under wraps for exactly this moment. Once it's let loose, there will be no recovering from it. I've seen him bury more people than I could count. There's no way I'm allowing him to add Boyd or Caleb to his tally.

The reality of the next hours, days, even years ahead, makes me physically ill. More so because of everything I'm losing than everything I'll be stuck with. Loss hurts more.

Even when you barely had a chance to hold on to it.

39

BOYD

Just One Yesterday

This afternoon has been particularly busy. After my work placement this morning, I was exhausted from using every ounce of brain power, but with only one other employee on the schedule, I knew I had to show up. Donnie is catching on, but he's still not capable of handling a busy shift on his own—nor should he have to.

In the midst of a lull in customers, I instruct Donnie to head outside to make sure there are no trash or lost belongings on the patio and empty the outdoor garbage. He nods and does as instructed, grabbing his coat and going out the front door. Not fifteen seconds later, the door chimes again. I assume he's forgotten a trash bag or something to complete his task, but I'm surprised to look up and see Sophie. Not usual composed Sophie. She's sporting red-rimmed eyes, puffy cheeks, and dishevelled hair.

I rush around the end of the counter to pull her into my arms. "What's wrong? Wilson, Caleb? Ashlyn, Celeste? Is everyone okay?"

She collapses into me with her hands covering her face. I fear the worst that something has happened to one of her loved ones.

"They–they're fine," she struggles to say through ragged breaths.

I don't feel any rush of relief hearing that. If that's not the problem, it's something else serious. "What is it? What's wrong?"

She tilts her head back to look at me and starts crying harder. I've never seen her cry before; it surprises me how much I feel her pain as my own, and I don't even know what is paining her.

"How 'bout I make you a coffee and you take a seat? Then we can talk."

She nods, but her tears haven't eased.

"Pumpkin spice latte? Side of sushi?"

That makes her choke out a laugh and crack a small smile. I twist behind me to grab a napkin from the dispenser and pass it to her. She dabs at her cheeks and I realize she's been crying for quite some time. That makes me more eager to find out what the issue is. I rush to make her a flat white, glancing at her with each opportunity, then join her at the table at the back of the café right as Donnie returns. He studies us both, so I flash him both hands, indicating I need ten minutes. Maybe more, but I sign his paycheques, so he's not going to berate me if I'm late.

Instead of seating myself on the opposite side of the table, I move the stool next to Sophie so I can wrap an arm around her. As soon as I do, she collapses into me again.

Several minutes pass before she speaks. "Henry is forcing me into an arranged marriage."

Nothing, and I mean nothing, could have prepared me for those words. "What?" My left fist tightens, digging my nails into my palm. I'm equal parts seething and crushed. "Did you tell him no?"

"Of course I did! But he doesn't take *no* for an answer. If I don't go through with it, I'm out on my tail."

"That's not the end of the world."

She sighs and sits upright, creating distance between us. Something that I'm afraid isn't just physical right now. "I'm well aware of your thoughts on the matter. Thank you."

"He has no right to do this. Someone needs to take him down. Teach him a lesson."

"I don't want to take him down. I wanted to rebuild this business, not dismantle it."

"The only thing you're building is a crypt for yourself! You keep letting him get away with things and wonder why it keeps happening." My voice is getting louder than necessary, so I take a breath to calm myself down. The fury pounding through me is not helping, though. "Trust me, I know that parents don't always make the right choices. You know that. Don't tell me you can't make a decision for yourself just because he's your dad. Wrong is wrong, no matter who is doing it."

"It's not a simple decision to just stick to what's morally right when it's business and the people you love at stake. There's a canyon of grey area and I'm stuck in it."

"It's not his business that's the problem, Sophie. Can't you see that? It's *him*." I rake my hands through my hair, tugging at the roots just to feel a sting somewhere other than my eyes. "I don't know what you expect from me, but I won't sit back and watch you waste your life catering to the whims of the one man in your life who doesn't care about you. Either you leave your job or we're done."

Her face transforms from teary-eyed and upset to flared nostrils and furrowed brows. "Just what I need, hmm? Another man in my life telling me what I should do. Another man to inform me that my worth starts and stops with *his* expectations of me. Perfect." She shoves her stool back, glaring at me with her puffy eyes. "So I guess we're done."

She stares down at me like she's waiting for me to change my mind or take my words back. But I can't. I meant what I said. If she's choosing Henry and his demands over me, then there's nothing to say it won't be that way forever. Beyond that, I can't sit back and watch her be treated this way and be okay with it.

"I guess so."

With that, she abandons me and her full coffee and walks toward the front door.

"You know what the irony is?" I call after her.

She does a quarter turn to look at me over her shoulder. "What's that?"

"You showed more loyalty to your made up boyfriend than you have to me."

That comment is harsh. I know it. She knows it. I told her I was past that, and here I am throwing it back in her face, just because I'm hurt. Understandably, she exits the café, into the fading light. I stare at the door for several minutes, hoping she'll turn around and come back inside. That she'll see what I'm asking isn't to have control over her, but because I want her to succeed and be happy. She won't be either of those things at *McNamara Enterprises*. And she certainly won't be if she's forced into an arranged marriage.

For a woman who pushes back against the patriarchy and misogyny with everyone else, it leaves me at a loss when she's willing to let Henry make such a huge decision for her life.

I can only hope that one day, she'll push back against him too.

But for us, it will probably be too late.

The morning after. A phrase I've heard a thousand times, but never really paid any mind to. I've never woken up hungover enough to stop me in my tracks. But this day, waking up knowing that Sophie will soon marry someone else, it's too much to process. Even harder to accept.

I've learned the best way to distract yourself from your own problems is to help someone with theirs. My brother has been moping around the house for months now, and it's time I do what I can to set things straight for him, knowing they're too late for me.

I peek into our shared office once I'm dressed and ready for work. I note the only line he's written under the *Study Methods* heading says, *I'll read stuff.* That is not promising progress on his PhD proposal.

"How's it coming?"

He spins his chair and exhales the longest breath I've ever heard. "Stuck on the synopsis."

I try to direct the conversation to his relationship woes, which makes me feel like a fraud. I have no right to be giving him advice in this area, but I do. For five minutes, we go back and forth, proposing solutions to his problem. He confides in me that he's in love with the woman he feels he can't have and thinks it's crazy to fall for someone so hard, so fast.

I interrupt him without hesitation. "It's not crazy." I know that for a fact because Sophie walked into my life in September and I'm pretty sure by November, she had taken up permanent residence in my heart. I loved her back then and I love her now, but I never told her. After falling so fast for Maggie, it only blinded me to big issues, and had I been more pragmatic, I would have seen them. Sophie knows how that story turned out and I was afraid if I told her I love her, she'd worry history was repeating itself. Now I'm wondering if I *had* told her, if her response to her father's demands would have changed.

While Holden is confessing everything weighing him down, I decide it's time for me to clear the air. For years, there has been tension between us and there hasn't needed to be. I swore to myself I'd fix this, and it's one relationship I can.

"I know we haven't been close over the past few years, and that's on me. I held onto resentment for no reason because I put my life on hold. But that was my choice. And to be honest, Dad getting sick was an easy excuse to drop out because I was barely passing my classes." I stare at my sock feet, embarrassed and ashamed of how I let my own insecurities poison our relationship. But this situation with Sophie has taught me that not all family relationships are equal, and we need to feed the ones that we value. "Taking that break renewed my focus and now I'm in a better place because of it. So I guess the point I'm trying to make is that I've always cared about you and wanted you to succeed."

He says nothing. He just nods, which I take as a cue to continue.

"One thing I've learned, though, is that success isn't about academic or career accolades. None of that means anything if you're not happy." I chuckle, understanding the irony in those words. I should have said the same thing to Sophie. "I don't know when I turned into a Hallmark card."

Holden stands and pulls me in for a hug. Something we haven't done since we were kids. We also exchange declarations of brotherly love and he apologizes for his sour mood the past few months.

"Nah, don't sweat it. I get it. More than you know." Before I blurt out anything else that will only compound his problems right now, I sweep my hands down my apron, mutter, "See ya later," and descend the stairs to carry on my normal day.

But there's nothing normal about starting a day with half a dead heart.

40

SOPHIE

Miss Missing You

eleste was kind enough to let me cry myself to sleep on her sofa. Boyd and I never had "the talk" to declare that we were official, so it's hard to call it a breakup, but my heart doesn't know the difference.

It's Friday morning and I should be headed into the office, but I can't face it today. I've *never* taken a sick day—not even as far back as high school. I'll power through any kind of flu or cold virus, isolating myself in my office, corresponding through phone and email. Nothing has ever gotten in the way of my work before yesterday. But heartbreak is a different kind of ailment to face. There's no over-the-counter medication to mask the symptoms, and they're far more detrimental than the sniffles.

A knock at Celeste's door at 8am jolts me upright.

She comes out of the kitchen, spry as ever, with Wilson trailing behind her. "Now, whoever might that be?" She asks, but I can tell she knows the answer.

I swallow the lump in my throat as I watch the door swing open. I don't want it to be Boyd. My life's course is set out before me and I don't have enough say in the matter that I want him tied to my sinking ship. My family's luck with avoiding shipwrecks ran out in 1914 when Thomas stepped on American soil.

Henry is angry about us dating, and if he'll go to such lengths to punish his own daughter, I can only imagine the evil schemes he'd cook up to torment Boyd. If he can get out unscathed, then this is the sacrifice I need to make.

But when I see who is standing on the front step, I realize I do wish it was him. Not that I don't love my best friend and brother, but Ashlyn and Caleb aren't who my heart wants. Too bad its wants aren't up for discussion anymore.

I stand and walk to the door. They both greet me with sympathetic smiles, though Caleb looks a little more angry than Ashlyn.

"Hi, little brother. Ash."

They step inside and I give them both a hug, reigning in my tears. Wilson jumps up at Caleb for some half-hearted ear scratches, but he gives Ashlyn a wide berth.

"Aren't you supposed to be at work?" I ask.

"I told them I had a gynecologist appointment. No one asked questions."

"Maintenance of your nether region is always a good option to avoid questions. That happens to be Andy's favourite excuse for me when I'm running late."

We both chuckle until I look at my brother's face and he's not laughing. He's not cringing at our discussion either, which tells me he's tuned us out and he's focused on the reason he's here. I can assume Celeste called him and explained what happened.

Like a good hostess, Celeste welcomes Caleb and Ashlyn inside for coffee. She's always been a tea drinker until Boyd taught her a few coffee making tricks. Now she's a convert, and it's just one more thing that's tied to him forever. Like my shower. And carousels. And Boston.

Ashlyn follows Celeste into the kitchen, in what I assume is an intentional move to give me and Caleb a moment.

"Please tell me you're not going through with this," Caleb pleads as he drops onto the sofa.

I take a deep breath and sit beside him, then Wilson jumps up beside me. "You didn't see his face, Caleb. I don't have a choice."

"Of course you have a choice. This has gone too far. I'm going to talk to him. Tell him this isn't the seventeenth century, and fathers can't marry off their daughters to some well-to-do business associate."

I place my hand on Caleb's, trying to calm him. He's a passionate guy and does have a temper at times—though it's nothing compared to Henry. This situation isn't something hot-head Caleb can fix, though.

"It won't do any good. No offence, but even if he respected your opinion, he'd just throw the blame back on you for not taking over the business like he had planned."

"Let him blame me. I don't care. Have I ever given you the impression I *care* what he thinks about me?" Caleb's voice raises in pace and volume as he grits out each word.

"It's not just you at risk, though. He knows about Boyd. He said if I didn't agree to this, you'd both face the full force of his wrath. So if I have to do this to keep you both out of his crosshairs, so be it." I choke up again, forcing out the reality of my situation.

"Soph, you'll always be at his mercy if you let him get away with this. Each time you let him control you, it gives him more power against you."

"I'd rather be at his mercy and take the brunt of his anger than pass it off to two people I love." The words spill out so fast, I can't stop them.

My brother heaves a resounding sigh. "What did Boyd say?"

"I didn't tell him," I confess, looking down at my fur baby, stroking his ears.

Caleb turns his body so he's facing me. "That you love him, or that Henry threatened him?"

It's a lot harder to keep my composure when he's looking at me, but I won't cry over this anymore. "Neither."

"I may not know him well, but I think he'd—"

"Am I interrupting?" Ashlyn peeks her head around the wall that separates the kitchen.

I glance at Caleb, who looks like he's about to reply, so I answer instead. "No, not at all."

Ashlyn takes a seat in one of the two armchairs opposite the couch, leaning forward so her elbows rest on her knees. Now is not the time to notice the impressive cut of her biceps, but it's impossible not to. "Tell me what's going on. Why are you doing this to yourself?"

Immediately, my body tenses, causing Wilson to perk up. "I'm not doing anything to myself."

"Oh, babe. You are. You're so wrapped up in what Henry says and demands of you, you forget that you're almost thirty years old. Beyond that, you have the ability to succeed in any role you choose, but you keep choosing this."

Ashlyn has never been one to pull punches, but this one is straight to the gut. A sucker punch I didn't see coming, but feel the full force of it. Here I thought my brother and best friend were showing up to be a support system. This isn't supportive at all.

"Great. Another person to tell me what to do with my life. Do this, Sophie. You're doing this wrong, Sophie. My decisions are always better than your own, Sophie. Please, tell me what else I can improve on. Should I message everyone in my life for approval on my underwear each morning? Haircut? To wax or not to wax?" My anger is reaching a level it hasn't approached for years. Normally, I can keep my cool, but after the last twenty hours I've had, my cool has been obliterated. "I wasn't expecting you to walk in here and plan a bachelorette party. But I really don't need anyone else making me feel like crap for trying to protect people I love. You haven't had a front-row seat to what Henry is capable of your entire life. I have, and I won't subject anyone to it if I can stop it."

Ashlyn doesn't react to my tirade. She just leans back in the armchair and stares at me with a stoic expression. "Finished?"

I look at Caleb for confirmation that she just asked me that. He looks far more uncomfortable than he did when Ashlyn mentioned the gynecologist.

"Do you agree with her?" I demand, staring at my brother.

He shrugs one shoulder. "You know I do, Soph. You know there's no love lost between me and Henry, but I also think you give him too much."

"Too much what?" I stand, ready to march back to my house and close the door to the outside world.

"Everything. You care too much about what he thinks, give him more credit than he deserves regarding his business— which, by the way, he's built from being a bully, not a smart businessman—and you definitely give him too much power over you."

Again, all I'm hearing right now is everything I've done wrong. It's wrong of me to want to love my father. It's wrong of me to want to protect people I love. It's wrong of me to work hard for a company I care about. Nothing I do is right, and I'm tired of trying. "Well, excuse me. It's not easy for all of us to turn our backs on our families and go do whatever we feel like. Thanks for stopping by." I storm off toward the door with Wilson hot on my heels.

My brother tries saying something behind me, but I can't process anything else today. I just want to go home and hide away with the one male who doesn't make me feel like a perpetual disappointment.

41

BOYD

Back To Earth

May sixth. According to Professor Benton, that's the day Sophie is supposed to get married to a douchebag, Derek Knoll. I'm not sure why he shared this information with me when I touched base with him yesterday, but it's been sitting in my head like a ticking bomb. Exactly twenty-eight days from now, the woman I love will be married... to someone else.

It's hard to put into words how much that hurts. When things ended so terribly with Maggie, I had a hundred other distractions to keep my mind busy and more important things to spend my emotional budget on. Now, all of my thoughts are consumed by Sophie.

"I can call Tessa in. She's been asking for more hours," Monica suggests.

I shake my head, realizing I just spent several minutes polishing the same spot on the back counter. "Thanks, Mon. Leaving now will just give me more time to think... and I don't want to think."

She shouldn't even be here today. It's her day off, but she stopped in to check on me. I want to appreciate that gesture, but her pitying eyes only make me feel more pathetic.

"Not up for discussion. Phoenix has tryouts for the summer league in ninety minutes. You're coming with us." She pulls her phone from her coat pocket and dials a number.

I tune out her discussion, minus when I hear her ask Tessa to cover my shift.

"Settled. She'll be here in thirty."

Her words are muffled as I stare into space. The entire world feels like it's closing in around me. Every voice I hear sounds like Sophie. Every person who walks in the door with hair the same shade just about brings me to my knees... and it's a very common shade, it turns out. My heart all but stopped two days ago when I saw a copper labradoodle running at the park. Its goofy way of bounding instead of a graceful run most dogs have was so similar to Wilson, I couldn't bear it.

"Boyd?" Monica shouts, snapping her fingers.

I blink myself back into focus, shaking out the muffled sounds clouding my head. "Sorry." My throat closes before I can choke out an explanation. Probably because I'm too embarrassed to confide in Monica and tell her how much I'm hurting. But my eyes aren't so good at keeping secrets, because without permission, they start to leak.

"Oh, come here, you big softie." Monica wraps her arm around me like a momma bear.

The gesture makes me feel like a child—a six-foot tall child with facial hair and a business degree.

I pull myself together after a few seconds, leaning out of Monica's embrace. Why am I always so set on dwelling on heartbreak? I let Maggie's dismissal haunt me for years. Sophie helped me get beyond that, and now I'm even worse off. There's no way I have enough of my heart left to consider ever giving it to someone else.

"I love her, Mom. And it hurts."

"Give it time. It'll get easier."

That sounds unlikely. It's been nine days since I saw her last and it hurts more now than it did then. Now that I've come to terms with the fact she's not going to come through this door, run into my arms, and tell me it was all a big misunderstanding. Reality is sobering, and I'd like to remain drunk on love.

Tessa walks in the door before I can reply. How long was I staring into space? It's a good thing it's Saturday and painfully slow. Another memory of Sophie's visit with Ashlyn surfaces. The weather was much the same, and foot traffic was minimal. But I need to convince myself she's not showing up anymore. Not even for a flat white.

"Everything okay?" Tessa asks, her eyes lit with concern.

"Yeah, all good," Monica answers. "Boss man just isn't feeling well. Thanks for coming."

"No worries. Looks slow, so I can still get some homework done." She pats her backpack and Monica talks to her for a few moments as I trail into my office. My obsessed brain pictures Sophie backed up against my desk, her blouse button undone, panting. I blink away the vision of her, rip off my apron, and grab my coat to exit as fast as possible. There's too much of her in these walls. Monica is right; I need to get out.

I thank Tessa on my way out the door, Monica trailing behind me. We walk the ten minutes to her place to pick up Phoenix, who is anxiously waiting in his soccer kit. He looks so grown up. Like he's ready to look at girls as more than targets in dodgeball. I don't want to be the cynical old man who warns him away from women, but I never want him to feel like I do right now. He doesn't need to be bogged down by my relationship woes, though. This is a big day for him.

"Ready, Captain?" I ask, clapping him on the back.

He hesitates to answer. "I didn't know you were coming. Mom said you were working."

Well, that's a crushing blow to my ego. He looks upset that I'm here.

"Yeah, she called Tessa in so I could come. Do you not want me to?"

"No, no. Of course. I... was just... surprised." He bends down to pick up his duffel bag, hoisting it onto his shoulder. "Ready."

We walk to the rec centre hosting tryouts. There are hoards of kids lined up to register, which is a good thing, so they'll have several full teams and make a more competitive season. Phoenix has aspirations to pursue soccer in the future, so playing the same group of a few kids won't sharpen his skills much.

I squeeze his shoulder after Monica's got him registered, then he ventures off toward the group of kids waiting to be assigned pinnies. Monica and I find a spot to watch in the indoor soccer field that has bleachers all the way around. We sit third row from the bottom, just left of the centre line on the far side. Kids start filing onto the field, wearing different coloured vests to distinguish their groups. They'll run through different drills, then get divided up amongst the coaches based on jurisdiction and skill level.

Phoenix runs onto the field, which is easy to spot, because he's about four inches taller than most kids his age. His sandy blond hair bounces as he jogs along the perimeter to warm up. We wave and shout at him as he goes past.

He waves back, but his eyes don't stop searching the crowd. He continues his trail, and I notice him wave again when he gets to the corner nearest the entrance. My eyes search the people in that area and land on her.

Sophie. What is she doing here? I clutch Monica's arm because I know if I don't ground myself, I'll float over there like my soul is being called home.

"What?"

"She—she's here," I stammer.

The panic in her voice is immediate. "Who? Maggie? Where?"

All I can do for twenty solid seconds is shake my head and stare. Finally, I offer some reassurance. "Sophie."

"The little bugger. Phoenix must have invited her. They exchanged numbers when they made the new playlist for the café. It never crossed my mind he'd contact her."

It doesn't look like she's seen me. If she has, she's a lot better at hiding it than I am. Her eyes are focused on Phoenix, and she randomly claps and smiles. But even from here, I can tell she's hiding pain in her eyes.

The entire tryout passes without me looking at the field once. My eyes were locked on her the whole time. It's not until she stands to leave that I realize it's over.

"I have to talk to her," I declare to Monica, and leap into action, bounding down the bleachers. My heart picks up speed as my feet do, which could be because of the effort I'm putting into catching up to Sophie or the thought of seeing her.

I exit into the rec centre lobby, searching for the familiar head of brown hair. She's disappeared. I look toward the large sliding glass doors at the main entrance, just in time to see her walking into the parking lot. My feet stall in place. My brain has finally caught up to what I'm doing, and can't come up with anything to say if I catch her. Still, I force myself forward, jogging to the door. I just need to stop her from leaving, and I'll figure the rest out later.

But as I make my exit from the building, I watch her SUV pull onto Queen Street. The hurt I was being suffocated by earlier today is nothing compared to watching her leave again.

42

SOPHIE

It's Hard To Say "I Do," When I Don't

Marrying a man I dislike—that's a generous way to describe my feelings toward him—is bad enough. Our names and lives forever linked. Long down the line, when Caleb's future great-great-grandchildren use one of those DNA kits to trace their ancestry, there I'll be beside Derek Knoll, and our wedding date will only tell a miniscule part of the full story.

But if he keeps talking over me, the date on the other side of *his* dash is going to be a lot sooner than he thinks. We haven't spent a moment alone—thankfully—but he's taken it upon himself to be fully involved in *McNamara Enterprises'* daily happenings, which means he's joined me for my current meeting and doesn't know when to keep his mouth shut.

"Sophie," he beckons.

Through gritted teeth, I reply, "Yes, Mr. Knoll?"

"We can do that, right? Add the rest of their list onto their shipment?"

I stare at him for a moment, having an *are you serious* moment. Considering the clients in front of me belong to a cosmetic company and the product they're requesting is a restricted ingredient, adding it to an existing order isn't an option.

"It's not a straightforward request, as I've explained. *Repeatedly*. It requires a strategic sourcing consultant to seek out specialized products, and shipping processes differ. No, we can't just add it to the ship."

He stares back at me with a stupid look that gives me the strong urge to drop kick him. If his IQ drops any lower, he'll be on par with a tulip. I swear, if he says one more stupid thing, I'm going to start watering him.

I spend the following five minutes arguing with Derek, trying to convince *my* clients that what he's suggesting isn't possible. Right now, Derek looks like the hero and I look like the one who can't execute his genius plan. If only it were easy to disregard ship manifests, legal requirements for importing goods, cost, and timeframe. Things would be so much easier if I was a genie who could blink their wishes into existence. But I'm not. And by the end of this meeting, the only thing *I* want is to blink myself out of this room.

When my clients leave, I have no words for my future husband. Not polite ones, anyway. I exit the room and march down the hallway back toward my office. Footsteps sound behind me and I don't have the energy to suppress the groan begging to escape.

"Why couldn't you just get them what they wanted?" Derek calls from ten feet away.

I stop outside of the women's washroom and turn to face him. "Because what they want is a restricted material. Your anthropology degree may not have explained to you about the laws and regulations surrounding shipment of hazardous materials, but surely you must have learned about what happens to populations consuming toxins."

"What?" His irritating face scrunches and he tilts his head like Wilson does when he can't understand my side of the conversation. On my dog, it's cute. On Derek, it keeps bringing back a violent streak in me that could have warriors on *Mortal Kombat* cowering.

I grumble at him rather than replying. He'll comprehend grunts and hand gestures better than words.

"You should have just made it happen, Soph. You didn't even try."

His use of the one syllable of my name makes my skin crawl. That's reserved for my brother and... Boyd. As if letting him go wasn't hard enough, Phoenix invited me to his soccer tryouts last weekend and Boyd was there. I ran out before I could bump into him and I'm not sure if he saw me, since I avoided looking at him at all costs, but it resulted in me driving home in tears.

Derek will never replace him. No one is ever reopening this vault I call a heart. So there's no way I'm letting his use of my nickname slide.

"I'm going to say this once, and I hope you get the message. Do not *ever* call me Soph again. You can call me Sophie, Miss McNamara, or the bloody Queen of Sheba for all I care, but you will never call me Soph. Next, there's no point in 'trying' what you suggested, Derek, because I have no interest in getting arrested for smuggling illicit materials into the country." I step toward him and slow my words to a speed he is more likely to understand. "There's a difference between importing goods and smuggling controlled substances. Only one of those is in my job description. Understood?"

His stupid face is back. The one that just looks stupid because I resent his existence. "Geeze. What's got your panties in a bunch? Are you on your period or something?"

I clench my disgusting office coffee in my hand, and tell myself not to pour it on his head.

He shrugs off his comment, dismissing the conversation entirely. "I was thinking we should spend some time together. Alone."

"No." That suggestion doesn't even require consideration. Hard pass. I'd rather call up my buddy Chad and have him run me through an AMRAP until I drop dead. At least he had redeeming qualities. He did something just to be nice. I doubt Derek could claim that he's done that once in his life.

"We're getting married in less than four weeks, Soph."

When I say it takes every ounce of restraint I possess to stop myself from slapping him, I mean *every* ounce. If this conversation continues much longer, there will be violence in this hallway. So to protect my reputation from being further sullied as being an irrational, unhinged woman, I walk away.

Andy is at his desk as I pass, so I mutter through clenched teeth, "Do not let him in my office or there will be bloodshed."

My dutiful assistant pinches in his lips to hold in a laugh. "Got it."

I shut the door behind me, collapsing against it and listening for Andy to use some colourful terms to tell Derek off. He doesn't disappoint and alludes to us coming as a packaged deal, so once Derek and I are married, he gets Andy too. He deserves a raise.

With Andy's comments forcing a little laugh from me, my blood pressure starts to decrease. My jaw unclenches and my shoulders drop from their positions around my ears. I take deep breaths at my desk until all the tension from the last sixty minutes disappears.

Then I get a text message.

Mom: *You need to pick a dress.*

Just like her husband. No small talk. No asking how I'm doing. Zero discussion about how I feel in this scenario. Of all the times she's chosen him, this has to hurt the most.

Sophie: *Fine. Anything else?*

Mom: *It wouldn't kill you to be happy about this. Choosing to be miserable won't make anything different.*

Such sage advice from a woman who has 'chosen' to be happy in a decades' long marriage to a man who controls her every action. The woman who has no control over her own wardrobe, bank account, or address. She's just along for the ride.

And the stupid thing is, I know that's the same path I'm headed down and there's nothing I can do about it.

43

BOYD

We Were Doomed
from the Start

My four months of work placement are almost over, and they've gone by in a blur. I have two and a half weeks left, but it no longer feels important. My words to Holden ring true: success isn't about academic or career accolades. None of that means anything if you're not happy.

I'm not happy.

Not even sitting in the crowded stadium with Phoenix at my side, waiting for his beloved Toronto SC to take the field. He's jazzed about the team he got chosen for in the city league, but we haven't broached the topic of Sophie being there. Whether he intends to invite her to future games is a mystery at this point. I'm not really sure how to discuss it with him.

He sips his massive soda, and I gulp my overpriced, flat beer. There's an awkward air between us that has never been present before.

Before I can cut into it, Phoenix blurts, "I didn't want to choose sides."

I look over at him, but he's staring straight ahead, so I can't gather any insight from his expression. "Choose sides for what?" That's an ambiguous statement, considering we're here for a soccer match.

"Mom and Dad. I know what he did. Mom doesn't know I know, but I have for a long time. I didn't understand what cheating meant when I was younger, but… yeah." He releases an awkward laugh, still focusing on the field. "He made me choose. Last time I saw him, he said I had to pick him or Mom, so…"

"What?" My fist clenches around my Solo cup, sloshing some beer onto my lap. "He said that?"

Phoenix nods. "Yeah. I was five the last time I saw him, and he told me if I picked Mom, I'd never see him again."

"Have you ever told your mom this?"

He shakes his head. "She was pretty torn up over things already. I chose her and that was that. But it stinks." He takes a big swallow and his eyes flutter closed.

I throw my arm around him, both furious and heartbroken his deadbeat dad said that to his five-year-old son. "His loss, man."

"That's not my point." He finally turns his head to look at me. "You've been like a cool extra dad to me, so I don't miss him. But Sophie showed up, and I saw how happy she made you."

My throat tightens at the mention of her name. I take a pull of beer to help. It doesn't.

"Then she made me happy too. She's cool. Easy to talk to. I can see why you love her so much."

"I never told you I—"

"Dude. I'm thirteen, not stupid." He rolls his eyes. "Again, that's not my point."

His point is quite elusive, because I don't know what he's getting at.

"What's your point, then?" I ask, trying to encourage him to spill.

"I didn't want to choose sides," he repeats. He takes another gulp of his soda while I'm left processing his words. "I don't know why you guys broke up. Mom wouldn't really tell me, but I didn't want to have to choose."

The third time he makes that statement, I finally understand. He invited her to his tryouts because he didn't want to pick one of us over the other. I might have known him a lot longer, but she obviously made an impression on him in the short time they spent together.

"I'd never make you choose. If I had it my way, it wouldn't be an issue, but I lost my say in the matter." That was a terrible thing to say. I lean my head back and look up at the grey sky, internally cursing myself for implying it's her fault. "It wasn't really her choice, either."

"Aren't you guys adults?" He thrusts his chin forward and narrows his eyes at me. "How is it not your choice? I mean, with my dad, he chose to do what he did. But how do two people who want to be together not have the choice? If you're telling me I'm going to grow up, have to pay my own damn bills, and still not get to make decisions for myself, I don't want it." His eyes bulge and he turns to face his feet. "Don't tell my mom I said damn."

I chuckle, and it's the first time I've had a decent laugh for weeks. "Your secret's safe with me, bud." It takes me a few seconds longer to figure out how to answer the rest of his rant. "Sometimes, when you're older, things get forced on you and don't leave you with much of a choice at all."

He scans the field and glances up at the time on the scoreboard. "I know if she could have, she would have chosen you."

And that one sentence makes me question everything about how things turned out between us. Maybe there's more to the story than she told me. But how will I know if she won't tell me? Why wouldn't she talk to me so we could decide together?

As the soccer teams run out onto the pitch, I find myself lost in another haze. I'm staring at the field, but my eyes are vacant, not processing anything from the outside world. My thoughts replay the entire conversation Sophie and I had the last time we spoke.

"It's not a simple decision to just stick to what's morally right when it's business and the people you love at stake."

What did she mean by the people she loves at stake? What did Henry threaten her with? Maybe in her mind, she had to choose sides, and got stuck on the one she didn't want.

Cheers erupt around us as the Toronto SC score at the thirty-four minute mark. The players, who have been running for half an hour, whip around the field and gather in a huddle. The sea of people in royal blue shirts filling the stands are roaring and the loudspeaker blasts a Queen song for all to hear.

Phoenix jumps out of his seat, cheering his heart out. "Did you see that?"

Not when it happened, but thanks to the benefits of video replay, I do now. "Yeah, Captain. That'll be you someday."

His smile grows twice as wide.

I don't know when he grew up so much or when he got so wise, but I cling to his words. *"I know if she could have, she would have chosen you."*

So I pull a cowardly move to ease my own aching heart, hoping it will help hers too. I tug out my phone and draft a message. My finger hovers over it until the game is nearing the end.

The scoreboard is tied 1-1, when I hear Phoenix say, "You gotta take a shot, man." He's looking at me, not the field.

Now's the time to take my shot at moving on.

Boyd: *I respect your choice.*

Except, if I had my choice, I wouldn't move on at all.
Boyd: *But I miss you.*

44

SOPHIE

The Pros and Cons
of Breathing

Ashlyn and Celeste are two very different personalities in two very different stages of life, but they're each such an important part of mine, I need them here for this moment. Thankfully, they have both forgiven me for my tirade the last time we were together. Neither one of them support my decision, so that makes the already dark rain cloud looming overhead feel significantly more dreadful, but at least they're here.

"Try this one." Ashlyn holds up a bedazzled muumuu with puffy chiffon sleeves.

"That's hideous," I reply.

"Exactly." She places the garment back on the rack. "A bride should feel excited for her wedding day and a beautiful dress can reflect that. But for you..."

She has a point.

"Well, then we should find something as constricting and uncomfortable as possible that will make me miserable the entire day. We can reflect that. One that requires an adhesive bra, because those things are another level of torture." I chug the entire mimosa the boutique offers, quickly reaching for a fourth. Not sure what the protocol is, but I'm finishing the tray.

Celeste re-enters the area Ashlyn and I are in, with two dresses I'm assuming are for her. They're both black, which can't be a coincidence. "What do you think of these?"

I scan both dresses, not particularly excited about either of them. Then again, I'm not excited about anything lately. "Whichever you're more comfortable in. There's no point in all of us being miserable."

She places them both on a hook outside of a change room door. "At least I'll have something to wear to the next funeral I have to attend."

This ceremony might be called a wedding, but it feels like a funeral.

"Real talk." Ashlyn steps away from the rack and squares me to her intimidating frame with one hand on each of my shoulders. "What do we have to do to talk you out of this? I'm down to go beat the living snot out of Derek. Or Henry. Bust their knee caps or remove their teeth until they get the message. Whatever."

"Yeah, girl. I've got your back." Celeste raises her hand, which Ashlyn meets with a high five and transitions easily back into conversation.

"I know you think you owe your father something. Your family. Your employees. Whatever. But you don't owe any of them your life. You have too much potential and you're too incredible to spend the best years of your life in a loveless marriage at a loveless job."

"Word." Celeste nods in agreement.

"Did you just say 'word'?" Ashlyn faces Celeste, sporting parallel twin lines between her brows.

"I'm hip too. I can hang with you young cats."

There's so much happening right now. Between the boutique employees buzzing around, the brides trying on sample dresses, my thoughts about this marriage—and Boyd.

With Ashlyn and Celeste further watering my seed of doubt, I'm not sure what to make of anything.

I sink onto a tufted bench, leaning against the blush coloured wall. "I don't know what to do."

Ashlyn and Celeste both look relieved to see my defeat. They each move to sit on either side of me. I tip the entire contents of my drink into my mouth, begging it to offer me some peace.

"Child, I know I've made my opinion clear, and I'm not saying any of this because I want to make you doubt what you feel is the right decision. But do you really think this is right? That this is the only option?"

I take a deep breath in and out. "No, it's not right... but it is the only option." This conversation isn't a surprise. I knew it would come up, but each time I have to justify my own decisions, it takes a little more of my resolve. "This is just easier."

"Do you know what your father really says when he tears you down?" Celeste asks in an abrupt turn of the conversation.

I open my mouth to speak, because the last thing I want is to hear Henry's words repeated, but she cuts me off.

"He *says* you're not good enough. You're not worth the space you occupy. But what he's really *saying* is 'your greatness intimidates me and my fragile ego can't handle being overshadowed.' He's *saying*, 'your light is brighter than mine, so I have to dim yours until mine looks brighter.' He's *saying*, 'your gifts are too valuable, so I have to shame you into being afraid to share them.'"

Her words create such a visceral reaction in my body, I feel the urge to vomit—which could also be because of the rapid-fire drink chugging. Everything she said holds so much truth, and I know it does, that I'm sickened by my inability to combat Henry's control.

But he's still my dad. The man who gave me life. He may not have supported us emotionally growing up, but he contributed financially. So maybe my cowardice is just undeserved loyalty.

I've played out scenarios in my head thousands of times where I tell my father off. I tell him exactly how I feel about him and his cronies. I tell him where to shove his company and his terrible golf game. But I've never had the courage to do it. Sure, I'm not in a great situation right now, but there's a strange sense of security from complying with a narcissist's demands, rather than upsetting them and being a target.

Yes, I wish I had Boyd's courage to face off with my father and take whatever fallout comes. But it's not a cut and dry decision when the person is family. And I certainly wouldn't sic him on someone else I love intentionally.

"I have to do this, Celeste." Another wave of defeat and shame consumes me as I say that out loud. It's one thing to think something, but it's another to voice it and put those thoughts out into the universe. Thoughts carry more weight once other people hear them—like they become one step closer to reality.

"It's really hard for me to watch you throw your life away like this," Ashlyn adds.

For a fleeting moment, I fear she'll give me the same ultimatum Boyd did. Granted, from her position, I'm not being forced into a legal contract with a new best friend. She's not being pushed out and replaced.

"But I'll be by your side. Just say the word when you're ready for someone to lose their fingers. I have extensive knowledge of human anatomy from years at the hospital."

The three of us laugh, but Ashlyn's is a little maniacal, making me realize she isn't kidding. I reach back and sweep each of their arms into mine, hooking them both and pulling them to stand. The second I do, the alcohol hits me all at once and I wobble. My remedy to the problem is to grab another glass.

If I have to walk out of here with a wedding dress, I want to be numb to what it represents.

Twenty minutes later, I'm drunk in the change room, pulling a dusty blue chiffon number over my head, straightening the white lace overlay. My phone chimes in my bag hanging on the back of the door.

I take it out, wondering if it's my mother checking in on the dress shopping she insisted on but refused to attend. It's not.

Boyd: *I respect your choice.*

My breath catches when I see the name and attached message. What does that mean?

Boyd: *But I miss you.*

I don't try to decipher it. I can't, because I'm once again reduced to tears.

Ashlyn shouts from the other side of the door, "It can't be that bad. Let us see."

Instead of replying, I drop onto the plush ottoman in the corner and start blubbering like a drunken fool. Ashlyn nearly takes the hinges off of the door to get inside, but an associate comes to unlock it before she puts her raw strength to use.

I can't breathe. This material is suffocating me. This room is wringing the air from my lungs. This future staring at me is strangling the life out of me. "I–I can't…"

Ashlyn and Celeste rush to my sides.

"What is it, darling?" Celeste asks while gently tugging the zipper down to free me from this fabric prison.

"B–Boyd." I point to my phone, hoping they'll understand.

Ashlyn picks it up from where I dropped it on the floor and turns the screen on. She tilts it to show Celeste, who then starts rubbing my bare back.

Ashlyn pulls the door closed, then returns to hoist me up with one arm under each of mine. "Come on, train wreck. This isn't your stop."

It's so Ashlyn to make me laugh with a harsh reality check. My two dear friends work to get me out of the dress I'll now forever associate with Boyd and return me into my own clothes. By the time I'm dressed, I've composed myself. I haven't been drunk often enough to learn I'm an emotional drunk. Lesson learned.

"We don't have to do this right now," Celeste says, opening the door.

"No, it's okay. I want this one." I clutch at the dusty blue dress my friends peeled off me, convinced it's the right choice. Maybe it will lead to another meltdown on my way down the aisle when I realize it's not Boyd waiting for me, but it feels like this gives me a small piece of him on the way. After all, he has my heart.

45

BOYD

Caffeine Cold

My shifts at the café are becoming fewer as the weeks tick by. I've done a good job of bogging myself down with other responsibilities at my work placement to stop feeling. But that finished yesterday.

Sophie never returned my text message from more than two weeks ago, and still every time she crosses my mind, I feel sick to my stomach at the thought of her becoming another man's wife. Thinking about someone else coming home to her every day. Making her laugh. Wiping her tears. Celebrating her wins.

But what turns my stomach the most is that with this arranged marriage, she's liable to end up with someone who does none of those things. Someone who treats her as a prop. A stepping stone. The one thing she said she feared when I first asked her out.

It doesn't make sense. For thirty-two days, I've analyzed and weighed everything I know about Sophie against the situation we're now in, and I can't come up with an answer.

I need answers. But most of all, I need her to be happy.

Monica pulls me aside after my third order error—there's a big difference between a regular latte and an iced latte. "What is up with you?"

I feel stupid for confessing that I'm still hung up on Sophie. Judging by Monica's face, I don't have to say it out loud.

Sometimes I forget that she's been my friend since I bought this place. Plus, she's a mother. If, over the last thirteen years, she's developed skills anything like my mum's, I should know better than to try to evade her questions.

She continues re-making the order I screwed up, leaving me to lean against the counter like an obnoxiously large, dust-collecting ornament.

"She's stuck in my head, Mon. It's been weeks and I just... I..." A lump forms in my throat, so I have to swallow it down to continue. "I still love her."

"Well, duh. That's not a surprise to anyone around here. Trust me. What I can't understand is why you're letting her go through with it." She passes the impressively made drink over the pickup counter to the toe-tapping patron who waited longer than necessary.

When she spins back to face me, I stare at her, questioning how obvious it's been to people around me. "There is no 'letting her' go through with anything. I don't have a say."

Something behind me catches Monica's eye. A wave of hope floods through me as I spin around, hoping to see Sophie walking through the door. That hope is doused by the arrival of Celeste and Ashlyn, who both look like they haven't slept for a month.

"Boyd, dear, could we talk to you for a moment?" Celeste asks with a tentative smile. The spunky, outspoken woman I've come to know and respect is neither of those things today.

I glance at Monica as if I'm asking her for permission.

"Go on. Maybe you do have a say." She waves me off and returns to the cash register. "Plus, you're just getting in the way."

I roll my eyes behind her before turning to Celeste and Ashlyn. "Can I get either of you anything? A tea?"

"No thank you, dear. We won't be staying long."

The nausea I've been grappling with for days threatens to boil over. I'm not sure what exactly has been the cause. Nothing has changed since Sophie walked out these doors. Other than time is ticking closer to her impending nuptials this weekend, and she disregarded my text message, making her position clear.

I sit on the stool opposite the wall, with Ashlyn and Celeste on either side. "What can I do for you ladies?" I clear my throat, trying to play off the fact my voice just squeaked out like a prepubescent boy. Even Phoenix sounds more masculine than I did just now.

"Well, we're not really sure, to be honest," Ashlyn replies.

"Our sweet Sophie is depressed. And I don't use that word lightly. She's putting on a good front, going to work, trying to prove her worth, but she comes home and sometimes she doesn't even pick up Wilson until an hour later. I can hear her crying through the walls, and she doesn't want to talk to anyone."

My stomach gurgles as my anger and upset reach a boiling point. I never assumed Sophie was happy with the arrangement, but being depressed is another matter. "What can I do?"

"Go see her. She was happy with you," Ashlyn adds without hesitation. "She accepted her fate because she was afraid if she chose you, Henry would ruin your career before you even started."

I lean back on the stool, but there's nothing to catch me, so I grab onto the table, glad it's affixed to the wall. She's doing this because of me? Didn't she realize that losing her would be worse than not having any career opportunities? I can live with owning a café and making coffee for the rest of my life… I can't live without her. I won't let her do this.

Words fail me. My mind is racing and my stomach ache has turned into a surge of adrenaline. I slide my stool back, stand, and stare at a ring from a cup dried on the table. What will I say? How will I change anything? What if she doesn't want to see me? Doesn't matter. I need to try.

"Monica, I'm leaving."

"Good." She smiles at Celeste and Ashlyn. "It's about time. Am I right, ladies?"

I'd roll my eyes again if I weren't so eager to leave. "Can you get someone to clean that table?" I ask as I pull out my phone to order a ride-share.

"Put that away. A knight in shining armour can't show up in an Uber. I'll take you." Ashlyn pushes open the front door with ease and waves at me and Celeste to pick up the pace. It feels like we're launching a revolution without coming up with a battle plan.

"Sophie doesn't need a knight in shining armour. But I won't let her throw her life away trying to be mine." I march down the sidewalk with intention, feeling like the ominous grey clouds overhead are somehow a prophetic manifestation for what's coming.

When we reach Ashlyn's shiny black Mercedes, I slide in the back, draping my legs to the side to fit in behind the passenger seat. There's a litany of gym gear in the back, including three pairs of shoes, towels, hand wraps, extra tank tops, knee braces, and a container of protein powder. Everything is just thrown on the floor or seat.

"Sorry about the mess. On the bright side, you never know what'll come in handy." Ashlyn weaves through west-bound traffic, glancing at me occasionally in the rear-view mirror.

"Thanks for this. I appreciate the ride."

Part way to Sophie's office, the 'what ifs' start running through my head. What if she refuses to say no to this marriage? What if she gets more angry at me because she thinks I'm trying to control her? What if she's mad at her friends for coming to speak to me again? But it doesn't take me long to calm the racing thoughts with logic. If someone I cared about was suffering and needed someone to step up on their behalf to fix things, I wouldn't hesitate to do it. I *have* done it. Now Celeste and Ashlyn are doing the same thing. I can't ignore their pleas. Because, like Sophie said, not every situation is black and white.

Sophie deserves so much more than a life trapped in a marriage under someone else's control. So even if she doesn't choose me, I at least want her to choose herself.

We pull up in front of the St. Clair Avenue high-rise, and Ashlyn double parks beside a forest green Subaru.

"Go get your girl. I'll find parking."

I wasn't aware this was a group expedition, but if I can't get into the building, I may need their help. With a nod and a thank you, I jump out of the passenger side and into the drizzling rain.

Before I reach the door, my heart stalls.

Me & You

"Andy?" I call through the intercom system.

Instead of replying, he pops his head through my door. He used to wear a smile when he entered, but for the past few weeks, the mood here has been so sombre, I don't think any of us have smiled within these walls. Not since Andy told Derek about him being a bonus in our marriage.

"Yes?"

I try to force the corners of my lips upward, but even with all of my effort, the right side of my mouth reaches a neutral position. The left is stuck in a permanent frown, like I've had an emotional stroke with physical consequences. "Can you set up a meeting with Derek? It's about time I talk to the guy and get some paperwork signed."

My father had his lawyers draw up extensive contracts that all protect his business. Not once did he consider adding in stipulations protecting the things I've worked for, and he certainly didn't consider protecting me. I took it upon myself to have my lawyer draw up an agreement to cover both.

"Sure. I'll touch base when I get him scheduled." Andy turns to leave.

"Hey, Andy?"

He looks back over his shoulder, but doesn't respond.

"Thank you… for sticking by me. I appreciate you."

"We're a package deal, remember?" He winks at me, but all of his usual pep is gone. His indifference crushes me.

Ashlyn and Celeste are upset with me, though they're still trying to be supportive. Caleb is furious with me and both of our parents, but he promised he'd still be at the wedding for my sake. The only one who hasn't changed toward me is Wilson.

Andy sends an email with a calendar alert saying Derek is coming in at 1pm today, and we're to meet in the conference room midway between mine and my father's offices. That gives me two hours to ready myself for the final step before I walk down the aisle in four days. My throat closes at the thought. Not the thought of walking down the aisle, but at Derek being the person at the end. For a brief moment, I allow myself to imagine Boyd waiting at the end as I walk down in my blue and white dress. My heart races with anticipation instead of dread. It's a distinct difference.

But that can never happen.

I just hope my heart gets the message soon.

I sit at the conference table next to Derek and lay out the contracts my lawyers have drawn up. I may not have much—a car, a condo with a hefty mortgage, and Wilson—but those are all things worth protecting.

Derek pans the paperwork spread before him, but makes no effort to read them. Instead, he shoves them to the side, leans back in the executive chair, and kicks his feet up on the mahogany table. "The only thing we need to discuss is our wedding night."

"I beg your pardon?" I stare at this idiotic tulip, waiting for him to elaborate. What exactly does he think is going to happen? I'm being forced into this marriage. Whether we consummate our sham of a relationship is not my concern. "I wouldn't even touch you if you needed CPR."

"Your dad told me you were uptight, but I thought you'd loosen up by now."

"Oh, you mean in one of the sixty minutes we've spoken in the last seven years?" I've spent my life dealing with Henry's wrath, but I've never wanted to stoop to such evil acts as I do against my future husband. I'm going to open a Nature Valley bar in this man's bed the second we say 'I do.' Put hair removal cream in his shampoo. Swap out his stupid coffee whitener for crushed Alka Seltzer. Pure evil.

He scoffs. "It's not like you've tried. I might be your favourite person and you just don't know yet."

"Derek, I don't need to spend time with you to know I don't like you. I'm so confident about that, I can assure you if you were on life support and my phone was at five percent, I'd unplug your ventilator to charge it." I glare at him, to let him know I'm not kidding. "And I'll be your wife, so I'm within my rights to do that. Tread carefully."

"You know, it's this ice queen attitude that's the reason your father is making me the CEO."

I spin my head around like I'm straight out of *The Exorcist*. "What did you say?"

"Henry is making me the CEO. That's why I agreed to this. But now I'm wondering if it's even worth it."

My emotions flick through the entire catalogue in a matter of seconds. It was one thing when I considered Henry hiring a *qualified* man in his place down the road, but Derek? The guy with the anthropology degree who I'd bet he paid people to do his assignments for? The one staring at me like the only thing he's interested in is our wedding night?

Is it worth it? Is the potential for changing policies ten or fifteen years down the road enough to keep me coming back to this day in, day out? Is my loyalty to the other women in this office worth trading my personal hopes and dreams? Is my fear of my father worth giving up on the relationship that brought me genuine happiness?

No.

I don't reply. I also don't sign a single piece of paper. There will be no crossing the t's and dotting the i's. No putting the final touches on our business arrangement. The lingering voices in my head for the past several weeks that told me not to do this are now louder than the ones telling me to suck it up and accept my fate. The collective voices of everyone who loves me are drowning out the one that has dominated my life for almost thirty years.

The cycle ends now. No matter what the cost. I know Caleb will understand. I hope Boyd will too.

"Andy, my office. Now!" I demand as I walk past him.

He's through the door before I even round my desk. "That bad, huh?"

"I need a box."

"A box? Like a gift box? A shipping box?"

"A moving box." I drop in my chair, waking up my computer so I can clear my personal files. "I quit. I'm done."

His green eyes bulge. "Really?"

"Really. Can you please find me a box?"

Andy literally runs out the door. I've never seen him move so fast, even on days I told him he could leave early. He returns three minutes later with two sturdy banker's boxes. "I got one for myself, too."

A flash of worry crosses my mind when I process his words. It quickly morphs into a smile. "Are you sure?"

"I've been waiting for this day for three years."

"You've been working here for three years."

"I know. I promised myself I wouldn't leave you here to fend for yourself, but I don't think I really helped with the fending."

I abandon my computer task to walk around, take a box from him, and give him a side hug. Not only did I stay and put up with the toxicity seeping from this building's pores, but Andy did too. Instead of feeling like my decision was noble, it feels selfish. "You've been an amazing assistant and a good friend. I'm sorry I stayed for too long. I always wondered why you didn't quit."

Andy dismisses my apology with a waft of his hand. "Hurry up and pack, would you? We might make happy hour somewhere."

Ignoring the fact happy hour isn't even a thing here, I giggle and move back around my desk. It helps ease some of the fear of telling Henry my decision.

It takes me fifty minutes to clear all passwords and personal information from my computer, pack up my things, and draft a resignation letter. Andy had an equal amount of things to deal with, so we both finish around the same time.

I exit my office with shaking hands, struggling to carry the box of picture frames, various phone chargers, two sweaters I forgot I owned, and some other miscellaneous items. It's not that the box is heavy, but it's hard to grip with trembling fingers.

Before I go to Henry's office, I detour through the three floors our company occupies and inform each female on our staff that I'm leaving. I don't go into detail why, but office gossip probably filled them in weeks ago about what was expected of me. Each one of them is supportive, but not as willing to jump ship as Andy. It makes sense. Most of them have families and responsibilities they need to care for. I try not to let the guilt of leaving them behind change my mind. Some of them even assure me that their direct bosses aren't so bad, so while they know they'll never advance in the hierarchy, they're not treated like second-class citizens daily.

It's a relief, but also a tough pill to swallow. I was so dead set on female empowerment and sticking it to the man, the only person I've stuck it to is myself.

Meredith, from our sales department, who I've worked with on several occasions, is the most emotional. "We're going to miss you, but I'm happy for you. You're a girl boss, Sophie."

I smile at her, trying to express my appreciation for her support, but I don't want that distinction. "Just a boss. It's time for me to just be my own boss."

Andy offers to come with me to Henry's office, since he wants to hand in his resignation letter as well, but this is something I need to do myself. I grab his letter and amble down the hallway, curling the papers in my hands. The delicate placement of my feet reminds me of nights I used to sneak into Caleb's room and didn't want Henry to hear me.

With each step, I gain more confidence. I'm not a child anymore, and what I want matters. More than that, what I *deserve* matters. And I don't deserve to be auctioned off to the highest bidder.

"Is he free, Joel?" I ask when I reach his reception area.

"Let me check."

How this man demonstrates such a sunny disposition after working with my father every day is beyond me. He gives me permission to enter, so I take a resolving breath and walk forward to face my fate. I need every ounce of courage I possess to maintain my commitment to leaving.

Maybe I should have called Caleb.

No, I can do this.

"What's this I hear about you calling Derek down here to waste his time?"

No 'HI, how are you?' No 'Are you well today, daughter?' Henry doesn't waste time on things like his children's well-being—a trait my mother has inherited. Also, the fact Derek came to my father to tattle is another indication that this is the right choice.

"Sorry. I probably should have told him the wedding is off before I walked out."

Henry lifts his head with his ever present scowl adorning his face. "I beg your pardon?"

My nose scrunches at the realization I sound like my father sometimes. "I'm not marrying Derek." I relax my features and replace the look of disgust with one of conviction. "I'm also leaving *McNamara Enterprises*; effective immediately."

"You signed a contract."

"No, I didn't. *You* signed a contract. My investment in this business or in that marriage never mattered enough to you to get me to sign it. I never had enough value for you to consider having me sign a thing. So I hate to tell you, Henry, but you're on the hook for anything you signed. Not me."

I've flip-flopped with referring to Henry as my father, Mr. McNamara, or by his name, depending on how I viewed him in a given situation. Sometimes I grant him enough importance in my life to call him my father. Other times, when we're in the presence of employees or clients, I've maintained professional boundaries. But now, and forevermore, he'll be nothing more than a first name.

Henry stands, leaning over his desk with his fists pressed against it on either side of his paperwork. "Little girl, you are not cut out to survive in this world. I'm doing you a favour by marrying you off. What, you think you're going to run back to that barista? Believe me when I say he'll never get a job in this town. And now you, you can guarantee you won't, either. I put up with you because you're my daughter, but if you walk out the door, I won't even make that claim anymore."

I swallow the lump in my throat. Logically, I always knew that my worth to Henry was relative to what I could do for him. How I could benefit his life, rather than just for being my own person with strengths and talents that differ from his, but aren't less valuable. Hearing him claim he'll disown me if I choose my happiness over his demands doesn't upset me anymore. Because I'm excited to share my value with people who appreciate it.

"You've already pushed one child out of your life. Why not both? You're a shining star as a parent, Henry. This enterprise you've built isn't going to mourn your loss someday. And after how you've treated people—family—as commodities you can import and export from your life as needed, I doubt anyone else will either."

In what I'll describe as the proudest moment of my life to date—even more so than graduating university with honours—I exit Henry's office to the sounds of his berating insults. But I don't listen to a word he says because none of it matters.

This day marks the start of me living my own life.

47

BOYD

I Am Thinking It
Must Be Love

Sophie is exiting the lobby with Andy at her side, each carrying a box. She's smiling. Laughing. Walking with an air of pride in her steps. She looks nothing like the depressed soul Celeste and Ashlyn described.

There's something about her level of happiness that fills me with regret for coming here. She's not lost or sad without me. Not even the drizzle falling can douse the radiance she's exhibiting.

She gives Andy a peck on the cheek and he turns in the opposite direction. Sophie tilts her head to the sky and closes her eyes, allowing the raindrops to fall on her face. She straightens and opens her eyes, which land on me. She's always been like a magnet for me. I'm drawn to her with no hope of pulling away. Her north to my south pole is a perfect complement.

My feet lead me to her with no conscious order to do so. Her magnetic force drawing me in.

"Hi," she greets, gifting me with her genuine smile.

"Hi."

"Small world. How have you been?"

"Awful," I admit. "Dreadful, really. You?"

Her smile falters as she swipes rain from her face. "Whatever's worse than dreadful."

"Soph—"

"I love you," she blurts, not dropping eye contact. "I should have said it before... told you that. It just..."

I don't know if I should be happy about that or if it's going to be another element to contribute to my heartbreak. If she's marrying someone else, I can't... "What's in the box?"

All remnants of her smile disappear, making me want to blurt the words I've longed to say for months. She steps back a foot, teetering on her heels. "Stuff from my office."

The file box doesn't look heavy, but I take it from her to hold. Ashlyn and Celeste appear from around the corner.

Ashlyn is using one of her many tank tops as a rain cover and swapped out her heels for sneakers, which looks odd with her business attire. She steps toward us, tucking her wet tank top in the crease of her elbow. Her questioning eyes bounce between me and Sophie. "Don't hurt yourself there, big boy. I'll take that." She takes the box from my hands, resting it on her hip, holding it with one arm. Show off. "What are you doing out here? What's with the box?" she asks Sophie.

Her mouth widens into a broad grin, creasing the corners of her eyes. "I quit."

Ashlyn shrieks at the same time Celeste shouts, "Hallelujah!" and throws her arms up to the sky.

I'm in shock, processing what this means. Once the women stop celebrating, I focus on Sophie's joyous expression. She's reminiscent of Sophie from the Boston Common Carousel. The picture of unbridled happiness and joy I've looked at an embarrassing number of times.

"You quit?"

She nods, her eyebrows raised in the centre of her forehead. "I did. I told my dad I wasn't marrying Derek, either."

Relief. Excitement. So many questions. It all floods my system at once. I wobble, feeling lightheaded, until Sophie steadies me with her calming touch. One point of contact. One hand on my arm, and I'm brought back to Earth.

"I love you too. I'm sorry I didn't say it the minute I knew. Things might have been diff—"

"Boyd," her stern voice interrupts me.

I look into her eyes, asking her to continue without words.

"Kiss me."

The moment our lips connect, I'm lost in sensory overload. The rain falls, soaking into my scalp as she runs her hand through the short part of my hair at the back of my head. Everything else is Sophie. She tastes like vanilla lip balm and bad vending machine coffee as I trace my tongue over her lips, begging for access. Her eager whimper drowns out the foot and vehicle traffic around us. My hands trace her satin blouse, revelling in the silky fabric that clings to her skin. She smells like citrus, flowers, and coffee. The perfume she's always worn. It smells like coming home.

I don't know how long we stand there reconnecting physically. Emotionally. We break apart when a crack of thunder signals the sky opening up, and water pours down in a deluge.

"I've always wanted to kiss you in the rain," she says, clutching her hands around my neck and leaning back, allowing the rain to pummel her flushed skin.

"Let me know whatever else is on your list. I want to check off every one."

"Come on, love birds. Let's take this reunion somewhere else, eh?" Ashlyn shouts over the sounds of the city in a downpour.

I smile at Sophie. She smiles back. In sync, with her hand in mine, we dash toward the parking lot.

Ashlyn and Celeste hurry back to Ashlyn's car parked thirty feet away. I guess they were in enough of a hurry to find somewhere dry, they didn't want to waste time to say goodbye. I can't blame them. My clothes are soaked through.

We open both doors on Sophie's SUV and hop inside, both heaving a sigh of relief when the doors close.

Instinctively, I grab Sophie's hand again, grazing my thumb over hers. Looking at the blush-coloured nail polish that matches her entire condo and my favourite dress. Absorbing how it feels to touch her soft skin and have her in my presence again. I just want a moment to breathe her in and confirm this is real, not some frenzied fever dream.

"He's going to make things hard… for both of us. He'll use his contacts to blacklist us both."

I suppose our moment to just enjoy reuniting has passed. "Anyone who values his opinion is of no use to me. Plus, there's nothing wrong with being baristas forever."

She laughs, squeezing my hand. "No, there's not." She turns her head and tilts it to lean on the headrest. "Besides, I'll love you in any career."

I close my eyes, receiving her words like a gift I want to commit to memory. Words I'll never tire of hearing. Words that validate my own intense feelings for this woman.

I lift her knuckles to my lips, placing a gentle kiss across the middle two. "I love you, Sophie. Even unemployed."

Her cackling laughter fills the car, competing with the sound of the weather. The rain beats down on the windshield at such a furious pace, the *McNamara Enterprises* sign in front of us is blurred. It's almost poetic. Sophie is beside me, clear and in focus. *McNamara Enterprises* is muddled and will soon be in the rear-view mirror.

She presses the ignition button and flicks on the windshield wipers. "Ready?"

I revel in the question we've asked each other countless times before. This time, it holds so much more weight. It doesn't just mean am I ready to go. She's asking if I'm ready for whatever the future holds.

"Absolutely."

43

BOYD
Epilogue

I'm Like a Lawyer

It's official. Today was my call to the bar ceremony. I shook hands. I recited an oath. And now, I've got all the certifications I need to move on. I have spent six years working toward this moment, yet I feel like my biggest accomplishment is the smile on Sophie's face.

"I'm so proud of you. I mean… not that I have any claim to anything because you did all of this before I showed up, but I'm so—"

I cut her off with a kiss. Timelines don't matter. When she came into my life doesn't matter. She's here now, and I hope she never leaves. "I love you."

She giggles, which adds to the vibrancy of her flushing cheeks. "I love you too. Come on. Our reservation is at seven and we can't be late." She grabs my hand and tows me to her car. "Your gift is in the back."

I halt my steps and look around her SUV to where she's standing at the trunk. "How did you…? You didn't have to do that."

"You're welcome." She scoffs, but gives me an even brighter smile as she opens the tailgate. "I wanted to. Open it."

I tug on the gold wrapping paper that she's obviously put a lot of effort into.

"Boyd, rip the paper." The glare she's giving me says we're flirting dangerously close with our reservation time.

I do as she says, tearing the paper down the middle, exposing a professional grade personal espresso machine.

"Now, you can put it in your office and you won't have to deal with subpar coffee at your new job."

My eyes bounce from the appliance to her. "I could have just used a French press."

She slaps my shoulder, laughing. "I'm not waiting for that to brew espresso when I come to visit you in your fancy new gig at *Rutherford*. And a French press doesn't steam milk. Call it a selfish gift."

I wrap my arms around her again, pulling her in for another quick kiss. "Thank you. I love it."

She boops my nose like she does to Wilson, then pulls away. "Come on. We better get a move on." She tosses me her keys and hops into the passenger seat.

Little gestures like that mean the world to me. Not because I want to drive, but because she's comfortable enough with me to give up control. I hop into the driver's seat and head south to *Hibiscus.* On the way, we pass the office building I'll be reporting to in two weeks' time. *Rutherford Consolidated.* A finance company specializing in mergers and acquisitions. It will be a stark contrast to my positions as student and manager of *Just Add Coffee*, but I'm excited for the challenge. Plus, I know the café is in good hands with Monica as the new manager.

We pull into an underground parking lot, catch an elevator to the twelfth-floor restaurant, and we're quickly seated at a table for two by the window overlooking the waterfront. A server comes immediately to take our drink order and make some menu suggestions.

It's not until our drinks arrive that I really take in the opulence of the restaurant and the view. Once upon a time, this would have bothered me. This level of extravagance is something I'd turn my nose up at because it reminded me of the lavish lifestyle Maggie expected. But I don't think about her anymore. And when I consider doing these things with Sophie, I look forward to experiencing everything.

"Is it weird you're here as a customer tonight?" I ask, refocusing on her.

"Not really. I'm mostly in the office, so I don't come out here a lot."

Since Sophie stormed out of *McNamara Enterprises* seven weeks ago, she's been working for Caleb, taking charge of his shipments and deliveries. It's right up her alley and has kept her from stressing about finances. Henry's reach must not be as wide or powerful as he thought, because between me, Caleb, and Sophie, none of us have felt the brunt of his anger yet. Rumour has it that after Sophie left, a lot of the junior executives and all the female staff weren't far behind. *McNamara Enterprises* is floundering, and it feels like sweet justice.

"It was nice your family was able to come today. And Monica and Phoenix." Sophie curls up the corner of her fabric napkin, her eyes bouncing from one thing to the next.

My nerves get the better of me, seeing how on edge she is all of a sudden. I can only assume the worst. "How was my mother? Did she say anything to you?"

"Oh, she was fine. You made her sound like a grizzly bear. She's more like a wombat."

I laugh at her characterization, happy my mother behaved today. "I'll tell her you said that."

"Boyd, don't you dare!" she shouts before covering her mouth with her hand.

Apparently, my mother wasn't as sweet as Sophie let on. Or maybe wombats are a savage species and I'm just not familiar with many wombat attacks, so I misunderstood. I don't get the chance to ask, as our server returns to take our order, and Sophie asks her to let Caleb know we're here.

As soon as the woman leaves, Sophie blurts, "I'm going back to school."

I choke on the sip of soda water I'm downing. After a few seconds, I reply, "Really? Have you talked to Caleb about it?"

She narrows her eyes at me, and I quickly understand my mistake.

"Not for permission, Soph. Just because of your job here."

Her face relaxes, and she takes a sip of her wine. "Not exactly, but he knew this wasn't permanent for me. It was a pity job that took a little work off of his plate. I can still work a few hours a week. Even if I do online courses, my schedule will be really flexible. Plus, I finally organized his office, so it should make his life easier."

I can tell the more she talks about it, the more excited she gets.

"What are you going to take?"

She looks unsure of herself as she says, "Human Resource Management."

I reach across the table, taking her hand in mine. "I'm proud of you, Soph. Not that I have any claim—"

"Stop it." She laughs. "Yes, you do. For a decade I watched Caleb prioritize his own dreams and goals, not bothered by whatever Henry said. I was jealous of him in a way... resentful, maybe. I always felt my dreams were tied to one job. One place. But you came along and helped me see that there were more important things worth pursuing. So I want to do this. I like the business world, but I want to be in a position I can ensure everyone is treated equally in their job." She strokes my palm with her thumb. "You made me realize I owed it to myself to figure out what *I* wanted." Her gorgeous smile that lights up my entire world is on full display. "Plus, Andy is going to take courses with me, so we'll be together again."

This woman across from me is so incredible. I could waste time hating Henry for how he treated her or feeling sad for the amount of time she's been suppressed or shamed into staying quiet. Instead, I'd rather put my energy into helping her shine as bright as she can.

Our server returns with our plates of food, followed by a smiling Caleb.

"Boyd, congrats, brother," he says as he places a hand on my shoulder, giving it a gentle squeeze. In his other hand, he pulls a gift bag from behind his back, setting it on the table.

"What's this? You shouldn't have, man."

"It's nothing, really. Hopefully you get a kick out of it. I'm sorry to cut this short, but as you can see, we've got a full house." He winks at me, then leans down to give his sister a quick hug and kisses the top of her head. "Enjoy."

Without a chance to reply, he's off again.

"Open it." Sophie bounces in her seat. "I want to see what he got you."

I do as she instructs, first pulling out a card. The message inside says *Congratulations on your graduation. Thanks for making my sister happy. Now you can make me happy too.* That's... mysterious. I'm almost afraid to open it now.

"Open it!" Sophie repeats with more enthusiasm.

I reach my hand around the tissue paper and pull out a box. I open the top and slide out a small stainless steel coffee carafe. The words *to activate lawyer mode, add coffee* are etched on the side. I chuckle, recalling our conversation from months ago. There's a second matching box, so I do the same, tugging it out, and find the same thing, but with *this chef is hotter than this coffee* etched into it. My laugh is a little louder reading that one. I turn it to show Sophie, and she rolls her eyes.

"I don't even know what to do with him sometimes."

With that out of the way, we eat our meal, allowing our conversation to flow freely, talking about Sophie's new plans and everything we have to look forward to. We share dessert because Sophie claims she's been dying to try the baked Alaska she's seen multiple times but didn't want to eat the whole thing alone. As delicious as it is, there's nothing I won't share with her.

We wrap up our meal and head to the elevator. It's still early as far as the city dinner rush goes, so we get to ride the elevator alone. As soon as the doors close, I look over at Sophie. She flutters her lashes. Licks her bottom lip. Tilts her head down. All telltale signs she wants me to kiss her. So I do. Long and loving and passionate until the elevator dings and the doors open.

Before we step out, I tell her, "Our future is bright, Sophie McNamara."

She smiles up at me. "The best part is, it's ours."

THE END

If you enjoyed this book, please consider leaving a review on Amazon or the retailer's website where you purchased the book from. I love hearing from my readers.

If you'd like to hear from me, find all of my links here: linktr.ee/TiffanyAndrea, including some free stories and social media links.

AFTERWORD

If you finished this book feeling like the storyline with Holden and Boyd's family was a little mysterious, I'm sorry. I'm writing this series so that each one can be read as a standalone. They're each on a similar timeline, so they overlap, and I don't want to give away what happens in one book in another. So, in this book, I only included what applied directly to Boyd. If you're curious about Holden's story and the family drama on the Edwards' side, you can find that in *Ay Chihuahua*. I may be biased, but it's an adorable story too.

Moving on.

As always, to my readers, thank you. This author journey is a wild one, and can be a roller coaster of emotions at times. It can also be very isolating and make you question a lot about who you are, what you want to represent, and what you're putting out into the world. I like to think that I create stories that will not only make you laugh, but make you think, too.

No situation is ever black and white or obvious to people outside of those experiencing it. If you've ever dealt with a narcissist, you may have sympathized with Sophie for not wanting to "anger the beast". But if you've been fortunate enough not to have close encounters with one, she may have frustrated you.

But the entire point of this story was to show the power of love. She was stubborn and scared and trying to do the selfless thing in her mind, so even though others in her life hated the situation she was in, they continued to love her. Boyd's love for her never wavered once he knew the real Sophie. There's such beauty in that. Eventually, that love was enough.

So, I hope this story helps people pause to reflect on their expectations of others, because it isn't always an easy answer. Like I always tell my kids, you can dislike or disagree with someone's choices and still love them.

I certainly don't want to turn this afterword into a psychology lesson or sound like I'm preaching about a situation you may or may not encounter, so this is all I will say on the matter: At the end of the day, lead with love and compassion.

Be like Wilson.

SPECIAL THANKS

First, I have to give a shout out to my beta readers. Sara, your keen eye and romance expertise are second-to-none, and knowing each book has your seal of approval gives me the confidence boost I need to press that final publish button. I'm forever indebted to you.

Rebecca and Sarah, the most supportive, talented sister duo in the southern hemisphere, you both helped me so much in getting this book over the line. Your supportive words and feedback were immensely helpful in getting this book out into the world.

Of course, I can never skip over the support and encouragement from my husband and daughters. They listen to me ramble about plot points—even though my girls think romance is disgusting—and whine when I'm overwhelmed. They're my greatest inspiration and loudest cheerleaders. You three are my whole world. (But don't tell Steel that. He'll never forgive me.)

Lastly, as with a lot of my books, I chose a musical artist as the story's inspiration. For this one, it was obviously Fall Out Boy. They may be seen as an early 2000's emo band, but their music has so many layers and talks about so many different things. I adore them so much, and can often be seen driving around with their music playing in my truck. A lot of their early music, had a similar theme of the guy who wants the girl but can't have her. So in this story, I took it one step further and made it so they wanted each other and couldn't be together for a while.

Luckily, in romance novels, the guy always gets the girl in the end.

So, as always, here is my ultimate Tell-Tail Sign playlist, which can be accessed through the book page on my website at linktr.ee/TiffanyAndrea. You can also follow my Spotify account at @Burdenofproofreading.

Coffee's For Closers
Eternal Summer
Ghostbusters (I'm Not Afraid) (With Missy Elliot)
Beat It (Michael Jackson Cover)
The Take Over, The Break's Over
Alone Together
XO
What's This?*
Dead On Arrival
Tell That Mick He's On My List Of Things To Do
Of All the Gin Joints In All the World
It's a Small World*
Hot To the Touch, Cold On the Inside
"From Now On, We Are Enemies"
Alpha Dog
Wilson (Expensive Mistakes)
I Don't Care
Calm Before the Storm
The Kids Aren't Alright
Start Today
Don't You Know Who I Think I Am?
Grand Theft Autumn/Where Is Your Boy?
Growing Up

Stay Frosty Royal Milk Tea
Irresistible
Sugar, We're Goin Down
Saturday
The Last of the Real Ones
Moving Pictures
Champion
The Mighty Fall (With Big Sean)
One and Only (With Timbaland)
Young and Menace
America's Suitehearts
City In a Garden
Snitches and Talkers Get Stitches and Walkers
Just One Yesterday
Miss Missing You
Back to Earth (With Steve Aoki)
It's Hard to Say "I Do", When I Don't
We Were Doomed From the Start (The King Is Dead)
The Pros and Cons Of Breathing
Caffeine Cold
It's Not a Side Effect Of the Cocaine, I Am Thinking It Must Be Love
I'm Like a Lawyer With the Way I'm Always Trying to Get You Off (Me & You)
<u>Special Mentions:</u>
What a Catch, Donnie
Centuries
The Phoenix
Dance, Dance
Immortals

*Indicates song is not available on Spotify Canada at the time of publishing

You Are Enough Series:
We're All a Little Broken: Book 1 (Zara's story)
We're All a Little Overwhelmed: Book 1.5 (Zara's extended epilogue)
We're All a Little Guarded: Book 2 (Chelsea's story)
We're All a Little Tired: Book 2.5 (Chelsea's extended epilogue)
We're All a Little Scared: Book 3 (Isla's story)
We're All a Little Determined: Short Story Collection (Available free on my website)

This women's fiction series focuses on various aspects of mental health and overcoming trauma. It addresses anxiety, depression, panic disorders, miscarriage, adoption, grief and loss, racism, discrimination, and more, but in a light hearted way that will also make you laugh. The entire series is set in Muskoka/Bracebridge, Ontario.

A New Leash on Life Series:
This series will consist of twenty interconnected standalone romances of various genres, each featuring a cuddly canine companion.

Total Bull (Angel and Damian)

Ay Chihuahua (Dina and Holden)
Tell-Tail Sign (Sophie and Boyd)
The Pugly Truth (Hannah and Caleb) *Coming 2023*
Pitty Party (Oscar and Frankie) *Coming 2023*
Chemistry Lab (Hollis and Myer) *Coming 2023*

Dear Sister, Never Again: This women's fiction novella was shortlisted in Wattpad's annual novella contest. It explores the journey to realizing DNA isn't the only thing that makes family.

Suburban Watchdogs: This nonsensical comedy features four longtime friends and their slobbery dog on a mission to save their town from being overrun by a trio of bumbling criminals.

Con Artist: This standalone romantic comedy follows the story of an FBI agent tasked with investigating an art theft ring. The only thing his number one suspect makes away with, is his heart. *February 2023.*

Trip and Fall: This standalone road trip romance follows two twenty-somethings who each have a different reason for wanting to leave town and explore the countryside. One out of a sense of wonder; the other, a sense of desperation. Will they find more than the adventure they were looking for? *Summer 2023*

Sign up for my newsletter, access my website, or follow me on social media to keep up to date with new releases and sneak peeks.
Linktr.ee/TiffanyAndrea

www.ingramcontent.com/pod-product-compliance
Lightning Source LLC
Chambersburg PA
CBHW060907210726
48293CB00006B/1990